From Beyond the Grave

Edited by

Michael J. Evans

A
Grinning Skull Press
Publication

FROM BEYOND THE GRAVE
Compilation Copyright © 2013 Grinning Skull Press

The Skull logo with stylized lettering was created for Grinning Skull Press by Dan Moran, http://dan-moran-art.com/.

ISBN: 0989026906 (paperback)
ISBN-13: 978-0-9890269-0-1 (paperback)
ISBN: 978-0-9890269-1-8 (e-book)

DEDICATION

To the memory of those who have passed from this life.

CONTENTS

ACKNOWLEDGMENTS

This anthology would not been possible without the help of a number of people. I would like to thank Michael R. Danaitis, Jr., Ida D'Emilia, and Theresa Dooley. I humbly appreciate your contributions, without which I would have been lost. To all the authors who submitted stories for this collection, you made the decision process very difficult. And lastly, to the contributors who appear in this collection, thank you for entrusting your work to my care. I hope you're happy with the end product.

INTRODUCTION

What happens after we die? That is one of life's greatest mysteries.

There are some who believe that death is the end, that when we die, that's it. There's no Heaven, no Hell, nothing. There are those who have died, "gone into the light," and come back, and they are convinced there's an afterlife where they will be reunited with loved ones already gone. There are those who believe the soul, or spirit, leaves the body and moves on to another plain of existence, be it Heaven, Hell, or some other place. And then there are those who believe some spirits are trapped on our plain for whatever reason: They might be scared and confused because they don't know they are dead; they might not want to leave behind a loved one, so they stay and try to protect those they cared about in life; or they might wish to avenge a wrong that was done to them while they were alive. These are our ghosts. Sometimes you can see them, sometimes you can hear them, and other times you just *know* they are there. You catch movement out of the corner, but when you turn to look there's nothing there. You hear a voice in the room, but there's no one in the room with you. Or maybe it's a scent—a perfume or cologne—that fills the air, reminding you of someone from your past.

The stories you are about to read are ghost stories. They tell of tortured souls, vengeful spirits, malicious entities that exist only to cause harm to others. They tell of dead children, murdered spouses, people wronged by those they trusted. They tell of spirits bound to a place because of things they did in their past, wrongful acts they committed against others. And they tell of love.

When I first set out to compile this anthology, I challenged the authors to scare the crap out of me, but they did more than that. Yes, they sent chills down my spine, but they also moved me in ways I wasn't expecting. Adam Millard and Brent Abell offer up heartbreaking tales of loss, while Rose Blackthorn, Mark Leslie and Carol Weekes, and Jennifer Word serve up the chills with more traditional ghost stories. Each of the authors included in this collection touched me in some way, and I hope they speak to you in a similar manner.

Happy Hauntings!

Michael J. Evans

FROM THE DEPTHS
ROSE BLACKTHORN

When she opened her eyes, she could see nothing. It was dark and cool, and there was the sensation of barely perceptible movement, as though she were floating in luke-warm water. She shook her head, and then yawned, trying to force her ears to pop. It was so quiet, she reached up to see if there were plugs in her ears.

She could feel… nothing. Not her arms moving, not her hands touching her head. Her long hair didn't tangle around her fingers. A quick indrawn breath was completely silent. No air expanded her lungs, her diaphragm didn't flex. She turned quickly—at least, she attempted to turn. The subtle sensation of movement didn't change, the view didn't change. She should have been gasping for breath, her heart pounding in her ears, but it was so still and dark.

"Shannon," she said. "My name is Shannon." The sound of her voice did not vibrate in her ears, neither from within nor without. But she could remember the sound of her voice, and it comforted her. "What's happened to me?"

She concentrated, trying to feel her own body. She tightened her muscles, trying to feel the warmth in tendons stretched taut. After a long time, while she stretched her limbs with all of her effort, she was rewarded with a new sensation. Her surroundings were growing cold.

It might have been minutes, it might have been hours, but the almost imperceptible feeling of movement began to yield a change. It was still dim, but no longer an unrelieved darkness. The color of the world was a deep midnight blue. Shannon looked up, and yes, above her it appeared to be lighter. As though becoming aware of the difference was the trigger, she felt herself moving upward toward a blue that was almost celestial. Higher still, and the color changed to aqua-blue, and then blue-green, and then teal, and then emerald.

"Water," she said, but her voice still did not sound. It was only the memory of her voice that she imagined. "I'm in the water." Now that there was some light, she looked down at herself to see what she was wearing. Her body, which she could still only tenuously sense, was misty and transparent. She seemed to be wearing a sheer nightgown as fragile as she was. She held her hands up in front of her face. Her nails were long and painted with some color that she could not determine in the watery light. A pair of rings circled the ring finger of her left hand, interlocking bands with diamonds, hard, solid, and glittering like ice.

She touched her face, expecting the pressure of cold fingers, but there was only the distant frisson of an unfelt chill. "How did I get here?" she asked herself. She could not remember.

She was still moving upward, the light becoming brighter, almost painfully bright. The surrounding temperature was colder as well, and if she could have, she would have shivered as though lying naked in the snow. Unexpectedly her head broke the surface of the water. She wanted to gasp for air, to fill her lungs with it, but had no more success now than in the deep waters.

She looked around, her eyes beginning to adjust to the bright sunlight that filled the air. She was perfectly still in the water, not bobbing with the waves as she would have expected, but when she willed it, she was able to turn in a circle, giving her a 360° view of an unending expanse of water. In one direction—she did not know which—there was a low shadowy bank that she assumed was land. Turning a little farther, she was surprised to see a boat not far from her. There were people on the deck moving around, soft bursts of static, and voices. She was not able to make out any of the conversation.

When she found herself moving toward them, she was no longer surprised. It seemed her desire was all that was required for her to move wherever she wanted to go. Swimming was no longer an activity she need pursue.

"Mister Petras, they've found something," a low male voice said, carrying clearly across the open water to Shannon. She was only a few yards from the boat now. It looked to be some kind of police or rescue ship.

She moved closer, and her wish to see better was enough to lift her from the water onto the deck of the ship. She waited for one of the uniformed people to turn and ask her what she was doing there, but they did not notice her.

"Not alive though, right?" another voice said, and this one she recognized. "I'll never forgive myself, never!"

She moved sideways, clearing the wall that blocked her view, and saw him. Simon sat on a low bench, a blanket draped over his shoulders. His dark hair was tangled and unruly, as though he'd washed it but never combed it out. There was a sparse growth of scruff along his chiseled jaw and across his upper lip. He had not shaven. It was not like her husband to be seen in public in such a disheveled state. He was always meticulous about his grooming.

"Simon, it's not your fault," the woman beside him said, her hand taking his in a comforting grip. Shannon knew her, too. Brenda, her best friend for years, ever since high school, was dressed as though ready for a photo shoot. Her strawberry blond hair was pulled back into a simple twist, and there was not a hair out of place. Her makeup was flawless, her clothing the definition of understated elegance. The expression on her perfect face was a mask of concern and grief. Her eyes, however, seemed to sparkle with excitement.

"We argued," Simon returned, pulling his hand from hers so he could press his palms to his face. "She didn't want to go sailing. I wouldn't listen; I tried to cajole her into enjoying herself. If we'd just stayed home, this never would have happened!"

"Captain," a voice called, and the uniformed man who'd been talking to Simon walked away. Shannon moved closer, feeling nothing but that same icy cold. There was no anger, no sorrow, and no joy at the sight of her husband.

"You're doing great," Brenda whispered softly so no one could hear her but Simon—and their unseen eavesdropper. "Keep it up, baby."

"There should have been a better way to go about this," he replied from the corner of his mouth, his hands still over his face to better portray the grieving husband to any who might be watching. The anxious tone of his voice did not match the role he was playing.

"It's in the past now, so you might as well stop worrying about it," Brenda said, putting her arm across his shoulders. "Just a while of playing the grief-stricken husband, then you can collect your inheritance and the insurance money, and we can start enjoying ourselves." The smile on her lips was perfect, like everything else about Brenda. But Shannon could see the greed behind it, something she had never noticed before.

"How sordid," Shannon said. Again, her voice was silent, but Brenda flinched and glanced around quickly.

"Did you hear that?" Brenda whispered. Before Simon could reply, the captain returned.

"Mister Petras, I'm terribly sorry, but we need you to identify the body."

Simon got to his feet slowly, moving like an old man, and walked with the captain to where the divers had just returned. As Brenda prepared to follow, Shannon spoke again.

"This was your idea, wasn't it?"

Brenda flinched as before, turning quickly to look behind her. Her perfect mask was cracking, her brows drawn together, her eyes flickering back and forth nervously as she tried to determine from where the voice was coming.

"You were my friend," Shannon added. At the way Brenda twitched, her wide eyes looking right through the specter of the friend she could not see, Shannon felt something new. The cold was diminishing, and heat was beginning to build deep inside her. "At least, I thought you were."

Brenda moaned, and she hurried over to join Simon with the small crowd at the aft of the ship. There were two divers, several policemen and crewmen, the captain, and the distraught widower standing around a pale figure lying on the deck.

Shannon followed, listening to her husband speak through hitching sobs. "Yes, that's her. That's my Shannon." He half-knelt, half-collapsed beside the still body. "Sweetheart, my Shannon," he wailed.

The captain nodded, and one of the policemen mercifully pulled a white sheet over the corpse, covering the pale, bloated face. Shannon had gazed down numbly at the familiar features and was mildly surprised that she had no reaction looking at her own body.

"I'm sorry, sir, but if you could just tell me what happened?" one of the officers asked, pulling out a tiny recorder. "You don't have to go into great detail, sir. Just what happened, as best as you can remember it."

"Can't you see that he's in shock?" Brenda broke in, trying to return to her role as comforting and protective friend.

"I understand that, ma'am, but we still need to take his statement," the officer returned politely.

"It's all right," Simon said, appearing broken and exhausted with grief. Shannon moved closer, not wanting to miss anything. Perhaps his words would jog her own hazy memory. "We went sailing yesterday afternoon. We don't usually stay out overnight, but we'd both been drinking, and we were tired." As he spoke, he rubbed his eyes, the absolute picture of desolation. "There is a cabin on the boat, all the comforts of home if you will. So I furled the sails, and dropped anchor, and we went to bed."

The policeman glanced at the captain, who was listening intently to the story, but said nothing as Simon went on.

"As I said before, we'd been arguing. Shannon—Shannon wanted to start a family, and I wasn't ready for that. Not yet," Simon continued, his voice becoming thick as though he were fighting back tears. "So when she left the cabin and went up onto the deck, I just figured she needed some space, some time to calm down."

Shannon listened, her head cocked to one side. She was remembering now. Part of what he'd said was true. They had been arguing. She did want to have a baby, and he had refused. They had been drinking, that was true as well. But she hadn't gone up onto the deck to get a break. They had both gone up on deck when their argument was interrupted by the sound of an approaching motor.

"After a while, when she didn't come back, I went up to check on her," Simon was saying, his eyes bleak as he gazed out over the open water. "The water was a bit choppy, worse than it is right now. All I can think is that with her being upset, and having a couple of drinks, she lost her balance and fell. I don't know how long before I came up on deck it happened, I never heard her cry out or anything."

"You don't think Missus Petras might have, well, committed suicide?" the officer asked as gently as he was able.

"Absolutely not!" Brenda broke in vehemently. "Shannon would never do such a thing! She was a very strong person who loved life. A simple argument with her husband would never have made her contemplate suicide."

"Of course, of course," the officer said, obviously not wanting to offend. "It's just something I have to ask." He turned back to Simon. "Can you tell me what happened then?"

"I searched the boat, top to bottom. When I was sure she was not on board anywhere, I jumped into the water," Simon recounted, his voice oddly flat and sounding as though carefully rehearsed. "I dove, hoping to find her, but there was nothing. So I climbed back on board and tried the radio. I couldn't raise anyone, and my cell had no signal. So I did the only thing I could—I sailed back to port and called the police."

"Liar," Shannon said, moving to stand just behind her best friend. Brenda started, and Shannon smiled. She didn't know how, but the woman could hear her, even if no one else could. Even if she still couldn't hear herself.

She remembered everything that had happened, now. First, the rather ugly fight with Simon, and then the sound of a motor approaching their boat. Going back up onto the deck, and seeing the other boat, a fast, sleek, open-bowed model. Brenda had called out to them and come aboard with Simon's help, pretending this was a spur-of-the-moment surprise. For the first time, Shannon had seen—really seen—the way Brenda looked at her husband. She had seen the way Simon touched Brenda's hand; they were obviously more than friends. When she had turned to confront Simon with her epiphany, she'd felt the sting of a needle in her neck.

Seconds later she was in the water, unable to move or call for help. She had slowly sunk beneath the surface, her last sight the water-obscured tableau of her husband and friend in a passionate embrace.

"You will always remember me, and never forget what you've done," Shannon said, noticing suddenly that the body's left hand remained uncovered. The matching rings, engagement and wedding bands, were not to be seen. There were no rings on any of the fingers. "You're a liar, and a thief," she added, knowing suddenly that the platinum and diamond bands her friend had coveted were even now in the pocket of her stylish jacket. Shannon looked down at her transparent left hand, where the rings seemed to have weight and substance. On instinct, she thrust her hand into Brenda's pocket.

Brenda jumped, stepping backward and twisting her ankle on her ridiculously high heel. Before anyone could help her, she fell, landing with a *thud*. When she hit, the two stolen rings fell to the deck and spun in tandem toward the dead body. Diamonds glittered in the sunlight.

Simon glanced from the rings, to the sheet-covered body, eyes widening.

"Excuse me, ma'am," the polite officer asked grimly, his little recorder still running, "But where did those come from?"

* * *

The scandal was huge, the trial a media circus. It had taken only hours for the lovebirds to turn on each other, each one hoping to make a deal by implicating the other. The prosecutor was able to prove that Brenda had brought the needle filled with drugs to knock out Shannon. He also convinced the jury that she had taken the rings off her paralyzed friend's limp hand in a fit of jealous greed. But Simon was not to get off without his share of blame. He was the one with the strength to lift his drugged wife and carry her to the rail, where she was dropped, helpless, into the cold water. And he was the one with the most to gain, financially. He was the only heir to his wife's substantial estate, and it was common knowledge that he'd come from humble beginnings.

In the end, Brenda was sentenced to death for her premeditated part in the affair. Simon, perhaps because of his good looks and a final tearful collapse in the courtroom, was given life in prison without parole.

Shannon stayed with her husband. After all was said and done, she knew who was to blame. Brenda had been a false friend with greed in her heart, but she had not had to work too hard to convince Simon that life would be better if his wife were dead. Shannon had loved him while she was alive. So she would devote herself to him now in death.

His cell was small and secure. But there was no way he could keep her out of it, as she could pass through the walls and bars at will. It took a little time and perseverance, but after a while, he could hear her as well as Brenda had. She whispered to him, waking and sleeping, about the life and dreams they had shared. She wondered aloud at the children they might have had, of watching them grow. When he tried to ignore her, attempting to protect his slipping sanity, she drew self-portraits on the floor in seawater. She had drowned in the sea and carried it with her always.

Eventually, with great effort, she was able to appear to him. The first time he saw her, face pale and haggard, hair in wet, twisted ropes that hung to her waist, he broke down again.

"Shannon!" he wailed, backed into the corner of his bed as far as he could go. "I'm sorry, Shannon!"

She shook her head and climbed onto the mattress beside him, leaching cold saltwater into his blankets. "You don't know yet what sorry is, my love."

* * *

"Have you heard about the artist?"

Tommy James was starting his first day at the prison. Jack Harris, a guard who had worked there for fifteen years, was showing him around. "The artist?" he asked.

Harris nodded, walking down the long hall with barred doors on each side. "Yeah. He was some rich society guy, killed his wife about ten years back. Got caught, like an idiot."

Tommy tried to remember; ten years back, he'd been in middle school fighting off a case of acne and a crush on Melissa Jensen.

"His name's Simon Petras," Harris said, turning a corner. "It was pretty big news back then. But he's starting to get famous again, for something else. He claims he's haunted."

The older guard stopped in front of a cell. It was a bit larger than most, with a double window taking up the outside wall. The window was made of reinforced glass, and there were bars on the outside as well, but the cell was well lit. Sitting in front of an easel, Simon was working on his latest painting. After years of practice—what else did he have to do with his time?—he had become more than just proficient.

"Always remember and never forget," Simon muttered to himself without turning around.

"Go on in and take a closer look," the elder guard said to Tommy.

Tommy stepped into the cell, quickly taking in the paintings scattered around the room. The one on the easel, a little more than half finished, was of the same subject as the rest. "Who is she?" he asked softly, feeling a chill run up his spine.

"She is me," Shannon whispered into his ear, and smiled when he twitched. Each painting was of Shannon. Face pale, eyes dark and slightly sunken, long hair hanging wet and tangled to her waist. Sparkling on her left hand was the interlocking pair of diamond rings.

THE CHAMBERMAID'S SECRET
ADAM MILLARD

She'd fallen in love with Pendleton Manor the first time she'd seen it. Pulling up to the magnificent oak doors—the carriage rattling from side to side over the cobblestones beneath—Anita Drake kept staring, entranced, at the majestic façade. It was, she'd thought, something plucked straight from a fairy tale; one of the many enchanting stories she had once read to Isabella. As she'd clambered down from the coach, she'd wondered whether she was deserving of such an appointment. Sure, she was a competent chambermaid, but that had been in households half the size of Pendleton, with fewer bedrooms. It wasn't that she doubted her ability; it was more that she couldn't fathom her good fortune.

Three months later—that coach, receding into the distance, seemed like an eternity ago—and she would kill to be anywhere else *but* Pendleton. The master, a roguishly handsome and yet disgusting creature by the name of Tom Collingwood, had done nothing but reproach her in every duty she performed. *The sheets aren't crisp enough; the shelf in the master bedroom has a thin film of dust upon it; there aren't enough pieces of coal in the scuttles...* the list was endless, and Anita was finding it almost impossible to maintain her usual air of elegance. There were only so many, "Do your duties properly, woman!" a lady could take, and Anita was at the end of her tether.

And yet, it wasn't the sanctity of her *own* mind she concerned herself with. It was that of...

"Has anybody seen that wretched chambermaid?" Collingwood's discernibly gruff voice echoed along the hall just beyond the door to the nursery. There followed a series of replies, each meeker than the next, as various members of the house offered their honest opinions as to her current situation. Mary Thurston, the haggard old cook, whispered something to the master, as if she didn't want Anita to hear her backstabbing in progress, and the master stormed across the hall to the nursery, bellowing, "I've been looking everywhere—"

The door suddenly flew open. Anita was, as was her wont, polishing the shelves. She had removed each of the books and neatly stacked them upon the freshly made bed that dominated the center of the room.

"Anita, did you not hear me calling?" Collingwood barked. Of *course* she had, and he knew it. This was one of his little games; he liked to see his staff squirm. The more Anita panicked, mumbled, and became agitated, the more excited, happy, and evil he became. She wasn't about to give him the opportunity.

"I *did*, Master," she said, continuing to scrub the shelves as if they were much dirtier than they actually were. "I called out to let you know where I was. You mustn't have heard me over the sound of the staff's surreptitious whispers." It was clever, but she immediately regretted it.

Collingwood stepped further into the room, inspecting it. In fact, he was looking for something he could chastise her for. She often wondered why she was still in his employ. Wouldn't it be easier to appoint someone with whom he got along? Surely, if he despised her so much, he could hire a replacement and send her on her miserable way.

But she knew he had no intention of letting her go. It was too much *fun*, for she bore the brunt of his rage, his sardonic and cutting remarks, not to mention the workload.

He reached down and snatched a book up from the bed. "Anita, do you have any idea how much some of these books are worth?"

She shook her head, momentarily ceasing her frantic polishing.

He sneered, as if she was something he had had the misfortune of stepping in whilst walking the terriers. "*This*," he said, holding the book aloft, "is a *first-edition* Hardy. Here you are treating it as something the Robin's pushed through the letterbox."

"I apologize," she said, feigning remorse. "I had no idea they were so valuable. I'll make sure they are returned to the shelves in exactly the same condition they were when I fetched them down."

Collingwood sighed, clicked his tongue. "You see, Anita," he said. "You just don't *think*, do you? I pay you reasonably, do I not?" He didn't allow her to respond, which was probably for the best. "In all my years I've never met such a useless chambermaid, and I might *look* young, but I can assure you that I've got enough years under my belt to spot deadwood when I see it."

There it was. The cutting remark that brought her to the edge of tears. She'd tried her damnedest, told herself not to let him affect her with his contemptuous inferences, and yet she could feel herself welling up inside. *This* was why he didn't dismiss her. *This* was why she was almost certainly his most useful asset.

"And I've been informed by a member of the staff that you continue to keep your own door locked throughout the day." He frowned, knitting his dark eyebrows together to form an ominous shadow upon the bridge of his nose. "Why, pray tell, do you persist with these ridiculous games? I've told you, on twelve separate occasions, that the privacy of all staff is maintained so long as duties are not compromised. Mister Devlin has not been able to clean the windows in your room for over a month. It really won't do, Anita." As he finished, he flicked his head; there was, she knew, no point in arguing with the man.

Her room was locked during her absence for good reason. She didn't want the staff poking their beaks into her business. Besides, it would be almost impossible to explain away the décor, the trinkets and toys scattered haphazardly around the place, the miniature clothes strewn everywhere. Questions would be asked as to why she possessed items that were clearly of no use to her, and then there would be further investigations that could lead to all manner of misfortunes.

Anita curtsied, though what she really wanted to do—and perhaps *should* have done—was kick the wretched bastard in the nether regions. Satisfied that he'd achieved what he'd set out to, he nodded before twisting on the spot and marching from the room. "And put those books back where they belong, woman," he said over his shoulder.

And then he was gone. The clandestine whispering of the staff could be heard beyond the master's receding footsteps. All trust that she might have had was gone; they were, it seemed, all out to get her. One thing was for certain—and just the thought of it made her shudder; if they were trying to oust her, the whole episode would not end well.

There came a sudden chill. The books upon the bed began to move; pages flicked rapidly, seventeen volumes (apparently first editions, or so *he* says!) all singing in perfect unison. The hairs on the nape of Anita's neck pricked up. If she wasn't used to this by now, it would have terrified her.

Then came the voice. The sweet, angelic babbling that only she could hear or understand. She listened carefully, before replying with, "I *know*. Just, *please*, don't do anything. I need this position."

More whispers. Anita glanced nervously around the room, hoping the owner of the voice decided to make an appearance. It didn't. Anita paid heed to everything that was said, though she hoped most of it would be forgotten shortly after. She didn't like what she heard, but had she expected anything less?

"Please, just calm down. I'm okay, and I'm very good at letting it all go over my head." Anita didn't like the sound of her own voice. She was practically pleading. "Really, I shan't let him, or any of it, bother me."

The first-edition Hardy suddenly levitated from the rest of the stack. Anita watched, bewitched, as the tome hovered dramatically for a few seconds. She had no idea what was happening until it was too late. The book—the incredibly rare and expensive book that was, Anita had no doubt, signed and dated to the master of Pendleton, or one of his relatives—was quickly torn in two. Half of it went one way; the other half in the opposite direction. Anita was too aghast to do anything but watch as loose pages slowly floated down to the bed.

There was one final whisper, and then the leather-bound cover fell from the air, no longer supported by invisible hands. *She* was gone, but *she* was angrier than she had been in a very long time.

Anita dropped to her knees and sobbed, for she knew what was to come.

* * *

The days following the confrontation in the nursery were miserable. Anita didn't know who to trust, and everywhere she looked the staff was pointing, or staring, or whispering to one another about her. The severity of her isolation was only further proved when the head gardener, Wilfred Bamshoot—a man with whom she had shared many a long conversation—purposefully avoided her whilst she beat the dust from the rugs. She had waved to him, caught his attention, but he had pretended not to notice and went about his journey to the large shed at the bottom of the garden, ignoring her completely. Anita, in that moment, felt as if her internal organs had been torn from her. She was hollow; just a shell with nobody to turn to.

It was so bad that Anita lost her appetite. If she couldn't trust anyone, she certainly wasn't going to eat the food prepared for her. Who knows what goes through some peoples' minds? Mary Thurston was an old hag, almost witch-like in appearance; would it be so difficult to believe her capable of concocting some intricate poison and slipping it into Anita's meals?

What annoyed Anita the most was that she had done nothing to deserve *any* of it. The staff had no real reason for the way they had opted to treat her, and Master Collingwood only liked to show his fierce side to maintain some sort of order. She was a scapegoat, and others were simply playing along because while the master was affronting Anita Drake, he wasn't tormenting any of them.

Well, Anita had made a decision not to let it get to her, and she was ultimately succeeding, although at times it didn't feel like it. However, she wore a brave face and went about her errands as always. Pendleton was a big place, thus it was easy to go missing if you so wished. There were days when she might pass a person in the hallway, but that would be it. And so she believed that, given time, it would all dissipate, or Collingwood would find somebody else to trouble, leaving her be.

A day later, the most terrible thing happened...

* * *

Anita dragged the sack of coal across the path. It was starting to get dark, and this was her final task of the day. Outside it was chilly; winter was on its way, and more coal was necessary to keep the temperature in the house comfortable. Under normal circumstances, Anita wouldn't be expected to shift such a heavy load, but Wilfred was still doing his utmost to avoid her and was nowhere to be seen.

She stretched, her back audibly cracking. It was then that she spotted the shadow approaching her from the house, marching down the path with a gait that she instantly recognized.

She curtsied, although at the pace Collingwood was moving she could tell it would do her no good.

"What could I possibly have done, now?" she quietly asked herself.

The master had a face like thunder. Anita could see he was biting his lip, waiting until he was close enough to unleash his wrath upon her. He was, she noticed, holding something in his left hand. As he lifted the book towards her, it fell apart.

It was the first-edition Hardy from the nursery. Collingwood had found it, although Anita had done little in the way of concealing the irreparable book. She knew it would only be a matter of time, and yet she didn't think he would find it so soon.

The master reached her, and without speaking—his face contorted into something malevolent—he slammed the book so hard against Anita's face that she was knocked over. She landed on the damp grass beside the path, her face tingling from the strike, her pride stinging along with it.

"What the *hell* did you do?" Collingwood roared. He was like some unholy beast, summoned up with no other purpose than to strike fear into all men's' hearts. "You *destroyed* it, you selfish whore!"

Anita was scrambling around in an effort to clamber to her feet. The shock of Collingwood's attack had rendered her legs useless; it was like trying to stand on strings of jelly. Along with her fruitless flailing, she found she lacked the function of speech. The man had hit her so hard, so cunningly, that she had been stripped of her voice. All she could do was watch as Collingwood's tirade continued.

"Not only have you ruined a very expensive artifact, but I had Wilfred open the door to your room. What the hell is the *matter* with you, woman? There are toys *everywhere*, and children's' clothes. I've been suspicious of you since your appointment, Ms. Drake, but now I discover that you've been harboring a child whilst in my employ?" He raised the torn and tattered book as if to strike her once again, and Anita shrank into herself, covering her face, which had already turned a very unnatural hue of purple. When nothing happened, she removed her hands to find the master grinning. Could it be that he was actually enjoying this?

"So where is it?" he asked, glancing around the garden—down toward Wilfred Bamshoot's potting shed. "Where are you keeping it?"

There was no *it*, but that didn't mean the way in which Collingwood referred to a child was any less offensive; he was talking as if it were a dog or a pet rodent.

He watched, somewhat nervously, as Anita finally managed to struggle to her feet. Her face burned from the impact of the leather, but she had suffered worse—a lot worse—from previous husbands and male acquaintances.

"I have no idea what you're talking about," she said, forgetting to call him Master, not that it would matter after this evening.

"Oh, don't play Simple Sally with me," he said, growing more frustrated by the second. "Your quarters are filled to the brim with childish trinkets and stuffed animals. Wilfred found a child's drawing with the name Isabella scrawled on it. *How*, woman, did you think you could keep this from me?" His face was almost as red as Anita's, though she wished he could feel the amount of pain she was in.

Anita was about to retort, cleverly, about how the clothes and toys were hers and that she liked nothing better than to pretend she was a child again, when the wind kicked up something rotten. No, it wasn't the wind. Anita knew *exactly* what it was, for she could hear the incessant whisper of the approaching voice.

This was bad; very bad, indeed.

Anita watched as Collingwood frantically glared around the garden, overwhelmed by the strange atmospheric developments. Such was the force of the ungodly energy, Collingwood took a few steps back to maintain his balance. A miasma of leaves, loose dirt, and small insects whipped up into the air; the master, Anita was quite pleased to see, looked positively terrified. The final few pages of the ruined book he was holding flew up and disappeared amongst the debris.

"What's happening?" the master gasped, taking a few more steps back. If he wasn't careful, he would end up in the pond, surrounded by reeds and fish whose breeds Anita couldn't even pronounce. His eyes were wide as his brain worked hard to conceive the anomaly.

"Don't do it!" Anita screeched, spinning on the spot and almost tripping over the coal sack she had been dragging along the path. There was no placating *her*; the assault from Collingwood had sealed his fate.

The master was suddenly launched into the air, his feet trailing behind him like ribbons. If he made a sound in protest, Anita didn't hear it. Backwards he went, landing face down in the fish pond.

Anita pushed through the impossible wind in a vain attempt to reach him, but it was no use. The man had already ingested the filthy water in his panic, and was flailing around, trying to keep from drowning. Even through the semidarkness, Anita could see the fish darting around, looking for somewhere safe, away from the sudden intruder. One—a Japanese Koi, she was pretty sure it was called—leapt out of the pond and nestled in amongst the surrounding shrubbery, flapping its way to a certain death the same as the master.

Anita turned away, not wishing to see the final moments of the fish's demise, which said something for her feelings towards Collingwood, for it was apparent that she could have watched his suffering until the very end.

After almost a minute, the master was still. The rippling water surrounding him began to settle. Somewhere off in the distance a fox mewled.

"You shouldn't have done it," Anita gasped, fighting back tears that were in no manner meant for Collingwood. "You've ruined everything... *once again!*"

But she knew from the unnatural silence and stillness all around that she was, once more, alone.

And then came another mewl; though this time it was indubitably human. A woman—Mary Thurston, the possible poisoner of Pendleton?—screeching as if she had seen a ghost. Anita's breath caught as she realized the backstabbing old cow might very well have.

She rushed towards the manor, fearing the worst.

* * *

They were all dead; each and every one of them slaughtered in some method inextricably linked to their duties. Mary Thurston was propped up at the kitchen hob, her head swallowed entirely by a vat of boiling jam. Crimson gore dripped from her sleeves and hem, and if it wasn't for the sickly sweet smell of raspberries, Anita would have mistaken it for the old hag's viscera.

Wilfred Bamshoot was in his quarters. He'd been reading a book about artichokes when the hoe had penetrated his back. He was still seated in his chair, arched backwards as if he had attempted to remove the tool shortly before succumbing to the darkness. The pole jutted out towards the door, almost pointing in an accusatory manner. *You did this! You and your little dead daughter!*

The master's butler, Terence Grovener, was folded double at the foot of the stairs. In his right hand he held the silver tray used to regularly serve drinks to Master Collingwood and his guests. Though Grovener, it appeared, had saved the final drink for himself. A crystal stem protruded from his throat; his usually crisp, white shirt was blooming with crimson flowers. Anita almost vomited at the sight. And then there was Mister Devlin, squashed by the window in her own room. It seemed he had finally taken the opportunity to give them a good wipe over.

And so it went, throughout Pendleton, bodies everywhere. Anita sobbed with each discovery. Some of these were good people, although towards the end she wasn't so certain. Still, they didn't deserve to die, not like *this*, not because of her.

Isabella was a fiery one, which was quite an understatement, Anita thought. This was the third manor to fall at the vengeful spirit's hands, and would not be the last. A chambermaid was good for only one thing: being a chambermaid.

Pendleton was burning quite nicely as Anita made her way down the long, cobbled drive towards the front gates. She had a small case of possessions—a few stuffed animals that Isabella requested—in one hand, and her daughter's frozen, invisible hand in the other. There was no point reproaching the child for her actions.

After all, she was only a child looking after her dear mother.

TEARS OF HEAVEN
BRENT ABELL

"Mommy, why is Daddy crying again?" Gail whispered, leaning over to her mother.

"Daddy's had it rough, baby. After everything that happened, he's just had a tough time getting through it," Melinda answered, running her long, thin fingers through her daughter's honey blonde hair. She let go of the bangs and wrapped Gail up in a tight embrace. Gail buried her face against her mother's slender shoulder and let out a small whimper.

A faint, sweet-smelling breeze blew through the park and Melinda used her thumb to wipe the solitary tear from her daughter's eye. Around them, children played and other people strolled by laughing and talking. Some stopped to check on the sad pair in each other's embrace, but in the end they all passed them by. Mother and daughter gave each other another big squeeze and turned back to observe Doug.

* * *

Doug sat perched on the edge of the bed, elbows propped up on his knees, his face cradled in the palm of his hands. Light sobs and sniffs escaped his mouth and nose. Salty tears formed a pool in his hands and drained away, dripping onto the stained carpeted floor. Doug shook and raised his head. Wiping his damp hands on his dirty, ragged sweat pants, he took a long, deep breath, and opened his eyes.

The room still looked the same as it did before, a godforsaken shit hole where people went to escape from life or to finally give up and die. A small lamp in the corner, *sans* lampshade, threw out a dim spot of light in

19

the dark room. Cockroaches darted out from under the bed and found cover beneath the chipped and faded nightstand against the wall where the clock blinked the same time. Snow hissed on the old television screen, calling out for the plug to be pulled. The dingy motel room looked more depressed than Doug felt. When he hit rock bottom, he hit it hard. Thinking about it, it didn't really hit him as much as it kicked him in the balls while simultaneously sucker punching him in the face.

Groaning, Doug went to the bathroom, and when he returned, he sat back down behind the beaten desk beside the old television. The pen and paper still lay there, mocking him. Every time he tried to write something, the words flowed through his mind, burned through his arm, but stopped short of transferring onto the paper from his fingertips. Doug didn't know writing a suicide note could be so difficult.

* * *

Sitting slouched in the plastic-coated chair; the past year swam around his head. The last drops of bourbon ran down his throat and landed in his stomach with a welcome burn. It had been days since he'd eaten, and without any food to absorb the alcohol, it roiled his insides and he felt bile race back up his throat.

Humph, how much better am I, always drunk and ready to die? I'm a poet and didn't know it! He thought with an ironic chuckle.

Since Melinda and Gail were killed coming home from ballet class one night by that worthless, drunken, sack of shit Eli Jacobs, Doug failed to see a reason to continue living. Every day when he looked up to the sky, he hoped they were happy wherever their souls might be. He hoped they couldn't see him unravel while he drank himself into oblivion, unable to put their memory to rest. If God did exist and Heaven is where good, innocent folks went when they died, he wanted God to spare them the pain of watching him fail to come to grips with what happened and lose himself in the never-ending litany of booze and drugs. If He let them witness his downward spiral, He, too, was a son-of-a-bitch. Gathering his thoughts again, he placed pen to the paper and finally began to write.

To anybody that cares (or whoever finds my body),
My name is Doug Clark. I am a widowed man who buried my wife and only baby girl at the same time. I looked to God for an answer, for a reason. All I found was the bottle. I can't go on any longer; I want to be with them wherever they are. Heaven, Hell, I don't care. I'm sorry for the mess; I left extra cash on the bed to cover

it.

Sincerely,
Douglas James Clark

Sighing, he reread the note and wadded it up. Tossing it in the air, it bounced off the other dozen or so attempts overflowing from the trash can. Like everything else in the last year, he failed, again. Snatching up the bottle and remembering he emptied it earlier, he smashed it down on the desk. The clear glass shattered and showered the floor.

He cried out and hung his head down, his body shaking from the force of his sobs. The loss and sadness cloaked him as he drifted off to sleep in a haze of booze and pity.

* * *

"Melinda, I wish you wouldn't bring Gail here to witness this tragedy. Doug is a mess and I hate to think what she thinks of her father now," the man said, sitting down on the bench next to them. The garden surrounding them was silent and he pointed to a box sitting in the middle of the cobblestone path. When a person strolled by, they kept their distance and passed without even a glance to the families gazing into their boxes. The men with the hoods stayed to the right of the path, respecting Melinda and Gail's need for privacy during their visitation.

"Hank, I love him and I want her to see how much he misses us. I don't want him to hurt, but it shows how much he loved us," Melinda muttered.

"He's my son, my blood, and the greatest joy in my life. Don't you think I ache on the inside watching him spiral out of control? That boy was all I had in the years after my lovely Jackie passed on. We missed her and seeing him down there like this after your death tears at me here." He pounded his chest above his heart.

"I wish I could have met her, she meant so much to both of you," Melinda said with a sigh.

"I loved her so, but there's nothing you can do while still in the flesh on Earth to change things," Hank shrugged.

"How long do we have to wait?" Gail said, reaching out to her grandfather.

"You know the rules, sweetie-pie," Hank replied. "He's not ready to join us yet." He smoothed Gail's golden hair.

"I want to hug my daddy!" she yelled and wiggled free from Hank's grasp.

"No honey, don't!" he called after her. Jumping up, he hurried to stop her from reaching the box.

Gail ran over to the box and looked in. Her father looked so small and helpless. Closing her eyes, she pictured herself in the doll house-like box, hugging her daddy. Drawing a deep breath, she focused long enough for her body to dissipate into a mist and her essence to seep into the box.

Diving toward his granddaughter, Hank reached out to grab hold of her before she faded away into the box to save her father, but his fingers passed through her arm as she dissipated. Hitting his knees, he felt the world unravel around him.

He knew all was lost.

* * *

Sitting back down at the desk, Doug picked up the gun and stared at it again. The .45 felt cold in his hands, even as his palms broke out into a sweat. The rush swelled in him and he stuck the barrel in his mouth again. Slowly, he closed his lips and bit down on the gun. The steel tasted tangy and the oil bitter. Hesitation settled in again. Doug dropped the gun from his lips and inhaled deeply. His breath caught in his chest, sensing something wasn't quite right. The curtain fluttered as though stirred by a breeze. He knew the air was off because it didn't work and hadn't since his first night here.

Glancing around, he felt the air grow cool and the hairs on his neck and arms rose until they pointed to the ceiling. On his right, a groaning bed spring cried out in the silent room. Cautiously turning his head, he noticed the indention in the center of the bed. It disappeared and the sweet sound of a child's laughter lightly called across the room. A loud pounding, like running, circled around him and he swung his head from side to side trying to follow the sounds. After a few trips in the circle, the room fell silent once more.

The fleeting scent of his daughter's lilac bath soap filled his nostrils. Doug reached out and swept his hands wildly through the air, trying to grasp anything in the empty space surrounding him, hoping that something would touch him back. His open palm touched something cool in the air beside him. His hand stopped and he held it perfectly still for a moment, picturing Melinda and Gail.

Flashes shot through his mind like an old movie, memories of the life he had shared with his family. Crying out from the sharp pain, memories continued to flood through his brain. Each moment of his life became a pricking in his soul while fleeting images of his wife and little girl filled him. As suddenly as it began, the sensation disappeared and the loneliness crashed back down around him.

Then he felt something wet splash on the back of his hand.

A small liquid drop, the size of a tear, ran down to his wrist, then fell from his flesh. On its downward journey the drop vanished into nothingness before hitting the floor. Curious, he touched his tongue to the spot where the drop touched his hand and an electric jolt shot through his body, burning every fiber of his being as he consumed the salty residue.

Like a flower on a frigid, frosty morning, what little hope remained within him withered and died. The darkness he embraced during the past year consumed him in one last bleak wave and his reasons for living vanished without a trace. With a new-found conviction, Doug picked up the gun again. In his heart he felt ready to do the only thing that made sense to him.

Quickly, he placed the gun back in the upright position, put up the tray table, and smiled. Doug sucked on the barrel twice in anticipation, and when the gun's seed exploded into his skull, his parting thoughts were about being with his family again.

* * *

Melinda cried out and Hank flinched, both watching Doug's head splash on the grimy yellow hotel wall in a crimson spray of brain, blood, and bone. In horror, Melinda looked away as the cockroach popped out from under the bed and danced through her husband's gray matter.

"No, no, no! It wasn't supposed to be like this," Hank muttered, shaking his head.

Melinda turned to him, "What do you mean 'supposed to be'?"

"He told me everything would be alright if we believed and followed the rules." Hank shook his head, trying to deny the reality of what he had just witnessed.

"Who, Hank?"

"*Him*, all we had to do was believe," he answered pointing to the sky. "He willed us to be together when Doug finished his journey. It wasn't going to be like this, Gail ruined everything. She violated the laws. She made contact! Now, she's doomed us!"

"What do you mean about Gail? What did she do, Hank?" Melinda frantically screamed at him. Rushing over, she pounded her fists into his big barrel chest, sobbing with each hit.

Reaching out, he grabbed her wrists and drew her to him. He placed a finger on her trembling lips to silence her. He let her go and led Melinda to the box to see the damage Gail had caused.

On the floor and walls of the box that looked like a motel room, the pulpy chunks of Doug's head slid around through the skin and hair to stitch itself together again. Soon, all the bits and pieces shook and started reforming Doug's ruined face. The crimson wall faded back to its normal dirty shade and the bullet sprang from the wall and disappeared in the gun's chamber.

Covering her mouth in startled realization, Melinda turned away, unable to watch any longer.

* * *

Doug opened his eyes and wiped the sleep from his tired eyelids. The cockroach ran past his foot and slid behind the TV stand, disappearing from sight. Looking over at the table, he saw the gun staring back at him. He got out of bed, sat down at the desk, and began writing his suicide note for the fourth time in an hour.

With slumped shoulders, he opened the curtains and looked out on a dead world and wondered where everybody had gone.

Seven hours later, after he felt his daughter's spirit with him, he pulled the trigger to join them.

* * *

Doug opened his eyes and wiped the drool from his chin. He did a double-take when the cockroach skidded across the floor and hid in the dark recesses of the dirty motel room. A sense of déjà vu danced in his thoughts. He got up and gazed out the window at the grey morning. The sun sat buried behind the clouds and the smog blanketed the city, a typical Los Angeles morning. On the freeway, nothing moved. He didn't see a car speed by for several minutes.

Maybe it's Sunday and everyone's still in bed, he thought and closed the smoke-stained curtains. Sitting back down, he put pen to paper and began to write his last words.

Seven hours later, believing his daughter had come to lead him away, he put the gun in his mouth. The bullet slammed through Doug's head and painted the wall in the pinks and reds of blood and brain matter.

* * *

Doug opened his eyes...

* * *

"Hell is repetition my dear," Hank whispered to Melinda.

Gail sat behind the bench under the weeping willow tree, her knees pulled up to her head, tears rolling down her cheeks.

"I made a deal to release him from his netherworld prison, but his physical contact with Gail broke the arrangement."

"What arrangement?" Melinda asked. She tried to hide the tone in her voice, but her anger, fueled by the pain of her husband's grisly end, only continued to grow.

"His suicide on the mortal plane left his soul in jeopardy for a millennia. All he had to do was redeem himself in Purgatory for a shorter time, now he is doomed to repeat the act in Hell for eternity. I have to pay my price now also. I laid my soul on the line to save him, and now my bill is due. Please, for Gail's sake, don't try the same thing. Leave us be and look after her."

Melinda turned and looked at him, "What price are you talking about?"

"Wailing and gnashing of teeth is my forever and ever, like my son now. I bet my soul that Doug could save himself. When Gail touched him and he tasted her tear, he felt her spirit and gave up. She made him want to die so he could be with you again. Now, I've got my own box as my reward."

One of the hooded figures bent over and placed an empty box on the path next to Doug's. Turning toward Hank, the figure bowed and walked away chanting. Inside the box, the blankness swirled and forms started to take shape.

Hank stood before them and screamed. Smoke poured from underneath his shirt and pant legs. His searing flesh popped and blistered as the flames licked up from the stone pathway, consuming his immortal body. He called out one last time before he fell to a pile of ash on the cobblestone walkway. The ashes swirled and blew around until the remains of Hank funneled into the box on the ground.

Melinda and Gail peered inside the box as Doug blew his head all over the wall again. Hank's remains reformed in the new box that appeared besides his son's prison and screamed at his personal Hell.

* * *

Seven hours later, Doug took up the pistol once again to end his life, while in the next box Hank reached out and failed to stop Gail from entering her father's tormented prison. A cloaked man stopped on the path in front of Melinda and Gail. Beneath the hood, Gail saw him smile at her and she gave a faint little wave in return. Afraid of the strange man, she grasped onto Melinda's leg and turned away.

The figure bent over and picked up the two boxes. He blew them off and placed them on the wall next to the pathway and continued on his way. The veil fell away from the wall and Melinda saw the rows of clear boxes stacked on top of each other reaching high into the eternally blue sky. Gail cautiously approached the wall and glanced in the boxes at eye level. A person sat in each box she peeked in. Most of them looked like a loop on the television, replaying the same scene over and over again. Cries and screams of agony echoed along the wall of boxes, each one a prison for some doomed soul.

Melinda walked over and gazed in on Doug and Hank one last time before turning and walking away, hand in hand with Gail, toward the gold cityscape in the west.

As mother and daughter strolled off into the cityscape's golden spires, Doug pulled the trigger... again...

... and Hank ran after Gail... again...

... over and over.

Father and son, side by side, bound forever in repetition.

ECTOPLASM
SCOTT M. GORISCAK

Moving day finally arrived late in June. Summer vacation had just begun. Mother was moving us to Pennington, New Jersey. After my grandmother's passing, Mom had inherited her house. So once all the lawyers were done processing the official documents we were set to go. Mom was able to transfer her job to Princeton, New Jersey. The movers were finishing packing the truck as our neighbors and friends were saying their goodbyes. I was born in Holcombe, New York, and lived a small-town life here. The people here were simple, hardworking, and friendly. It was all that I had ever known. I was going to miss it.

My mother was a single parent; I never met my dad. All I ever knew of him was that he worked on a mink farm outside of town when they were married. The marriage didn't last long and he was gone a few months before I entered this world.

My mother approached the car with a box in her arms and said it was time to go. I climbed in the back seat and buckled in between miscellaneous boxes of our belongings. I waved goodbye to my friends as Mom drove the car out of the driveway. Mom said it was going to be a long ride so she told me to get comfortable and relax. That was easy; I fell asleep after about an hour. By mid-afternoon we arrived at our new home.

I awoke as the car came to a stop. I remembered opening my eyes and seeing this big, beautiful house in front of me. I knew it well. Over the years we had visited Grandmother during summer vacations and on holidays. Looking up at it that day it didn't seem as big as I had remembered, but compared to our two-bedroom apartment, this four-bedroom house seemed huge. The house was yellow with white trim, and I knew

Mom liked it. She liked the color yellow. I got out of the car and walked around to the back of the house. The yard was as beautiful as I remembered. This was going to be great. I ran upstairs, going from room to room trying to decide which one I would choose for my new bedroom.

I watched the empty moving truck pulling away. Moving day was almost over. I was pretty tired when Mom called me to dinner. Mom and I sat down to have our first meal together in our new home. Mom had ordered pizza, and we ate in the dining room amid a jungle of unpacked boxes. After dinner I went upstairs to my new room and began to unpack. Fatigue reminded me just how long and taxing this day had been. After only a few minutes, I turned off the light and crawled into bed.

After about a week, mother and I were doing some weeding out in the garden when a man walked into our yard. We both stood up as he approached. With a big smile on his face, he said, "Welcome to the neighborhood." He reached out his hand to shake my mother's. He said his name was Michael Finnegan. Then he turned to shake my hand. A cold shiver went through my body as our hands met. His visit to our house was on behalf of his elderly mother who lived on the next road. He handed a letter to my mother that had been delivered to his mother's house by mistake. He further explained that this happened on occasion due to the fact that his mother's house and ours had the same number, and depending on which part-time mail carrier was working, the mail didn't always get delivered to its correct destination. He asked if there was anything we needed, and Mom told him that we were fine. He smiled and said goodbye. I saw him walk out of the yard and turn left toward the corner. I looked down for a moment then back in his direction. He was gone. I walked to the edge of the yard and looked down the road in the direction he had been walking. The street was empty. While I thought it odd, I dismissed it as nothing more than a swift departure.

The next day my mother surprised me with a gift, a Beagle puppy. I named him Cody. Over the next few days the weather turned cold and it rained non-stop. This forced Cody and me to spend lots of time exploring inside of the house. Mom said the house was built in the 1700s. The hallways were very narrow. They made me feel uncomfortably claustrophobic. The upstairs consisted of just the four bedrooms and a bathroom. The downstairs had a dining room, living room, family room, kitchen, laundry room, and a small room next to the bathroom. Mom said that it used to be Grandmother's sun room. She had loved to read in that room. I noticed that it had a strong smell of perfume and incense. I liked how the sun brightened it and made me feel warm, so I was also going to use it as a reading room.

Exploring the house got boring, so Cody and I went to the play room. As we walked into the room Cody kai-yayed like I never heard before. He ran from the room and hid under the couch in the living room. I went after him and pulled him out. I called to my mom and told her what had happened, and she checked him out. He didn't seem to be hurt, and she reassured me that he was fine. He started to play and wag his tail. I picked him up and again we started toward the play room. As I got near the doorway, he started to squirm in my arms and resume his crying. When I carried him into the room, he started to growl. I put him down and he scurried out of the room and up the stairs. It was then that I noticed the smell of perfume grow and linger in the air. I thought to myself, *That smells pretty. I wonder what mom sprayed in here to make it smell so nice.* Then a music box mysteriously began to play. I liked it, but where was it coming from? I turned around and went out in the hallway. I listened up and down the hallway to hear where it originated. It was coming from behind me, from the sunroom! I was starting to feel a bit uneasy. So I turned and went back into the room in search of the music's origin. I froze in my tracks.

Across the room, sitting in the chair, was an old woman. I didn't know if I was scared or just startled. I couldn't take my eyes off her. As I looked at her, she was studying me, and I could feel my blood cool as chills coursed down my spine. No matter how hard my eyes labored to see her—to identify her—her features kept going in and out of focus. Parts of her were there, and then they weren't. She was wearing a long dress that was buttoned all the way up to her frilly collar. Her long skirt, I guessed, would have reached her ankles, if she had any. She cast no image from her knees to the floor. She just sat there and smiled. I felt safe, but freaked out just the same. Looking at her, I couldn't make up my mind whether I was more excited or more frightened by the experience. I wanted to call my mother, but the woman vanished from the chair before my eyes. As the clouds crossed the sky, a light shimmered in on the now-empty chair.

I didn't really detect any sense of danger while she was present, but it was difficult to logically assess the experience. Truthfully, it had left me a bit shaken. Who wouldn't be freaked out by a visit from a ghost? It was probably better that I didn't mention it to Mom. I don't know how she might react. The possibility of my being punished ran through my mind, mostly because I had a history of making up stories, and Mom didn't appreciate it. I think if I had told her what I had seen, she would have thought that I was up to my old tricks again.

The music stopped suddenly as Mom walked into the room and sniffed at the air. She said the scent reminded her of her mother. I told her it may be from the flowers outside the open window. She said that couldn't be, that it smelled more like perfume. She shrugged and told me it was time for lunch.

In the next few weeks the apparition of the old woman manifested itself a few more times around the house. She never scared me or jumped out at me. She would just fade in and out as if she were checking on me. I never saw her outside the house, but at times I would look up at the sunroom windows from outside and would see her looking down at me. She would often wander the hallways. I always wanted to try to touch her, but I wasn't quite brave enough. There were numerous chances to see the spirit in different lights and angles as she traveled through the house, and while she looked familiar, I couldn't quite place her. My mother never said anything to me about her. I wondered whether she only revealed herself to me or my imagination was playing games. I remember many nights smelling her perfume and hearing the music as I was falling asleep. I couldn't see her, but I knew she was watching over me.

After about six weeks—I remember it was on a Saturday morning—I heard a knock on the door. I opened it to find Mr. Finnegan on the front porch holding a letter. "Good morning" he said. I returned the greeting. "Is your mother home?" he asked. I nodded, then turned and called for her. A moment later she came down the stairs. She smiled and said, "Hello Michael, what a pleasant surprise." I could tell she liked him by the way she was looking at him. She invited him in. As he walked past me I felt a cloud of coolness surround me and noticed some of the lights dimmed briefly.

In the weeks that followed, Michael was at our house more than he was away. I would come home from a friend's house to find Mom and Michael out in the yard or working on the house, either painting or cleaning. They really seemed to be getting along well. I couldn't put my finger on it, but something still bothered me about Michael. It wasn't until the other day when I caught him looking in our mailbox that I swear that I saw him remove a letter from it before he grabbed the rest of the mail and brought it to the door. I met him at the front door and he looked at me in a queer way, as if I had caught him doing something that he wasn't supposed to be doing. He smiled as he handed me the mail. I wondered if he had seen me looking at him as he went through the contents of the mailbox. He quickly called out to my mother as if he needed a distraction from my confronting him about his odd behavior. He continued past me toward the living room, where Mom was sitting watching television.

The next night I had gotten in late from a movie. I noticed as I walked down the hallway that my mother's bedroom door was open. I glanced in and was surprised to see Michael sleeping next to my Mother. He was over to the house a lot lately, but he had never spent the night before. I guess I had underestimated their relationship and my night out of the house gave them a rare opportunity for romance.

It was dark and it was late, so I really didn't trust what my eyes were seeing. Michael was on the bed closest to the doorway. When I looked in I had difficulty focusing on what I was seeing, but he looked transparent! I could see my mother through him on the other side of him. I moved slightly and the floor creaked beneath my foot. Michael's eyes opened and his body solidified. He looked at me and asked if I needed something. I replied, "No, I was just on my way to bed. Good night."

That was the beginning of many more sleepovers for Michael. In the days that followed I recognized the happiness in my mother's face and the spring in her step—she was definitely in love. I didn't want to spoil anything that was going on between them so I didn't bring up any of my suspicions about him.

I kept up the charade for weeks until I witnessed another incident that convinced me that there really was something wrong. I was sitting in the playroom when Michael walked by and stopped in the doorway. His words died midsentence and a look of horror came over his face. It was at that moment the smell reached my nose. The smell of perfume quickly flooded the room followed by the sound of the music. Michael left the room faster than the dog did. *What is going on with this guy?* I wondered silently.

After that incident it seemed that the frequency of Michael's visits decreased, and he never came near that room again. I also noticed that the old woman's spirit's visits increased. I was puzzled by the coincidence. What was the connection between the two? Her appearance seemed even fuller than before. I actually saw her full appearance, but only once. She was very solid that day, and wore her hair up in a bun tucked under some type of small, decorative hat. Her dress was long and dark; her shoes were laced up, but most of the time she was very translucent.

A cold winter night froze our pipes. It was then I began to realize that I wasn't just seeing things that weren't there. Mom called a repairman to the house. We waited for the plumber to arrive all morning. The house was cold. I sat at the top of the basement stairs and I peeked down to hear the plumber's conversation with Mom. They talked about basic plumbing problems until Mom asked if he had ever done any of the repairs on this house before. He looked around and said, "Oh yeah! This is the house that the lady swore was haunted. She lived here before you." I saw my mom's face turn white. The plumber asked her if she was okay. Mom hesitated, then answered that she was fine. I went to watch television so that she wouldn't know I had been listening. The repairman finished and left. Mom looked slightly shaken as she passed me and went up to her room. I wondered if she had also seen the apparition of the elderly spirit that wandered our house.

Sunday morning greeted me with the welcoming aroma of pancakes. I walked into the kitchen and found Michael and Mom at the kitchen table. They were holding hands and Mom smiled as she looked up at me. I sarcastically thought, *Great! They're getting married.* But I soon found out that my assumption was incorrect. "Michael and I want you to know that you are going to be a big sister." I forced a smile. I also felt relieved that I was getting a new sibling and not a new father. Not yet anyway.

A few days later I was walking home from school when I saw a number of pickup trucks parked in the driveway. As I got closer I saw that they were contractor vehicles. My mom was on the porch when I walked into the yard. I asked her what all the excitement was about. She said that she was going to have the sunroom redone as a nursery for the baby, but in the process of doing this the workers had discovered some termite damage. They determined that the work would be more extensive than they originally estimated. Mom walked me to the sunroom and showed me the plans she had, and I saw the men tearing at the walls and the floor.

Suddenly, Michael entered the room and pulled my mother aside into the living room. He looked angry. I followed to listen in and see if Mom needed me. I didn't hear how the argument had started, but I could hear the desperation in Michael's voice as it escalated. I moved closer to the living room door. The longer I listened the more confused I got. The argument was about the renovation my mom was having done on the sunroom. I thought to myself, *Why would Michael care about some construction work at a house that wasn't his?* Mom told him that there were signs of insect infestation and damage. The work needed to be done, and while she was doing the work she might as well upgrade it for the baby's nursery.

He fell to his knees and began to beg for my mother to abandon the work. He cried and grabbed her leg. I had never seen a man cry like that before. Then he said if she loved him she would stop the work. It seemed that my mother was moved by his words and tears because she turned and started to walk toward the door.

Then in a loud angry voice the word, "Stop!", echoed out. This voice stopped Mom in her tracks. My mother looked around the room. Michael's expression of desperation quickly changed to fright. My mother looked at me in disbelief. Then the voice spoke again, "In death as in life you're still a sniveling fool. Get up, you poor excuse of a man. You heard me!"

Then in the center of the room a faint glow appeared. It grew stronger as the moments passed. The light began to form into a defining shape. When the transformation was complete, we were looking at my grandmother. She was standing in the most peaceful of light. It was the tone of her voice and her words that cut through us like a knife. "Get away from my daughter, you parasite!" My mother moved next to me and put her arm around me, holding me tightly. "I'm sorry, dear, I didn't mean to frighten you," the apparition said to my mother, "but I am here to protect you from him." Michael stood and backed away.

"Did he tell you why he doesn't want you to renovate the sunroom?"

My mother shook her head.

"The reason is that his body is buried there. If you renovate the sunroom, the workers will discover his worm-ravaged carcass. When the authorities are notified to investigate, they'll remove his remains from here, and he'll be forced to cross over to the other side, and both he and I know he doesn't want that, knowing where he is probably going."

"Mother, how did his body get here?" Mom asked.

"Well, it's simple. I put him there after I killed him."

My mother let out a slight gasp.

"Don't worry, child. I'm not the monster that you are now picturing in your mind. It was all quite simple. This so-called man wooed his way into my life after your father died. I was lonely and he seemed nice. His guise of being helpful faded shortly after I let him into the house. He became possessive and overbearing. He insisted upon knowing my every move. He accused me of being unfaithful. It was when I broke it off and attempted to get him out of my life that he became violent. He wouldn't leave the house, and he struck me numerous times when I tried to call the police. He tore the phone from the wall. I thought that I was going to die right then and there. But what gave me the energy to fight back was you. During the argument you walked into the room. You were only about two years old. He was screaming at me and you began to cry. He turned his anger to you and pushed you to the floor. You cried even louder. I wasn't going to allow anyone to hurt you. I quickly scooped you into my arms and whisked you off to the bedroom.

"When I returned to the kitchen, I guess he had in mind that he was going to teach me a lesson. He struck me in the face with the back of his hand, sending me flying across the room and smashing my head into the counter. I had the advantage over him. I was mad as hell, and he didn't expect me to fight back. My anger grew, as did the welt on my head.

"My hands located a rolling pin. With my back to him, I heard his steps approaching. When I felt his presence within striking distance, I held the rolling pin tightly and swung it blindly as I turned. It struck him in the side of the head. It was the most disturbing sound I had ever heard, a dull crunching sound. He held his head as he stumbled backwards, screaming, and fell to one knee. I saw the blood stream through his fingers from the wound. I didn't want to give him the opportunity to recover and kill me. I hit him again. Then he screamed at me, even angrier than before. He reached out and grabbed my ankle. I swung downward and struck him on the back of the neck. The sound of the vertebrae cracking was hideous. He released his grip and fell flat to the ground. He was still alive, and then I heard his last gurgling breath. My back slid down the cabinet until I was sitting on the floor looking at what I had done.

"I got up, raced over to the sink and vomited. I don't know why I had that reaction because I felt neither sorrow nor joy. I felt relieved that we were safe. I don't know how long I looked at him, but I was there long enough to smell the scent of death creep into the room. I needed to figure out what to do with the body. I thought for a moment about calling the authorities, but I didn't want to take my chances of going to jail for defending myself. Then I thought about dismembering him and burying him in the back yard in multiple locations. I thought that was too risky. I might be seen or some of the local wildlife may discover him and dig him up. Besides, it seemed too involved to accomplish. I walked through the house. I went to the basement to inspect the walls; maybe I could hide him in the foundation of the house. It was as if God was listening and my prayers were answered. I found what I was searching for. There was a three foot access door at the north end of the basement that had been added as a crawl space under the addition on the house. That was it! I went back upstairs and grabbed Michael's legs. When I was dragging him across the floor I noticed the path of blood his head was leaving as I dragged him. I went over to the cupboard and pulled out a plastic trash bag, placed it over his head, and tied it with the shoe lace from my sneaker. That solved the problem of the blood staining the floor as I moved him. When I reached the top of the basement stairs, I rolled his body down, his dead weight providing the momentum I needed to get him where I needed him. I grabbed his legs and dragged him the rest of the way across the dusty basement floor to the access door. I opened it, crouched down, and pulled him. When he was all the way in and I was satisfied with his final placement, I began to pull at the soil beside him. I didn't stop digging until I created a grave sufficiently deep enough to hide his remains."

Then, without warning, Michael began to scream in agony.

"Oh no, it looks like someone found you. It's time to go now," my grandmother said. Michael began to fade right before our eyes, screaming until he was gone.

The voice of one of the construction workers distracted our attention away from Grandmother. "Ma'am, we seem to have a problem." He hesitated and stuttered. "We seem to have found a skeleton beneath the floor in the sunroom." My mother tried to look horrified. She told the man that she would call the police immediately. He left the room. We then both remembered about Grandma and looked for her, but she was gone! My mother called out to her, but there was no reply.

"Mother, what about the baby?" my mom screamed. Again, there was no response. That question reminded me that Mom was pregnant with Michael's baby. *How could that be?* There were other questions as well, like how did the body end up under the sunroom when it had been buried in the basement? Maybe she moved it later on. I guess we'll never know.

Mom went to the kitchen to call the police and report what the workers had found. I went to the sunroom and looked down through the floor to see the workers had used a backhoe to dig out the ground for the new foundation. The machine was about to dump its load of dirt when the men had discovered the skeletal remains in the freshly turned earth. It was an eerie site seeing it sit so neatly placed in the bucket of the backhoe, almost as if it had been tucked into bed for its eternal sleep.

* * *

In the months to come I never mentioned or brought up anything about Michael, or my concerns of complications relating to his being the baby's father. Her pregnancy seemed to be normal. I noticed her going through the usual motions of sitting on the couch reading, a book in one hand and the other resting on her belly as the baby moved inside her.

The day finally arrived. Mom's water broke. We jumped into the car and were off to the hospital. Mom felt the contractions increase in strength and frequency. It was fortunate that the hospital was close and the ride was short. She was rushed into a maternity room immediately. I waited outside when a nurse came out and said that my mother wanted me to be with her during the delivery.

It was about an hour later that a doctor and two nurses entered the room. The contractions were close, and it was time for my brother or sister to enter this world. The doctor was now controlling the speed of the delivery with his directions to Mom. It would only be a few moments now. The doctor told Mom to push. Three pushes later and the baby was on its way into this world. I was standing next to my mother, holding her hand and watching the doctor as he positioned himself. I knew it was time when I felt my mother's grip tighten. The doctor's hands reached out to receive the child. His expression changed from sober to dumbfounded. His eyes widened and his mouth dropped open. He looked as if he didn't know where to put his hands as they swayed from the left to the right. It was as if he had never done this before. The nurses screamed. A second doctor had walked into the room and saw the other doctor struggling. He quickly reacted, rushing to the other doctor's side and reached out to help.

I moved forward to see what was going on. I saw the four hands of the doctors juggling the baby in what I thought was amniotic fluid. I was terribly wrong. It was the baby! The baby looked like a normal baby, but its structure had the consistency of a raw egg. The doctors were struggling to keep it from slipping through their hands and falling to the floor. I could see the baby's shape and limbs, but it fell out of shape without warning and turned into an ever-changing, shapeless, gelatinous mass. The nurses were able to roll the infant delivery table alongside the doctors just before it slid through their hands.

As the two doctors stood over the table, they lost their fight to keep the baby in their hands and it slipped into the rolling basinet below.

The child's shape flattened and spread. The facial landscape of its features wandered beyond their normal boundaries. Its eyes and nose floated and moved around the confines of its head. One eye floated high, the other went below the nose, its mouth moved toward his right ear and turned. His left ear came to rest above his forehead. The doctors stood back from the delivery table, a look of horror on their faces as they looked down at this abomination of life. It began to cry.

PROGRESS

JAY WILBURN

He dropped open the barrel to his scattergun and thumbed one shot shell into each barrel and then locked the barrels back into the stock. He braced his back against the tree even though he could no longer feel it.

"Deep breaths," he whispered. "You're the man today. It is your fight today."

The men mounted the hill from the edge of the property. They had slaves with them walking their horses. Most of the white men walking in front were carrying hand weapons and hard-bullet guns. One of them was carrying a short-barreled, British riot gun.

Ten-year-old Benjamin Collin was standing alone amongst the tombstones of his family under the tree they called the Blue Dragon Oak because of the shape and shade of the branches and leaves. His left foot was sinking into the soft soil of his mother's grave. He was a riot of one, and he missed his mother more in that moment than all the days since her funeral in March, when the ground thawed after the bitter winter of 1857.

"Ben," the man in the lead called. "Go fetch your, Pa."

"He's out on business across the line in Virginia," Ben said.

"We must have just passed him on the road here," one of the men called. "How long has he been out of Kentucky, son?"

"Not your business," Ben shouted. "You lost the road. Track back to it, please."

The man in the lead said, "Ben Collin, watch your tone, boy. I'm Buck Chandler. Your Pa knows me. We need to search over your property for some runaways. Lower your fowler there and let us do our job."

"This is my family's property," Ben called. "You lower yours and turn about. You ain't looking nowhere without my Pa here."

"We got a right to search," one of the men yelled.

"Sounds to me like you're from Virginia. You got no rights on our property."

"They are here under my authority," Chandler said. "Don't make me take that barrel across your backside, Ben."

"That ain't how it works. You keep walking on me and I will show you."

The men stopped and stood across from the family plots.

"You can't shoot all of us," one of them said.

Ben braced the stock on his shoulder. "I don't got to shoot all of you. I drop Buck and you got no authority here. I can drop a couple more with the other barrel. I'm already standing by my mother's grave. My Pa will hunt down the rest of you afterward and they'll call him a hero for it."

"We know you're hiding slaves," Chandler said.

"We are not," Ben said. "One more step, Mister Buck, and I'll race you down to Hell."

The men on both sides of Chandler lowered their weapons and began walking backward. Chandler looked at the men retreating and sneered at the boy aiming out from the graves.

A Century Later

The brothers locked their arms around each other's heads and squeezed. When they could take it no longer, the younger brother drove his knee up into Benji's gut. The older brother grunted in pain, but didn't let go. Stoker drew his knee back to strike again. Benji pushed forward and broke a hole in the old plaster of the parlor wall. The faded wallpaper tore and they tumbled to the hard floor.

Stoker groaned. "Let go of me, Benji. We're almost fifty."

Benji climbed on top and wrapped his hands around Stoker's throat.

"Stoker, our father is turning in his grave over you trying to sell the land to the government. Traitor."

"You go to Hell." Stoker grabbed Benji's wrists to open up room to breathe. "It's only one road's width, you idiot."

Benji gritted his teeth as he pressed down. "Right down the middle… right through the Blue Dragon and our family's graves. How could you?"

"They will condemn it and take it if we don't sell it… get off me, Benji… get off."

Benji let go and started to climb off Stoker. The younger brother swung from the floor and clipped Benji across his jaw with a closed fist.

Benji bit his tongue and yelled. Benji threw his fist down twice. He connected with the orb of Stoker's eye once and the floor the second time. His knuckles came back bloody and misshapen. Stoker bucked his hips and then shoved his older brother off of him.

Stoker crawled under the cobbler's bench the Collin family had used as a coffee table since before they were born. He hit his head on the drawer under it as he went. He didn't fit as well at forty-five as he did when he was a kid escaping his brother's wrath.

Benji didn't chase his brother like he did when they fought as kids. He leaned back against the stiff cushions of the sofa that were crisp and yellowed from generations of smokers. He cradled his swollen knuckles and bit down on the inside of his cheeks. He was not going to recover as quickly at age forty-eight. When they were kids, their dad, Little Benjamin, would have had them both up by their ears and separated by now.

Their grandfather, Big Ben, would have done worse to end their squabble.

Stoker was up on his knees and leaning his eye on the nicotine-infused arm of the Admiral's chair with its plush upholstery stretched and held on by rows of tarnished fabric caps.

"It was this kind of nonsense that convinced Jolie to sneak off with the kids, Stoker."

"I doubt it," Stoker said into the arm of the chair.

"You do?"

"Yeah, I'm fairly sure it was spending half our lives struggling to break even on tobacco and the other half mashing corn into whiskey."

"Whiskey makes money," Benji said. "At least it did until Governor 'Happy' Chandler raised the tax on it last year."

Stoker dropped back on his butt with his back to his brother. "We weren't making real money on whiskey either since fifty-four... probably since dad died. The tax is just the death nail. It's 1957, Benji, and we'll be bankrupt before 1960."

"So you want to sell our family's land... a strip of land right through the middle of our fields... literally over the dead bodies of our parents and grandparents and..."

Stoker screamed into his hands. "And our great grandparents, and our infant sister and our drunk Uncle Marvin, and our own graves that just ain't been dug just yet."

Stoker heard his brother clamber to his feet and bark his shins against the cobbler's bench.

Benji shouted, "We gave up everything for this... everything, Stoker.

If that highway cuts through our farm, we are done. The Collin family... everything is gone."

"They will take it," Stoker said. "Eisenhower's earthmovers will not detour around our land and put a big elbow turn in the I-50 project for us. The cove is on one side and mountains are on the other. This highway will be good for Collin Cove, Kentucky, Benji... good for us... good for—"

Stoker heard the cobbler's bench topple over onto the wooden floor with a crash. The younger brother waited on his backside with his head down and his neck exposed. He waited for Benji to snap his neck or to smash the antique bench over the back of his head. He waited to see if his older brother had the nerve to finish it for the sake of the family farm. Stoker was afraid, but he was curious.

He felt the cold hands close around his neck. He was surprised that his brother was going to snap it after all. He was more surprised when his face was jammed forward into the wooden portion of the arm of the Admiral's chair. Blood blinded out his vision in his left eye. The chair fell and slid all the way across the room into the corner.

"Jesus, Benji," Stoker choked.

His face was pressed to the floor and he was held flat by his neck. The seam between two boards bit into his right cheek. Blood from the cut above his left eye ran down the creases in his forehead and over the bridge of his nose. He watched along the edge of the floor as the blood began to pool, but then seeped through the tiny gaps in the wood.

Stoker's airway began to close as the pressure spread around the sides of his neck. The tight fingers laced together in front and squeezed.

Stoker slid his left hand along the floor from his side. His fingers smeared through the blood, but kept going. He couldn't budge his head and he felt darkness closing in on the edges of what he could still see.

He ran his bloody fingers up against his neck. The skin was compressed and smooth. Parts of it were folded into tight lines. He felt his pulse throbbing in one of the arteries as he felt along the bare surface of his neck.

There were no fingers and there were no hands holding him. He was pinned to the floor by nothing. He raised his hand behind his head and grasped at the air. There were no wrists or arms.

As the world faded out, Stoker spied his brother across the room. Benji was against the wall. He was clawing at the wallpaper behind him. His fingers came within inches of the frame of their grandmother's painting that showed the farmhouse, the tobacco fields before half of them were switched to corn, and the drying houses in the distance.

Benji's feet kicked the side of the sofa in the air above the floor. As his heels connected with the wall where he was suspended, clods of dirt from the fields dropped away from the soles and the stitching of the material around each shoe.

As Stoker sunk into darkness, he was more curious than afraid.

* * *

Stoker felt far away as he woke up sitting in the Admiral's chair. He had been choked by Benji when they were kids, but never all the way out. He coughed and then regretted it when the inside of his throat exploded with raw pain.

He tried to blink the drying blood out of his eye, but the lid was pasted shut. He tried to reach up to rub it, but he couldn't get his hand to move. He opened his mouth to speak, and then closed it without trying. He swallowed over his dry throat several times.

Stoker started to remember Benji flying as he was blacking out. He looked up at the wall again. The painting of the farm was crooked on its nail. He always thought it was odd to have a picture of the house in the house. He knew his grandmother had painted it on the hill. If he could magically step into it and turn around, he would be looking at the poorly painted trunk and leaves of the Blue Dragon Oak.

Stoker saw the oblong puncture in the plaster and wallpaper where they had fought into the wall. If their father was alive, he probably would have whipped them even if they were forty and the man was full of tumors. If their grandfather was alive, he would have strung them up in the barn.

Most of their grandfather's lectures started with, "I didn't stand with my back to the Dragon when I was ten just so I could see..." They continued with a list of whatever crimes he had witnessed against property, family, or God. They ended with pain.

Stoker's fingers were going numb.

Little Benjamin was heavy handed as a father, but Big Ben played for keeps. The other kids down at the white kid's schoolhouse back when it was in the basement of the courthouse below the jail cells in Collin Cove had talked about their grandfathers letting them get away with murder. Stoker could picture the man murdering before he could imagine mercy. The kids in the colored school that had been over at Mrs. Cora's house thought Big Ben was an angel, bringing them supplies for schooling and toys for Christmas and birthdays to their fathers that worked the farm for the Collin family. Men came across the West Virginia line to work for Big Ben because of it.

Stoker saw the broader impression in the wall above and beside the couch. He eyed the distance from the floor to the damage.

He tried to stand but his wrists and ankles wouldn't come away from the chair. Stoker turned his head so he could look down with his good eye. The rope from the barn was coiled around his arms and legs, tying him to the Admiral's chair. He flexed his forearms and found no give. As he twisted his forearms, he saw the edge of the knot on the underside of the coils. It was a falconer's knot and a loop hitch that Little Benjamin called the Collin knot. Stoker had last seen it tied in the barn when he and his brother were punished for knocking a plow into the wall.

"Are you awake?" Benji asked, startling Stoker.

"Why did you tie me to the chair, Benji?"

Stoker groaned at the end of his question. He thought he could taste blood in the back of his raw throat. His head throbbed and his back hurt when he tried to turn his head.

"Look at me, stupid," Benji snapped.

Stoker felt himself about to cry again like he did when he was little. He lifted his head slowly and scanned the room. His right eye finally found Benji sitting in one of the kitchen chairs down the wall from the damage and the couch.

"Let me loose, Benji. I can't open my damn eye where you bashed my skull open."

"Look at me, stupid."

"I'm looking."

The arm of the chair creaked when Stoker tried to reach for his neck. He thought about trying to yank the arm of the chair loose and pictured himself beating Benji to death with it.

He looked up again and saw Benji's wrists looped and Collin knotted, too.

"What's going on?" Stoker whispered.

"You don't remember what happened?"

Stoker looked up at the wide dent in the wall and the crooked picture. He turned his head back to look at his brother. "Are we being robbed?"

"Do you not remember anything from last night?"

Stoker looked away from his brother to the front window. It was daylight. He looked up at the exposed bulbs in the hood above the parlor. The glass was broken. The stems were still screwed in and the twisted filaments showed through the jagged remains. Stoker looked down. The thin shards were scattered around the coagulated smears of blood on the floor. Other pieces were salted on the top of the cobbler's bench that had been set back up at an angle to the couch. Stoker saw fingerprints in the blood.

Stoker turned one hand over as far as it would rotate. Blood was dried brown across his palm and fingertips.

"Nothing that makes sense," Stoker mumbled. "I was out all night?"

"I thought you had a bleed inside your head or were in a coma," Benji said.

"You shouldn't have attacked me like that," Stoker grumbled.

"You still think I did this?"

Stoker looked at his brother tied to the kitchen chair. He tried to look over his shoulder at the kitchen doorway. His neck seared with pain that filled his shoulders and back. He turned his head back and squeezed his eye shut.

"What happened?" Stoker asked. "Are they still here?"

"Who? The invisible man?" Benji shouted. "I was up in the air like Superman for a half hour. I watched the chair drag in from the kitchen. The front door opened and rope dragged in from the barn. I was dropped in the chair. Before I could run, I got flung around the room like... a rag doll while you slept on the floor. Then, the rope tied me down."

Stoker opened his eye and raised his head. "I was choked out, you jackass. You always make yourself the victim even when you're not around. You are a selfish child, Benji. I hate you sometimes."

"Are you not hearing what I'm saying, Stoker?"

Stoker said, "You never stop talking, Benji... and you never start listening."

Stoker stared at the wall and the crooked picture of the farmhouse from the outside. He imagined himself looking through the stroke of blue for the window and seeing the Collin brothers tied into painted chairs in a painted parlor.

The picture scraped against the wall as it rotated on the nail. Stoker waited for it to fall. It came back level. The picture lifted slightly against the wall and then slid back down to rest on the nail.

"What in God's name?" he whispered.

Benji shouted, "You lifted off the floor and the chair picked itself up. I had to watch the whole thing while you were unconscious."

Stoker looked at Benji again. "Poor, poor Benji, having to watch me be beaten bloody and choked unconscious."

"I tried to get out and got knocked around, too... the back of my head got cut, Stoker."

Stoker laughed. "Typical."

"How is any of this typical?" Benji yelled.

"You're right, Benji," Stoker agreed. "Typically, when you run away, you succeed."

"What does that mean? And why are you saying this now?"

Stoker said, "You're trying to turn this whole highway mess back on me like I've just been sitting here relaxing and waiting for the general to come buy up our farm. I didn't run off to play football in college for a couple years. I was doing the work of two while you were flunking out."

Stoker heard glass moving on the floor. He looked down at the blood and broken bulbs. Nothing was moving.

"I didn't break your ankle, Stoker," Benji said. "I'm tired of being hung with every bad thing that ever happens to you."

"I worked the farm and watched out for your family while you were off at war," Stoker said.

He heard the glass again. Stoker glanced down. One piece was wobbling on its curved side.

"And was I relaxing on Nazi beaches, Stoker? Poor Stoker, had to stay home in his bed with my family while I was seeing the world, you spoiled brat."

The piece of glass slid and turned along the board. He stared at it until a greasy furrow dug itself through the caked blood. It reminded him of a plow cutting the earth, breaking the hard ground for tobacco or corn seed. The line was a finger-width thick. It was pulling through in both directions down to the wood of the floorboard. As the line reached bits of broken glass, the piece of bulb would be cast to one side or the other by the tiny, invisible plow. The furrow continued through the drying blood until it reached the edges of the smear on both sides.

"You got nothing else to say, brat?" Benji called.

"Did you see that?"

In the center of the trail through the blood, the board creaked and crackled. A crack formed in the exposed furrow like a scratch. It spread in both directions along the finger line drawn in the blood.

"What's happening?" Benji looked down at the floor from across the room.

Stoker looked up at his brother and back down at the floor. The board rose on one side of the crack and lowered on the other. The crack spread in sharp bursts along the floor board in both directions. When the split reached the end of the first board, a small, white scratch began to spread along the center of the next board. The first board separated up on both sides. The nails pried away from the crossbeams and dust wafted up from the crawlspace.

"What's causing this?" Stoker breathed.

"Is there something under the house?" Benji whispered.

Stoker looked down into the darkness, waiting for some monster in the crawlspace to reach its claw up through the gap. He looked over the break to the next board down the line. The scratch was clawing itself down deeper. Splinters were dug up from the floor one stroke at a time.

"This is happening on top," Stoker said. "What's doing this?"

Benji looked at the slow destruction across the center of the room. "Do you think this is about trying to sell the farm?"

"We're not selling the farm," Stoker yelled. "It's an easement for the road. We'll still own the land on both sides. They will use eminent domain to take the whole thing from us if we don't sell the piece they want. Damn it, Benji, did you learn anything in college before they kicked you out?"

The cobbler's bench screeched as it rotated back parallel to the couch. The broken glass on top bounced. A few pieces vibrated across and dropped off onto the floor.

Stoker breathed out through his nose.

Benji said, "You give away pieces and it's over, Stoker. We're going to farm with cars racing through the fields like the German Autobahn?"

Stoker stared at the table as he listened to the scratching spreading toward the walls along the floor. Even watching the movement through his one good eye, he was still grinding his teeth listening to his brother talk.

"Eisenhower was your man twice, Benji," Stoker growled. "He was talking about this freeway system during the election. Did you think he was kidding, dummy?"

"We can't make more money with less land," Benji said.

The crack reached the wall on both sides and split the baseboards. The floorboards pealed up away from the crossbeams. Cobwebs fluttered up in the opening. One black roach scuttled up over the moving boards and stalked across the floor over the bloody smear. Nothing else visible emerged from the floor.

"Your man is slapping his five stars on a fine, blue sign right on the side of... the side of I-50 between the corn and tobacco. Generals conquer land and your boy, Ike, has finished with Europe and he's starting on Kentucky." Stoker smiled as Benji looked down and heavy tears dropped into his lap.

"Shut up, Stoker," Benji said. "You never cared about this place or this family. You stayed because you were too much of a coward to leave. Don't blame me for still being here. I left and came back because I love what our family struggled to build and what they did with it. This highway is your excuse to finally escape. You were too scared to just go. You want this."

The crack traveled up the wall as flecks of plaster fell away through the broken sheets of wallpaper.

"You go to Hell, Benji," Stoker screamed and jerked against the chair.

It hopped once and the leg crunched back down on the head of the roach. Its back legs spasmed, kicking against its death. The arm of the Admiral's chair bent and pulled up slightly from the ancient glue in the peg slot.

"You go to Hell," Benji yelled, leaning forward in his chair.

Cracks spread out across the front glass of the parlor window. The crack on the other side began snaking across the ceiling.

"You chose this farm over your family. Jolie was miserable here and you were miserable being a father."

Benji snapped, "Shut your mouth, Stoker."

The crack reached the light fixture and the hood dropped down a foot, dangling from its exposed copper wires. The front glass rang as it washed out white. The crack spread up the wall above the window.

"I could see it on your face when you came back home from the war," Stoker sneered. "You'd rather have been killing Nazis than caring for those boys. You were relieved when you woke up one day and they were gone."

"I will feed you your teeth," Benji screamed.

The fixture fell and shattered against the floor. Most of the glass fell through the fissure into the crawlspace. The front window exploded into the room. Stoker hissed as it sliced across the back of his hands and over his cheek. He closed his good eye.

"This farm is already dead," Stoker roared.

Pieces of ceiling fell away around the floor. A split opened that looked up into Benji's bedroom, a room that used to belong to their parents. They heard the bed shift across the floor above them. Sparks spit out of the opening in the ceiling.

"You don't deserve this place," Benji yelled.

"I'm glad it's over," Stoker said with his eyes closed. "I hope they tear up every row and plow that damn dragon into the bodies. I hope they build a motel for poor, white, West Virginian trash. I hope it's full of hookers and communists and they forget how Collin Cove got its name."

Stoker felt the impact in his chest like a sledgehammer. He barked out all the air from his lungs as the Admiral's chair slid back across the floor into the wall. One of the arms broke loose from its peg and Stoker's arm fell limp at his side, still tied to the chair's broken arm. His eyelid came unstuck and he blinked both as he looked down at nothing.

He gasped for air. "Who are you?"

A piece of glass began to bounce across the floor. Stoker stared at it, trying to figure out if it was from the lights or the window. It left scratches in the floor as it slid toward his feet. The shard climbed up the chair leg, fraying the coils of rope as it went. It connected with the wood again. A deep line cut into the chair frame as it ascended the arm.

Stoker reached over with his free arm tied to the broken curve of wood and began pulling at the knot on the other wrist.

Sparks burst out from the ceiling again.

Benji called, "Stoker, what's happening? Do you think this is dad?"

Stoker kept pulling at the knot. "Did dad tie us up and threaten us?"

The glass traced along the coils of rope around his wrist. Two loops broke apart, giving Stoker some slack in the bond as he pulled the knot open. The sharp piece left the ropes and began traveling up the skin of his forearm. Stoker hissed in pain.

Benji caught a glint of sunlight off the glass slicing along his brother's arm.

Benji whispered, "Big Ben?"

The glass left Stoker's elbow. He got the knot loose and began unwrapping the coils from his wrist. The shard began cutting the upholstery as it sliced up the material behind his shoulder on the chair.

He leaned forward and began pulling at his ankles. He felt the glass gently cutting open the shirt over his back. He struggled with the rope as the shard bit into his back along his shoulder blade. The ropes broke along one ankle.

The glass pressed at his neck and did not stop. Stoker screamed as he felt the cold, invisible fingers closing again. Warm blood seeped from the wound under the cold grasp.

"Leave him alone," Benji screamed.

He rocked his kitchen chair and crashed into the floor. Benji bounced his head off the boards. The ceiling folded down, covering the painting over the couch. The bed and dresser crashed through two floors into the cold dirt beneath. Sparks rained down onto the sheets and the wires sizzled above their heads.

The glass shard dropped into Stoker's lap. He snatched it up and began slicing at the knot on his bound ankle.

Flame erupted on the bedding scattered in the crawlspace and smoke began wafting out of the broken section of ceiling.

The knot snapped and Stoker began pulling the coils loose. "The knot is always the weak point, you old coot."

Stoker heard the scraping across the room. He looked up and saw the cobbler's bench spinning through the flames. Stoker flattened and let the table smash through the remains of the Admiral's chair against the wall.

"So much for family." Stoker pushed up to his knees. He looked over at the broken window and then through the flames at his brother on the floor. Stoker ran and jumped across the gap. The fire made him groan.

At his brother's side, he began pulling at the knots on Benji's bonds.

"God," Stoker moaned. "That seems easier in the movies."

He had trouble getting the chair arm still tied to his wrist out of his way.

Benji raised his head off the floor. "Stoker…"

"Just get your arm loose," Stoker said. "We can work out our problems once we get far away from here."

"Stoker… no," Benji mumbled before he spit out blood.

"You still want to stay here after all this?" Stoker asked.

Benji's right hand pulled loose from the ropes.

"No," Benji said. "Behind you."

The rope that wrapped around Stoker's neck was singed and hot from the growing flames. Benji grabbed Stoker's wrist, but the rope pulled Stoker backward out of his big brother's grasp.

"Leave him alone," Benji screamed.

* * *

The picture snapped.

"I think we have it, Governor."

Happy Chandler stepped off the box. "That farmhouse would have been better than the tree. Please be sure no one finds out we're knocking that oak down. Where is the farmer? We want pictures that show us on the same side as the communities and landowners. Anyone know?"

"Sir, the property is bank owned. One of the brothers died in the fire."

"Perfect," Chandler said. "Let's load up and move down the route to the next farm before it gets to be 1958, shall we?"

"Yes, sir."

Chandler looked up at the long branch coming off the oak like a dragon's tail. Men were walking up the hill with shovels.

"What are they doing?" the governor asked. "Where's all that million dollar road equipment I spent Ike's money on?"

"They have to dig up the plots around the oak and move the remains and stones down to Collin Cove Baptist, sir."

"God, help us," Chandler muttered. "Aren't those bodies from the War of Northern Aggression? How much remains remain?"

"Well, like I said, sir, one of the brothers died in the fire before the family lost the farm this year..."

"Jesus, Mary, and Joseph," the governor whispered. "Get the press loaded back up quick before we end up with a story about paving over the dead."

Up on the hill, the workers carried their shovels on their shoulders as the governor and the press walked away below them.

"Should we start with the fresh one? The dirt will be loose."

"I don't know. Let's pry up these old stones first."

"We have to dig down for the bones."

"Says who?"

"Says Chandler... and the feds... and God, I'm guessing."

"I think we dug down six feet and found nothing left. Don't you guys remember that?"

"Sounds good to me, boss."

The shovel cracked across the foreman's face.

"What's wrong with you?"

"I didn't do that."

The shovels began smashing into kneecaps and skulls. One of the workers slammed face first into the trunk of the tree. He turned around and tried to run, but the shaft of the shovel pressed into his throat. He felt his trachea cracking.

Stoker looked up from the kid on the trunk into the branches. His father, Little Benjamin, was tied to the Dragon's tail under his arms. His mother was tied next to him, dangling from one wrist. Other relatives he had seen only in pictures were tied to other branches by their waists, legs, or arms. All of them were tied using the Collin knot.

All of them were tied with Collin knots except for Stoker. He was hanging from the Dragon's tail by a charred noose. He continued to claw at the knot behind his head, but ropes didn't have weak points for him anymore.

Stoker looked back down at the ten-year-old pressing the shovel into the worker's throat until the worker's living arms went limp. Ten-year-old Ben held the worker a while longer.

* * *

Down the hill, Benji stared out from the ruins of the house. He looked from the governor's vehicles weaving away on the dirt road to the action on the hill by the Blue Dragon. The worker's hands fell away from the shovel across his neck. He dangled from the tree as the other men lay across the family plots.

"Good luck knocking down that tree," Benji whispered. "He's been defending it for a hundred years now."

Benji looked down at the painting in his hands. It was charred at one corner, but survived better than the house. He tucked it under his arm and walked out from the opening beside the porch.

"If anyone can stop I-50, it's Big Ben," Benji muttered.

He looked back up in time to see the last worker slide down the tree. The shovel blade stabbed itself into the soil between graves.

COLD CALLING

LISAMARIE LAMB

It was probably because I was paying so much attention to the cat that I missed it. It was a skinny little ginger thing, and it had a pink nose. I'd never seen a cat with a pink nose before, which is why, as I walked up the blocky path to the front door, I was looking at the cat instead of where I was headed. I'm sure anyone would have done the same, especially as that damned cat was tap-tapping at the door with a quiet determination to get inside. I was fascinated.

I reached up and pressed the doorbell, all the while enjoying the cat's persistence. I knew how it felt. That door tapping and hopeful waiting— the life of a door-to-door salesman. Except the cat had nothing to sell. I had my paintings.

I only looked up after I'd actually rung the bell, and that's when I saw it. The sign, homemade and stark, stuck to the teeny tiny porch window with failing browning tape; *NO cold callers, NO hawkers, NO canvassers.*

That was me all rolled up into one crude, rude sign, and I'd already made my presence known. A long-fingered hand gripped at my heart and squeezed, my legs trembling with the strength of it, my bowels fluttering with the fear of being caught disobeying. I was good, I played by the rules, and I was terrified of being in the wrong place, in the wrong situation, or just generally in the wrong.

Could I have walked away? Yes. Oh, yes, but that would have been an awful thing to do. To ring a doorbell and run away, it was childish, silly, and cruel. I wouldn't be a part of that. And besides, what if the neighbors saw me? What if someone caught me? I had to stand my ground, I had to explain myself… I had to stop looking at the bloody cat and pay attention to what was happening.

Five, four, three—I counted down, and told myself that when I got to zero I would walk away, having waited long enough—two, one, zero. No one opened the door, so I should have walked away. I should have just left; the cat could fend for itself. Whoever lived in the end terrace house obviously wasn't at home. It worked out okay like that. It was the best outcome.

I didn't leave. The cat—all whiskers and feet, its body tiny, its tail, now that I looked at it, kinked and flicking about in the air and waving dejectedly—weaved around my feet, pushing hard against my calves and my ankles, dipping down low, that pink nose almost scraping along the path. Stupid cat. I decided I didn't like it; there was something too know-ing, too human about the creature, and the way it was trying to burrow into my skin, deep down into my very flesh, was unnerving.

And then it stopped.

And that was worse.

Something about the set of its shoulders, the sudden straightness of its formerly broken tail, the grin—yes, a grin. Cats can smile when they want to. I know you've heard of the Cheshire Cat. The grin on its furry face made my stomach clench and my hands sweat. My art portfolio, shiny and black, a burden on the bus with its thick plastic handle, dug into my skin, and the whole thing slipped from my grip. It landed with a splat and a slap on the ground, just missing a pile of something brown—I hoped it was mud but knew it was not. The cat didn't move. It glared. And then it threw a hind leg into the air and began to lick it, viciously, manically, as though the waft of air that had draped across it when the portfolio fell was contaminated and filthy.

When its tongue moved lower, towards its balls, I looked away. I looked to the side and up, to the front door, and that's when I saw her. An old woman. Ancient. So bent over that her hunched back rose above her dipped shoulders like a second self, casting a separate shadow across her face. Her hair was as thin as gossamer thread and whiter than snow, only not as beautiful. Not beautiful at all. She was staring at me with colorless, half-closed eyes.

Christ knows how long she had been standing there, watching me watch the cat lick its privates, but the expression she wore on her wizened face was not a happy one. It was not friendly. It was not welcoming. It belonged, I could tell, to the person who had stuck that stark sign up in the first place.

"Ah, hello, I'm sorry to have disturbed you," I said it in a high-pitched, reedy kind of voice, most unlike my own, yet it seemed to fit the moment. And I was sorry. Very sorry. I'd never been sorrier. All I wanted to do was not be there. I almost ran.

I wish I'd run.

But instead of running like a school kid, I stood, grinning awkwardly, red cheeks flaming bright with embarrassment and shame at having inconvenienced her. I bent down to retrieve my portfolio, not daring to look at the damage the concrete driveway had inflicted upon it, my body shying away from the cat, sure that if I touched it, it would let out with a yowl and attack me.

I thought, perhaps, the woman would do the same if I didn't get a move on.

"I pressed the bell by mistake," I added to fill the dangerous silence. "I didn't see the sign."

The woman sniffed, a long, hard, liquid sniff. She swallowed loudly. "It's not exactly easy to miss." Her voice was full of cobwebs, dusty from underuse, and after she spoke, she flicked out a tongue, cracked and yellowed with age, and licked her upper lip, which was hairy, whiskers sprouting from it just like her cat's face. As she ran her tongue across her lips, the hairs glistened with saliva in the sunlight.

I looked at the empty space to the side of her head and coughed, hoping that I wouldn't have to see anything anymore foul than that.

If I had known then... but I didn't, nor did I imagine anything worse.

I sensed movement, a slow and painful creaking of an arm being raised. The woman. This ancient woman. She lifted her hand and rested it heavily on my wrist, her fingers, gnarled and haggard, clamping around it, the long, jagged nails digging into my skin, making it sting and itch and crawl.

"You're selling something?" She nodded at my portfolio, and I heard her bones crack and creak beneath her thin skin.

And still I stayed where I was, rooted to my fate with my sense of propriety. "Oh, it's nothing. Just some art. Paintings. Nothing at all, I should really go—"

But by God, the crone was interested. Her grip tightened and she tugged me towards her, a tiny movement, so small that I wasn't even sure it had happened at first. Not until she did it a second time. And then she said the words I'll never now forget: "Come in, won't you? Have a cup of tea and a slice of cake, and show me why you're here. Sit down and have a chat with me. It won't take long."

It won't take long.

And I believed her, and although I was still embarrassed, and not a little sickened by the witch herself, I still nodded. How could I refuse? I had no pressing appointments, nowhere to be, no one to see, and I had paintings to sell. I never was a good judge of people. I never was a good judge of anything, so I allowed myself to be taken inside, into the deep and dirty darkness of the dingy, narrow hallway.

"Close the door, would you?" the old woman asked, and I did as I was told, pushing the door shut. It clicked heavily and the sound echoed in the dimness. The last thing I saw of the outside world was not the sun or the sky, or scudding clouds. It was not trees or birds or cars driving past. It was that mangy ginger cat, its tail twitching. It blinked at me as I disappeared inside, and for an instant I would have said that it seemed like nothing. Insubstantial. Ragged and doomed as though death were upon it.

A strange thought.

A terrifying thought.

As the image passed across my vision and seeped into my brain, I shuddered and my chest clutched together tightly, hardly allowing space for me to breathe. But breathe I did, and with enough breath I spat out words that were important to me at the time. "Your cat, is it all right? I mean, it seems a bit…" *Dead. It seems a bit dead.* "A bit sickly, perhaps."

The old woman snorted unpleasantness. "I don't have a cat."

And that was that.

I was left to wonder about it as she directed me to a sagging armchair in the dark living room. I sat, but as I did so I saw the stains, the holes, and the dirt. I didn't want to touch anything, and the more I looked around, the more I noticed the filthiness. The woman was just as filthy. Her skirt was torn, her tights laddered, and her blouse decorated with leftovers from numerous messy meals. Her fingers were black with grime.

The sofa was placed next to a gas fire that was humming on low even though it was only the end of summer without any chill in the air. A coffee table was directly in front of me, and the room was so small my knees pressed against it. Upon it were placed plates of cakes—Cherry Bakewells and French Fancies—and there was a pot of tea, still hot, on a silver tray. None of it was terribly clean.

"Are you expecting visitors?" I asked, innocent and uncomfortable.

"Only you," was the reply, which made no sense. Still, I reasoned, why should it? Why should it, indeed? Here I was, a stranger, asking questions and invading the woman's privacy, ignoring her quite clear instructions regarding interruptions, so why should she deign to answer me in anything but riddles? The idea that she was playing with me gave me a sense of relief; to know that she was fully aware of everything was good—I was not in the presence of madness.

I smiled at her. "Okay. All right. Only me then." The teapot, the glaze hazed with tiny cracks, the whiteness now a nicotine yellow, happily huffed steam and I pointed to it. "Would you like me to pour you a cup?"

The woman shook her head. "I don't drink tea. But help yourself."

She plumped herself down into the armchair opposite me and played with the hairs on her chin, stroking them, pulling at them, rubbing her thumb across the stubs of newly growing whiskers. In order not to see, I focused on making tea. There was no way I could wipe away the layer of dust in my cup without causing offence, so I did not. My stomach complained, and my throat constricted, but I continued regardless. I would be a good guest.

I went with milk first, as my grandmother had taught me, but I tipped too much into my cup in my anxiety and could do nothing about it without looking like a fool. Flecks of grey floated. Lifting the teapot gently, I held the lid on with one hand and poured with the other. Dark amber liquid trickled out, immediately turning a too-light beige when it mixed with the milk. I normally had sugar, but I hardly dared to spoon it in for fear of spilling the lot. Besides, I could see the spoon resting in the bowl had been used recently—or perhaps not so recently—clumps of brown sugar clung to it, and it made me hesitate.

I reached for a cake instead, hoping that would do as well as a spoonful or three of sugar in my tea. The old woman watched me, her eyes watering at the corners, and for a moment I thought she was crying. But then she smiled, her dried lips cracking and splitting and spots of bright blood popped up, sprinkling what was left of her teeth. "I got them in specially," she said, nodding at the plates of cakes. "For you."

"Okay." I hadn't taken a bite yet, and found that her words, as innocent and kind as they might have been, sent a shock of fear through me. What was I doing here? I had to leave, to breathe fresh air again, to feel clean. A fly buzzed on its back, dying on the tea tray. I started to replace the cake back down onto the table, but she stopped me, shaking her head and muttering, "Don't be rude, boy. Eat your food, boy."

"I'm sorry, I'm so sorry," I gushed, transported back to childhood with all its nonsense rules and hierarchy. I plunged my teeth into the thick, sweet icing, my gums aching from the sugar coating. My tongue swept the roof of my mouth to remove the pasty remnants. I don't know how I swallowed, but the stuff went down at least partway, lodging in my chest.

I drained my tea to wash it down and only succeeded in trapping it further as I spied the muck at the bottom of the cup.

"Now," the crone continued, "tell me about yourself. Your paintings."

I had forgotten about the paintings. The strangeness of the house, of the woman, the smell—musty and dusty—and the dirt was making me groggy. But her request brought me back, and for that I was grateful; if I was talking to her I wouldn't have to eat anything for a while.

"I paint imagination," I told her, sounding pretentious, but it was the truth. No rolling landscapes for me, no staid portraits. I transposed what I saw in my mind to the canvas and sold it. That is what I did and that was all I did. "Would you like to see?"

It was easier to show her than to explain.

The old woman considered the question. I saw her glance around her, checking the clock, or so it seemed. Who else was coming to this tea party? I hoped we were alone in the house, and then I wished that we weren't. I hauled my portfolio onto my lap and unzipped it, flinging it open and presenting the first painting. It was a swirling, whirling ball of flames, and in the middle of it was a face, crying out in agony, wanting to be free. "This one's called *Life*. It's rather dramatic. Not all of my work is like this." Except that it was; everything was over the top with colors and themes because that was what was selling. I didn't have a style; I painted what made money.

"Show me more."

I did. I turned over page after page of paintings, a palette of shades running from reds through greens and blues, purples to greys and black. She stopped me once. There was a deep red picture, the entire page filled with the one color, and on top, randomly spaced, there were stars of gold. At the very top, half hidden, was a hand. It appeared to be reaching down, through the redness, but had failed, the fingers beginning to melt away, dripping like candle wax, leaving a smear of yellow beneath them instead of the shadow that might have been expected.

"I like this," she declared, placing her own hand over the imagined one. "I'll take it."

"Are you sure? You don't even know how much." I was surprised, to say the least. It wasn't one of my better efforts, in my opinion, a rather quickly dashed off scribble done in a fit of pique one day when I had better things to do but felt guilty if I didn't create something. But then, there was no accounting for taste.

The old woman shrugged. She stood, every bone cracking and snapping together. "You have some more tea."

She shuffled from the room, a wake of dust motes left behind her. I tried to remember the colors, the light, the feelings, so that I could paint this scene later. It would be a good one. It might even be an important work.

Alone, I allowed myself to relax somewhat. I even leaned back against the crusty cushions and closed my eyes, the heat of the fire in such a small, close room making me sleepy. I remember being glad that I had made a sale. Sad that it was a poor painting.

And that was it.

That was the end for me.

I dreamt then, and I screamed in the space between awake and asleep. One person heard me, the old woman, dead so many years now, her body turned to dust and covering the house she had lived and died in, but she refused to come back. I had let her leave, and she let me have my nightmare.

In my dream, or out of it, I watched myself sleep. I saw the world turn as I dozed, my eyes flickering every now and then, and that's when I cried out to my somnambulant self to wake up, wake up, live, stop dreaming your life away! But it made no difference. I ran to the door, but my hand wouldn't grip the handle, it simply passed through it as though it was nothing. The cat, still outside, yowled at me, it alone knew I was in the house, it alone wanted to come inside, but I couldn't help it. I couldn't help myself.

When I returned to my sleeping body, I had aged. Grey hairs sprouted from my head, my face, lines criss-crossed my forehead and the corners of my eyes and mouth. My hands, once so lithe and long-fingered, once so artistic, were now crippled and cursed with arthritis. And still I slept.

My soul—I suppose that's what I was—crossed to the window, searching, searching. I could see the world, and I could see myself out in it. A version of myself. I stood in a gallery, my paintings surrounding me, being applauded. I had money, plaudits, awards... I was a great artist. And there, my true masterpiece. It hung resplendent on a wall all to itself; a painting of a room, small and cramped, dust motes floating in front of everything, sparkling, tea for two set out neatly on a low, dark coffee table. And at the edge of the canvas, just disappearing out of view, the hunched and folded back of an old woman. Her head half turned, a twinkle of her vicious eye, a smile on her evil mouth.

It was called *Destiny* and the world was in love with it.

If I had painted it, I would have been proud.

But I did not paint it.

I knew that. For how could I have? I had been sleeping for decades, snoring on a sofa covered in the grime of neglect and the remains of the old woman. And my soul, trapped as it was, could only watch as someone else lived my life. She had stolen everything. "I'll take it," were her words, and I had assumed she meant that painting, but no, she had meant so much more than that.

I understood it all and understood too much.

I returned to the living room to watch myself die. Wizened and wasted, bright white hair, what was left of it, and a sagging lip. My eyes leaked tears of age. My heart stopped beating. Old age. It takes us in the end. And after that dust becomes dust once more, as I did, as the old woman did.

And then there is nothing until the bell tolls.

When I awoke from death, it was cold and it was dark, and something was ringing in my ears. A bell. Distant sounding, but getting louder. And then cutting off abruptly. I blinked with rheumy eyes, mucus sticking my lips together, and saw a small living room, a fire, burned out long ago, a pot of old, cold tea, and a plate of moldy cakes. I reached out to them with old hands, unsure, wanting to know if they were real, and as I did so, they came alive, the silver shone and the tea was hot. The cakes looked fresh and whole again. The fire popped to life, a low heat emanating.

Just right for a visitor.

The ringing that had awakened me still clanged in my head, and I knew, then, that someone had made the same mistake I had all those years (or was it only days?) ago. A bright, fresh-faced young man at the door rang the bell and doomed himself because I would do as had been done to me. I would take his life. I would make it mine since mine was stolen so cruelly, and he could wait here in the dirt for his own visitor.

I stood, a slow and painful process, and I hoped against hope that whoever was at the door had not departed. Perhaps the cat would keep it occupied. Perhaps that is what it was there for, to lead the unwary up the garden path, and to allow for lives to be made from nothing.

Or perhaps it was just a stray cat.

Whatever it was, as I opened the door—my hands able to grasp the handle now, renewed strength in my ancient claws—I saw it, small, ginger, pink-nosed, weaving itself around your legs, its tail waving. It looked more alive now than the last time I had spotted it, when the door closed on me, and I felt a great affection for it, a reminder of my old life.

You were afraid of me, and I understand that. I am older than anyone has a right to be, even though I am still young. I am dead, even though I am still here for you. My friend. My soulmate. Myself.

Come in, won't you? Have a cup of tea and a slice of cake and show me why you're here. Sit down and have a chat with me. It won't take long. Don't mind the cat. I don't have one.

FACE IN THE WINDOW
MARK LESLIE & CAROL WEEKES

The dog usually barked at strange sounds in the night, but this time she simply sat up, the hair on her back bristling, and bolted up the stairs toward the bedrooms. Ron Nathan listened as her nails slid over the hardwood floors. Judging from the direction of the sounds, she was scrambling under his bed.

"Casey?" he called out to the terrier.

She let out a mournful bark, then went still.

"What the hell?" He snapped his paperback closed and placed it on the coffee table, glancing at the clock on the wall. It was a few minutes after midnight. He became aware of just how quiet the house was when the refrigerator clicked on in the nearby kitchen, making him jump.

Casey's actions had raised goose bumps on his arms because she never acted this way. Clearly, something significant had frightened his companion of five years. He understood that a dog's acute hearing could detect even minute changes well beyond the human auditory system, and he fought the urge to soar up the stairs after her and join her under the bed.

"Casey!" he commanded, hoping to entice her back downstairs so that he could pick her up and carry her outside and show her that nothing was wrong. The only times he'd seen her this frightened was when powerful summer storms shook the house with their crashing thunder. It was autumn now, the storm season long past. Occasionally someone would trek through his property, which cut a wide expanse between the woods and the road, or an animal would come sniffing around for food; raccoons mostly, sometimes foxes or coyotes. It wasn't an unusual thing around here. His house, what had been a neglected bed and breakfast Victorian affair dating back to the late 1800s, sat by itself on almost ten acres of land, most of it consisting of thick forest and a rambling field, one edge of which terminated at a robust flowing river.

Ron thought about the most regretful incident that happened a few nights ago—but that was over now.

He went to move towards the stairs and bedrooms when a crash from the back of the house made him issue a short, high scream. Casey emitted a low, rumbling snarl that carried all the way downstairs. He ran into the kitchen and onto the back porch to stare out across a yard that, despite the porch lamps, was swept in shadows.

Leaves drifted down from the maples and oaks festering in the yard. A harvest moon illuminated sections of the yard in long, gold slashes. A gust of wind whistled, picking up the leaves, breathing life into them once more and giving them one last ride before they began their slow decay and return to earth. It was a moist, but cool early November night, as if the season could not decide if Indian summer was over yet. For a moment he thought he saw a face forming in the swirl of leaves and grass. He blinked and it was gone.

Irritated, he circled the side of the house and discovered one of his trash cans toppled, the lid off and the contents—mostly meat bones, vegetable peelings, and soggy paper towels—spread over the ground.

"Damn raccoons," he said, glad for the sound of his own voice. Whatever had been here was gone, likely back into the woods. He re-placed the lid and stood up, perusing the house he had purchased less than two months ago. It had solid brick construction, gothic with its steeped window caps and heavy leaded stained glass. Its front sat hidden under the sweep of a full-length covered porch. Even in a town like Old Dundas, it had been quite a catch for the price, a mere $100,000 for a house with fifteen expansive rooms and a fully finished attic.

He went to turn back when the crack of a branch snapping from his right caught his attention.

"Hey?" He whirled to face the clot of shadows in the back yard again, and noticed what looked like the tail end of someone's plaid shirt moving past the west corner of his house. "You there! Wait a minute!"

He broke into a run, determined to catch the culprit rummaging around in his trash at night, and experienced a flashback to that other incident.

Things don't happen the same way twice, he thought. Still, he shivered. Similar incident—similar time, but this time the shiver had nothing to do with the weather.

He reached the corner of his house in time to see the back of a man sprinting with great difficulty towards the edge of the woods that led towards a creek, and ultimately, the distant river. The form looked familiar, wide, low shoulders, shaggy head, arms swinging in a simian manner... and the thought crossing his mind told him that what he was imagining was impossible. If only he could see a face, he'd know for certain—yet the idea of it terrified him.

"Lucas?" he called out, incredulous.

Trees swallowed up the form, replacing it with mysterious darkness and the sounds of disturbed birds.

He moved back inside, locked the kitchen door, and shut the curtains over the window above the sink. He went through the house doing the same in every room, feeling lost. On one hand, whoever it had been wouldn't be able to see inside now, but at the same time Ron wasn't able to see if the stranger returned. Consoling himself that Casey would let him know if the person came back, he found his shotgun and loaded it. He put the gun and the box of ammunition on a low trunk near his bed, then got down on his knees and gently pulled Casey out from her sanctuary. She was shaking and he could smell her fear like the wet, sodden odor of rotting fruit.

Nonetheless, he tucked her into bed, and, fully clothed, slid under the covers himself. When he closed his eyes he tried, unsuccessfully, not to think about Lucas Mallory, whose funeral was scheduled for the next day.

* * *

Lucas Mallory, one of Ron's nearest neighbors, had been a local town drunk. When Ron first moved into the house, Lucas would often stumble, drunkenly, onto Ron's property in the middle of the night, kicking over the garbage cans, tossing beer and whisky bottles about and just being a general nuisance. H would often pass out in the middle of Ron's yard and wake up around noon—leaves stuck to the side of his face—to stumble back home in search of another drink. Lucas' entire family had a reputation for bad drink, rape, incest, and creating trouble. The *trouble* turned out to be unusual, too, based more on town gossip than any fact Ron could discern.

"They're known for dabbling in witchy crap," John Lacey, who owned the local Sunoco in the center of the town, told him after Ron began having problems with the old man's midnight visits.

"Witchy crap?" Ron had asked, mildly amused. "How do you mean?"

John lowered his voice. "Witchcraft. Spells. Magic. Rituals. Don't laugh at it. There are others in this town who've gone to bed with their lamps on and their weapons loaded... not that it did some of them any good in the end. Guns can't protect you from the shadows of evil."

John slid the gas nozzle back onto the pump, shut it off, and made change for Ron's twenty. "No one knows why some of the stuff around here has happened—only that it happened. We tend to just leave it alone and continue on with our daily lives. Let me give you a word of advice. Don't fight with him. Just let him stumble past. Call the police if you must, but don't deal with him personally."

Ron snorted. "The shadows of evil? Come on, John. You seem like a reasonable man to me."

"Oh, I am that," John conceded. "It's them Mallory folk that ain't. You didn't know Norton Chisholm. His father owns that farm just up the road from yours. Well, one of Lucas' brothers—he has nine of them, all the devil's spawn if you ask me, and one sister—tried to use the Chisholm barn to conduct their rituals. They were killing chickens, of all things, spreading the blood over the doorstep to the farmhouse, near the barn. Farm animals began to die at first. Cattle giving premature birth, animals attacking each other and doing enough damage to warrant euthanasia. Then things began to happen in the house. An electrical fire, Norton's wife falling down the stairs when she felt *something* trip her in an empty hallway in the dark. All this after Norton discovered Gary Mallory trying to feel up some young local girl in the loft of that barn. He run him out, like anybody would have done, the girl crying and, as it turns out later, pregnant. She didn't last to see her pregnancy out, either. Car accident. I say it wasn't an accident. She was talking against Gary, telling everyone he raped her."

Ron frowned, pocketing the ten from his change into the fold of his wallet. "No one's living at that farm now."

"That's right. They moved out, but they can't sell the property. It ain't big enough to prosper like large farms these days. Big farms are corporations. There's the competition factor. No one around here would take it, even if it was a gold mine. It's a piece of land that comes with a weight. They couldn't sell it to a local for a dollar, and we don't get too many new faces around here. Take my advice: most people wouldn't talk to you about this. They're afraid of retaliation. So let's just keep this between us." He lowered his voice again. "And be careful."

Ron had driven home. Before he reached his house, he slowed his car and stared at the two-story clapboard structure less than a mile up the road from his place. The only thing that sat between them, on the opposite side of the road, was a small Presbyterian church and a small, dated graveyard full of faded stones. He'd gone in there the first week he'd moved in, curiosity drawing him to read the weathered epitaphs. There'd been some Mallory's, set off by themselves, away from the others. Perhaps they'd requested it that way.

"Just leave me alone," he said to the Mallory house.

Lucas was back two nights later, loud and carrying a half-filled beer bottle in his hand. It was Casey who heard him first, and she let out with a string of raucous barking. It was the beginning of it. He should have listened to John's words, but he'd been too angry, and the fury of the moment had carried it to its conclusion.

The beer bottle came whistling through his den window as if to announce, in no uncertain terms, the stroke of midnight, breaking antique glass and sending diamond-like shards all over the rug. Ron had gone racing out, spying Lucas swaying in the front yard, talking a stream of babble as if there were a group of people all hard of hearing standing before him. Then, his liturgy suddenly over, he turned and relieved himself in the yard, sending a steady stream of yeasty urine into the grass.

"God damn you, stay the hell away from me!" Ron bellowed at him. "Go on!" He descended on Lucas and the older man glared up at him, eyes looking like the hunted glare of a tracked wolf. Three days of peppery beard coated his face and throat. He'd spilled beer down the front of a flannel lumber jacket. He reeked of hops and unwashed filth.

"Piss on you," Lucas hurled at him. He hocked a wad of phlegm into his mouth and spat it out at Ron. It landed on Ron's cheek with a wet smack.

Enraged, Ron shoved Lucas with an open hand, sending him sprawling backwards onto his ass. Lucas's hands scrabbled madly in the grass and found a stray branch that had come loose from one of the big maples during the previous evening's storm. He flung it at Ron, whipping him hard on the side of the face. Ron recoiled in pain.

"Bastard," he snarled, losing his self-control. He booted Lucas in the leg, rolling him over the lawn. Lucas promptly vomited, but he managed to get up. He whirled and flung a series of wild punches in Ron's direction. Ron punched back, again and again, moving the drunk over his front yard towards the side of the house. Finally, smart enough to know he'd been bested, Lucas dropped his fists, turned, and ran.

"Get out of here!" Ron managed, despite a sudden sharp pain in his solar plexus. "I see you on my property again, I'll call the police." Lucas stumbled off in the direction of the woods. He debated whether or not to follow him and drag him back to the road, or just let him go. *Let the moron get lost in there*, he decided. Spending half the night lost in the woods might cure him of his destructive behavior.

Lucas didn't return home that night. Drunk and disoriented, he stumbled through the woodlands, roaming deeper where the light blinked out beneath dense foliage, to tumble into the tributary linking its way up with the wider expanse of the river.

Lucas' sister, Rebecca Mallory stood outside Ron's door the next morning.

"What did you do with him?" she demanded. She might have been in her forties or her eighties. Long, silver hair fell over her shoulders in knots. She wore a pilled dark green wool sweater pulled over a skirt and ankle boots. Blue eyes like ice chips burned out at him. "I know he was here last night. Tell me the truth, Mister Nathan, because I'll find out. I'll know."

He regarded her with disgust. "Get off my property—that's what I told him, too. Your brother's a drunk, coming around here and disturbing me. Last night he broke a window with a beer bottle. I should be the one at your door, with a bill of damages. I chased him off and he went into the woods over there. Don't worry, he'll come back to you, I'm sure. Unless he has a stash of liquor in the woods somewhere."

She didn't step back, but held her ground. "It's autumn. Nights are getting colder. I had a dream. I dreamt that Lucas is no longer of this world, thanks to you. I thought I'd talk to you first, just so you'd know."

Casey moved near them, growling. He shooed the dog away with his foot, prepared to physically remove her from the porch if she didn't back off. "So I'd know what?"

"That you helped kill my brother."

Ron discovered the body later that day while walking Casey through the woods. It had been their normal pleasant afternoon walk when all of a sudden Casey had picked up a scent and bolted past bramble and alder towards the water. Hustling along behind her as quickly as he could, Ron discovered a downed tree and the dimpled, pallid flesh of Lucas Mallory, his clothing snagged on a branch, his head beneath the water.

He screamed at Casey and turned back in the direction of the house to call the police...

... and found the Mallory woman standing in the leaves, watching him stoically. He hadn't heard her approach, neither had Casey. In a woods like this, with the ground covered in dry leaves and branches, that shouldn't have been possible.

"What are you doing here?" he yelled at her. "I came looking for him to see if he'd passed out anywhere." He shook, both from the crisp breeze that had dropped in degree overnight, and from an inner chill, remembering John Lacey's words. *Let's just keep it between us… and be careful.*

"It seems to me like you knew what you were looking for," she retorted reproachfully.

Ron took a step back, feeling as if her eyes were working their gaze between his garments and his skin, then between his skin and his muscle, like a winter chill.

"This isn't my fault," he told her. "I had nothing to do with your brother's death. I had the right to remove him from my property while he was being belligerent and destructive. He came in here on his own accord."

"There'll be a reckoning." She cocked her brow at him. "And not by the law. Mark my words."

"Are you threatening me now?" he asked her, incredulous. "Do you honestly think I won't seek legal counsel if this kind of harassment continues? As it is, I'm calling the police to report his death on my property. I've got nothing to hide. He threatened me and my property and I shoved him. I didn't drown him."

She drew her sweater closer to her body. Her skin looked transparent, like rice paper, in the thin ribbons of pale morning light working its way through gaps in the trees.

"Some things are beyond any help," she whispered. Casey began to growl again, her fur bristling along her neck and shoulder blades. Ron drew her closer beside him, holding onto her collar. "Some things that are seldom understood by most, and accepted by few. You'll come to know, in time." She turned and walked away from him. This time he could hear her footsteps breaking ground, grinding leaves to dust and leaving a shallow path in her wake.

"I don't want to see you or anyone affiliated with you on my land again!" he yelled after her. "I'll have you arrested for trespassing."

"They can't arrest what they can't see," she said, her head facing away from him, her voice seeming to come as a strand along the wind. She continued until the trees swallowed her. Casey sat down on her haunches and let out a single, mournful howl.

* * *

"Death due to hypothermia," Ron repeated the policeman's statement. "So, he didn't actually drown?" he asked the Constable. He relaxed slightly, although he didn't know why he should. He'd told the Constable about Rebecca Mallory's words. The officer had rolled his eyes while jotting down notes.

"His head went into the water after he'd died and the current dragged him partially under. His heart gave out. He had a blood-alcohol level of almost four hundred." He shook his head. "His system just shut down from the wet and the cold. You've told us everything now?"

"That's right." Ron had nodded. "I shoved him, we got into a bit of a tussle, nothing serious. He bolted into the woods before I could stop him, and I didn't feel I was in a position to go after him without a light."

"Did you afterwards?"

Ron hesitated. "No, I didn't."

"Did you think of calling us, just to do a property check?"

"I figured he'd make his way out again on his own. He was around so often I'd have been calling you half a dozen times a week."

The Constable shut his note book. "It's an unfortunate accident. The family's... strange. If you have any more problems, let us know. We'll go and talk to them."

"Thanks, I will." He shut the door and thought about the hollow look in the officer's eyes when he mentioned going and talking to the Mallory's. He might have said, "We'll strip naked and jump into a pool filled with razor blades" with the same look of conviction.

* * *

Four days later. After a long, restless night of tossing and turning, thinking about Casey's fit of panic and the figure running through his yard that looked like Lucas, the old drunk's funeral had taken place at the church across the road. It was as if the ceremony had been held there just to taunt him. Ron had stood in an upstairs window watching two sextons dig a hole in the pariah section of Mallory stones set off in their own corner of the yard. He drew the curtains when he saw the family turning to gaze at his house, the sister pointing.

He stood looking at the dark, silent mound later that same evening, watching it as the sun set beyond the tree line and the mound grew into nothing more than stony shadow. He told himself to forget about it—it was done. Lucas was buried and the family would have to deal with the consequences of a drunken old man's stupid decisions.

Casey had gone off her food that day and never strayed from his heels. Ron sat in the front parlor, a fire going in the grate, with Casey sleeping at his feet. He'd just switched on the television, found a midnight special program about cave bats on an educational channel that was just starting, when something solid hit the living room window.

He spun and saw something white and wet, like a hand stuck to the surface, sliding along the window; but it wasn't a hand. He saw the rubbery distended line of a mouth being pulled along glass, teeth sliding in soft screaming sounds, a single blue eye pressed hard so that the lid lay crushed.

Lucas.

He'd know that face anywhere.

Casey screamed, lips curling back from her teeth, ivory points extended into a feral attack. She lunged at the window, hit the wall in a resounding smack, then turned to flee to her safe spot under the bed. Ron's thoughts raced as the face slid out of sight below the sill, thinking of John Lacey's words, wondering about the possibility of a heart stopped due to hypothermia, but not dead... not dead enough to stop a desperate man from digging his way out of a cheap pine box, through five feet of freshly turned dirt. Christ, hadn't they done an autopsy on him, cut him open, verified him dead? He couldn't be back. Lucas had nine brothers, but Ron hadn't met them all. Could it be one of the brothers?

Out on the lawn there was nothing but the first crisp dusting of snow swirling beneath muted moonlight and no footprints beneath the window.

No footprints beneath the window?

"I'm going crazy," he whispered. He approached the window, his own feet making tracks in the snow, to find a hand print, stark and sticky, against the glass, and other things... the snail-slime slide of a cheek, the open print of human lips... their creases distinct. He leaned forward and recoiled, the stink of putrefaction clinging to the glass.

Liquids from a body breaking down.

He ran in and shut the door. He found the shotgun and shells in his bedroom. This time he left Casey where she lay, shaking and whining, and returned outdoors. He searched the edge of the woods, the fields, the entire expanse of his backyard. Nothing. Desperate, he crossed the road and marched into the tiny graveyard, pushing through the loose iron gate, past frozen flowers and the curled hulks of stone angels, to the Mallory graves. He stopped in front of the mound of dirt, white now in the snow. It was not disturbed. Not at all.

"What do you want from me?" he screamed into the night, to the silent church with its dark panels of windows providing no mercy, to the winter season and its symbolism of sleep and death, frozen, cold.

He turned on his heel and ran back home, the rifle frozen against his skin. He stood in front of the fire, the house locked, curtains drawn, rubbing his arms, but the fire could not warm him. It couldn't reach that inner, bone-deep chill.

* * *

Lucas came back again the next night, one full week after his death.

This time he knocked on the door to announce that the witching hour had arrived. There was no exclamation of a hurtled beer bottle or a face slamming against a window. Ron opened the door cautiously, peering out into the dark, expecting Rebecca Mallory or one of her clan. He wasn't completely disappointed, only terrified.

A man one week in the grave is a sight to see, even if the winter weather has frozen his skin and the level of decomposition. What had begun to rot lay dormant in its rigid state. Lucas' left eye had bulged to sit partially on his cheek. It had split open when he'd run it down the glass. His upper lip had parted in the center, exposing grisly muscle tissue and the dark purple of frozen flesh.

"What do you want?" Ron managed to say, lifting the rifle to Mallory's chest.

"My life..." Lucas' terrible mouth broke wind.

Ron stumbled back into the wall. "I can't give that to you. I—I didn't take it from you in the first place."

November gusts pushed the door all the way back, throwing Ron off balance. Lucas Mallory, black burial suit stiff with the cold, white shirt stained greenish from his fluids, stumbled into the room, and that was when Ron saw it.

The street lamp, a lunar disk of blue, shining through Lucas' ruined head. In the dark he looked whole, but in the light, what was supposed to be the safe light of reality, he moved, ghostly and ethereal. Ron lowered the rifle and dropped it. It wouldn't help him here.

"You have life and I want it."

Above them, in the safety of the bedroom, Casey shrieked. Wind gusted into the house, sucking out the warmth provided by the fire and replacing it with the acrid stench of old funeral flowers.

"You want me to die, just because you did?"

"No. I want you to live, so that I may also live."

Lucas swung out with hands that had once gripped the killing bottle, hands in which Ron could clearly see the old blue veins criss-crossing bone, and clutched Ron's head in a vice grip. He pulled Ron towards him and Ron began to scream. It was exactly what Lucas wanted. Lips like dried liver and tasting of brine moved over Ron's, sealing his mouth, sucking on him. Lucas blew into Ron's mouth, blew winter and hoarfrost and the stink of the grave into him, filling him. Lucas began to evaporate, but the cold stayed in Ron. The cold stayed while Ron passed out, was still there when he awoke to an empty room. Persisted despite the fire, blankets, and a bottle of brandy.

Casey growled whenever Ron went near her, biting at his hands. He found out why soon enough.

* * *

The mirror on the wall shows him that haunted face in the window every single time Ron looks into it. He stands close, examining the wrinkled weathered skin, his hands shaking and teeth chattering. The furnace blows a steady heat in the background to no avail.

His eyes are no longer completely brown. Pale, frozen lake specks of blue swim in them. Sometimes it looks like a trick in the light, if it wasn't for the persistent feel of skin beneath his skin, so cold, laying there dividing his own flesh and muscle like a thin glove. He can't shake it.

He opens his mouth and notices his teeth have yellowed considerably in less than twenty-four hours. His skin has begun to spot in brown tones, what people call liver spots. He hasn't shaved and his beard is speckled in salt and pepper.

"I hate you," he whispers into the mirror, and the eyes looking back at him grow hard, determined. The glass shatters.

He has begun to drink, too much.

He tried to kill himself with a knife last night, but his hand... no longer completely his hand, fought the urge. He was somehow able to fight back long enough to let Casey out, kai-yaying, into the night, to go wherever she would, before what he had become might hurt her. He wondered if death might ever release his own body, if and when it will come on its own.

Until then, alcohol is the only salve for his misery. Thank God that the hands allow him that small haven from the misery of knowing Lucas and he were joined eternally.

The doorbell rings and he knows it will be Rebecca and the rest of them. He knows they'll want to hold him, to feel past his skin to the cold beneath it, welcoming

Lucas home. He wants to scream, but Lucas ushers him towards the door, thrusts out the hand that opens it.

Then, Lucas makes him smile in welcome.

PHANTOM CHASERS
DAVID NORTH MARTINO

"The dead have been asking for you," Tanya said. She was a twenty-four-year-old college graduate, so fresh and full of life that her vivacious-ness contrasted with her morbid fascination for all things dark and beyond the grave, but she hadn't outgrown her gothic style. The paleness of her flesh juxtaposed with the darkness of her clothing.

"You're joking," Mason said. But she wasn't and he knew it. A small wave of fear washed over him, but he pushed it away and pretended it was exhilaration. He did love the chase, nipping at the heels of death, discovering what waited on the other side. Tanya also fascinated him. If he were just a little bit younger, he would have welcomed spending some time in a hotel bed with her instead of sitting in a small conference room that had been temporarily converted into a paranormal command center.

"Afraid not. I have proof. That's why I called you out here. E-mailing you the file just wouldn't do."

"Let's hear it." Now Mason felt real excitement. He had driven all the way from Rhode Island to Boston to hear the audio. If they were legit, the recordings would be perfect for an episode of his cable television show, *Phantom Chasers*.

Tanya called up the digital audio editing program on the computer.

"Here's the first one," she said. "I'll play it without noise reduction or any enhancement."

He listened and could almost make out a voice. Was it saying what he thought it was saying?

"And here it is enhanced."

We want Mason Strange.

Hearing his name made him jump. He didn't like that. He was a professional paranormal investigator. There was nothing to fear from the dead. All he had to do was profess his control over them and they would be powerless. But he still found it quite shocking.

"Are you okay?" Tanya asked.

Mason nodded, hoping his skin hadn't flushed to a paleness that matched her makeup.

"It's all very exciting," he managed. But his mouth felt dry and his palms felt wet. What was happening to him?

"They're calling you out," Tanya said. "I don't think they liked how confrontational you were with them last time. Has this ever happened before?"

"Oh no, this is definitely a first."

She played one more EVP, Electronic Voice Phenomena, recording.

We hate *Mason Strange!*

"I definitely have to go back there now," Mason said, trying to keep his voice steady.

"I don't know if that's the best idea," Tanya said.

Mason knew she was right. But he had a show to do and ratings to consider and besides… "The dead can't hurt me."

* * *

Mason could have approached the investigation in a different manner and still have an interesting show for his audience. He could have picked five or six team members and brought in a couple of professional camera operators, making the episode a bigger and more expensive production. The budget would have allowed for it, but he didn't think as many scares and thrills would be provided that way. Instead, he had opted to bring two other cast members. The group would consist of Tanya, who had become a fan favorite, and Jeff Baylor, whom the audience on the online message board had dubbed the scaredy cat. Mason thought of him as the Cowardly Lion—a big guy afraid of his own shadow. The three-person team would provide a sense of isolation and make it scarier for the viewers.

Mason drove them to the location in a black van with a *Phantom Chaser* logo emblazoned on the side. Tanya rode shotgun and Jeff sat in the back. Mason had already decided on a great title for the episode: *Mason Strange Must Die!*

If that didn't up the ratings a little, nothing would—and he needed that ratings bump. With all the interest in the paranormal and the success of his show, a handful of imitators had flooded the market and were vying for viewers' attention. A couple of these shows were decent enough, but most were hack jobs created to cash in on the fad. If they weren't careful, the whole industry would dry up and they would all have to get day jobs.

Two days ago he and Tanya had recreated her presentation of the EVP evidence to be used in the show. When he heard his name called again, he didn't have to act for the camera; it was like hearing it for the first time.

Now, with all the preproduction work completed, he could concentrate on tonight's investigation. Even in the daylight Danwich State Mental Hospital looked ominous. The gables and spires of the Gothic-style brick building, originally built in 1874 and finally closed in 1992, created a permanent façade of foreboding. Mason drove the van into the deserted parking area, finding a spot closest to the front door. They exited the van, each of them grabbing a case of equipment out of the back.

"Let's do this quickly while there's still some natural light," Mason said.

"Quick it will be, boss," Jeff said. He had already gone half a shade paler.

"You look like you're about to keel over," Tanya said to him. "Why do you do this to yourself?"

"What do you mean?" Jeff asked. "I wouldn't miss this for the world."

Mason fumbled with the keys the property owner had loaned him. He put the key into the lock and opened the door. With the mustiness flaring his nostrils, Mason walked in with his crew following close behind. The interior was exactly as he remembered it. The reception area was just a wide-open hall with a long check-in desk that reminded him of his local hospital. Black graffiti scrawled over the peeling white walls and under the dust on the cherry wood desk. A brilliant but dusty crystal chandelier still hung from the atrium ceiling, too high for the vandals to reach even with a standard ladder, but Mason could tell a few chunks had been knocked off, most likely by local teens throwing rocks. He tried the light switch on the wall. The production company had paid the property owner to turn on the electricity. A muted light shone through the dust that had settled on the crystal.

"We've got power," Tanya said.

"Jeff, you want to do upstairs?" Mason asked.

"By myself?"

"Oh, God," Tanya said and rolled her eyes. "I'll do it."

"Okay, I'll check on you in a few," Mason called to her as she trudged down the hall, equipment in hand, heading for the main staircase. She would only be preparing the first few rooms. He didn't feel the need to do an investigation of the whole building. He wasn't going to have to go to the dead; the dead, he was sure, would come to him.

"We'll still have to split up to get everything done in time," Mason said.

"I'll start here then, by the exit," Jeff said sheepishly.

"Good enough," Mason said. Jeff could really annoy him at times, but his personality lent an authenticity to the proceedings, as well as comic relief. As long as Jeff was good for the show, Mason would put up with him.

Mason grabbed his gear and headed past the desk and the main staircase and into the first room on the left. The Chief Attendant had worked for many years in this office. A heart attack claimed her in 1990, before an ambulance could arrive. A haunting black and white picture coated in dust still hung on the wall. It showed her standing with a little boy whose eyes shone vacantly, undoubtedly a former resident. A portrait of the stone-faced Superintendent had been propped against the wall, as if placed in the room for eternal storage. The story was that the atrocities committed by the staff of the asylum on the residents had kept them here in their own private hell. They were said to have become devils in their own right, keeping the souls of the residents confined in their eternal prison.

Mason grabbed a broom and swept the dust away. He then put an "X" on the floor with duct tape where he wanted the camera, set up a tripod, and then plugged in the extension cord and taped it to the floor so no one would trip. The tape wasn't sticking well, but he figured it would hold.

He continued his walk without incident, placing markers and equipment in the reported hotspots and the areas where activity had occurred during their first investigation.

Mason!

Mason stopped walking and held his breath. He felt cold and the hairs on his arms stood upright. His heart hammered in his chest. A voice had called to him, clear, distinct, like whatever uttered his name had a command over all sound. Mason wanted to call to it, interact with it, but he needed to save everything for the cameras and the show.

"Don't worry," he said aloud to the air. "I'll be back tonight and we can talk then."

Slowly, Mason climbed the stairs. He reached the top and took a few steps down the hall. Without warning, he found himself sprawled on the dirty floor. It took his brain a second to catch up and figure out what had happened. A cord had been stretched across the hall to reach an outlet. The tape had come loose and turned the cord into a tripwire.

"Mason, you scared the shit out of me," Tanya said as she ran in from the room to him. "Are you all right?"

"I'm fine," Mason said as he stood up and dusted himself off. "Sorry the noise scared you."

"I should be the sorry one," Tanya said. "I guess I didn't secure the cord well enough."

"It wasn't your fault. The tape isn't sticking to the floor. Make sure you use extra so that someone doesn't go ass-over-teakettle down the stairs."

Ghosts couldn't hurt them, but he knew their own carelessness could.

* * *

Showtime.

"This is Mason Strange and you're watching *Phantom Chasers*," Mason said into his mini digital video camera, the infrared night vision system washing his face and the surrounding area in a light green on the flip out monitor. He turned and looked toward Tanya's camera. "And tonight we're back in Massachusetts at the Danwich Mental Hospital to confront the spirits that have been calling me out since my last confrontation here. We will be locked down with no way out until first light. This should be an eventful and scary night, so please stay with us." He continued to look at the camera for fifteen seconds and then said, "Cut."

Mason imagined how he would splice the show together. He'd go right from his intro to the show's opening teaser. Then he would present the voice evidence. Most of the show would be their investigation. The final five minutes would recap the video and audio evidence—if they caught any.

From here on out they would keep their cameras rolling, only stopping to change memory cards and batteries.

"Okay, let's separate," Mason said. "Tanya, you start upstairs. Jeff, you have the reception area. If something happens, call us on the walkies. After about an hour, switch locations and round robin until the end of taping."

"You got it, boss," Jeff said with what Mason recognized as a hint of false bravado. Mason figured Jeff was about to piss his pants.

Just save it for the camera, Mason thought.

Mason made his way through the darkness, the screen of the infrared camera and the echoes down the hall his only guide.

He entered the Chief Attendant's office. It lay bare except for the stationary camera and a folding chair he had brought in. Sitting in the chair, he placed his camera in his lap, pointing it to the left side of the room. He removed a digital recorder from his pocket and pressed the record button. The red light turned on.

"EVP session. Chief Attendant's office. Mason Strange investigating," Mason said after he placed the recorder on his leg opposite the video camera. He kept the recorder's internal microphone away from his mouth when he talked so that his voice wouldn't be too loud during playback. EVP sessions could cause quite an earache if not recorded properly.

"I would like to ask that any spirits or entities in this room try to make contact with me. Talk into this device with the red light and I will be able to hear you," Mason said to the empty room. "Can you tell me your name?"

He waited in silence and apparently didn't get a response. But he couldn't be sure until he played back the recording. With any luck, something would respond with the clarity that he had heard earlier today. He continued asking questions and getting no replies. It was time to up the ante before moving on to a new spot.

"You called me out. Didn't you think I'd come back? Why don't you show yourself, or say something? Are you afraid? You're nothing more than a bully."

He waited through a moment of electric silence, sweat beading on his forehead. Then a crash and a scream. The riotous noise made him jump. It came from the reception area.

What's that Cowardly Lion up to? Mason grabbed his gear and made for the door.

"Jeff!" he called out, hearing a slight echo as he moved as quickly as he could. He watched the monitor's green glow so he could see what was in front of him. Mason's heart raced right along with his breathing. Up ahead he saw Tanya, also answering the call.

"Tanya," he said into his walkie-talkie. "I'm right behind you."

"Thanks," she said, her breathing labored. But was it with fear or excitement? He knew he felt a mixture of both.

When they got back to the reception area, they found Jeff squatting next to the entrance. Mason couldn't believe Jeff hadn't fled outside by now.

"Damn ghosts threw something at me." Jeff's voice held a tremor of fear. His breathing and his manner told Mason that Jeff wasn't lying. He seemed genuinely freaked out.

"What was thrown? Did you find it?" Tanya asked.

"I—I haven't looked yet."

"Let's stop right here and find out what it was," Mason said.

They all crouched down using their infrared-enabled cameras to search for the object in the darkness.

"There's so much debris, I don't think we're going to be able to say for sure exactly what it was," Mason said after a few moments of fruitless searching. "We should probably get back to our locations."

"No way," Jeff said. "I can't stay in this place after what just happened."

"You don't want to sit this one out. The fans are already calling you the Cowardly Lion. It's making the show look bad."

"Dude, there is no way I'm staying in this place by myself."

"Then go with Tanya." He could see Tanya's features tighten on the camcorder's monitor. She wasn't going to like this one bit, but he knew she'd deal with it for the rest of the investigation. "Tanya, why don't you and Jeff stay together downstairs and I'll go finish upstairs."

"Sounds like a plan," she said, but her voice sounded as tense as her expression.

Mason returned to the staircase and carefully ascended. At the top, he looked down to make sure the tape was still holding before stepping over the cord. He made his way to the room and crossed the threshold. A folding chair waited for him. He sat down and positioned himself for more EVP work.

A scream rang out—Jeff's voice. Mason sprung from his chair; the digital recorder clattered to the floor. He sprinted across the room and through the doorway. He turned to his left, ran for the stairs, and tripped. He heard his camcorder thudding down the stairs.

"Shit!" Mason said as he stood up, apparently no worse for wear. That's when he saw them. But how could he see them?

The stern-faced Superintendent, the Chief Attendant, and the little boy with the vacant eyes stood in front of him—but Mason could see by their ghastly pallor, and their translucent quality, that they were no longer alive.

"We hate you, Mason Strange," the Superintendent said. "We hate you for awakening us, and for the torment that it brings."

"How can I see you?" Mason asked. He wouldn't admit it to anybody else, but he was terrified.

"We're going to make you pay," said the woman. "Make you pay for disturbing us."

"You can't hurt me," Mason said, but even to his ears it sounded like a question. "The living have power over you."

"It is true, we can't hurt the living," said the Superintendent.

The young boy turned his head toward the foot of the stairs.

Mason crept closer, as close as he dared, enough so he could see over the railing and down the stairs. It hadn't been his camera that thudded down them. Mason saw his body sprawled on the dusty floor, his neck twisted at an odd angle—broken.

"But now that you're dead, we *can* hurt you," said the boy with the vacant eyes.

A long stream of shambling phantom inmates, clothing tattered, expressions frenzied, ascended the staircase. They came as if by some silent command, anger and resentment smoldering in their eyes.

"Welcome to our asylum, Mason," the Chief Attendant said, her voice dark with menace. "Welcome to the pain!" And with that, the three of them moved toward him, maniacal laughter rising from the horde of phantoms behind them. Mason uttered a scream that would never again be heard by the living.

HAUNT

JEFFREY KOSH

MIRRORS

Under cold, indifferent stars—I wait.

Wondering about Death and what it really is. For I have died, and yet I am reborn. Still, I am as confused as I was in life, amidst unknown shores of a gloomy, undiscovered country from which no traveler has yet returned.

With saddened eyes, I scour my surroundings, looking for joy, yet finding none. This is a mirror of where I used to live. Everything is warped, shadowed, and misty. Nonetheless, it rebounds in familiarity.

There, the bright towers of modernity, monument to Man's vanity and pride, impudently pierce the darkness-shrouded sky, mocking Creation and Creator at the same time; shiny windows hiding memories of fleeting ghosts. But they are just a parody, a reflection of what they are in the lands of the living. Or is it the other way?

Mirrors do not lie. They show things for what they really are, what they are made of. The windows have no glass, for they are just fleeting barriers that isolate Man from his siblings, providing a false veil of safety. There is no need to keep inside the heat in an everlasting chilly world. The buildings themselves climb up impossibly, fading away in heavenly abysses, so murky that no eye, living or dead, will ever fathom how high. The beams are not made of cast metal, so dear to modern Man, and the frames seem to writhe and contract of their own accord; a fastidious, pulsating beat impossible to ignore, yet unbearable to behold. They are made of flesh, these unliving travesties. Thick bluish veins transporting fluids from Somewhere to Nowhere. For no purpose, just a pallid imitation of ducts and cables; the lifeblood of city buildings in the living world.

And the inhabitants. Or better, the lack of. Pale lights brighten empty rooms, perpetually waiting for a master to claim hold, yet none will ever come, for the dead do not need the comforts of enclosed spaces. At least not those who are unbound to roam this dreary landscape.

Here, the crowds, endless assemblies of pallid figures, all transparent and faceless, they stumble around, crossing clogged thoroughfares, yet oblivious to each other's presence. Eroding carcasses of rusted metal and cracked plastic, automobiles and other vehicles clutter the road like standing tombstones in a cemetery made of macadam and shattered glass. Forever stuck in an eternal, yet unmovable, rush hour.

They are pitiful affairs, these creatures. The living.

They are as superficial as they are clueless; asking questions, yet dreading the answers. Wrapped in lies since birth, they stagger around the rugged path we call "life." The suffering of the human condition is best described by despair and unworldly hopes. So much of humanity afraid of Death desperately clings to illusions and creates imaginary places for its thoughts to linger. Yet, the stench of Death permeates everything it says and does. Humanity builds temples and memorials to it, a constant reminder of the ultimate fate.

Life, itself, doesn't last long, compared to the almost eternal ellipses of celestial bodies. Gulfs of nothingness surround us in that tiny spark of a dead, black night. Planets and stars will outlive the sturdiest Methuselah and remind us of our frail existence in a hostile, cold universe of indifferent, if not malevolent, demiurges. Nonetheless, Death is a rebirth, a passage through the veil of Ignorance burrowed out by Reason. It is not an end, but a new beginning.

Death is all and nothing wrapped in the shroud of a universe's decaying corpse.

And in this Deadland I exist only as a whisper.

However, I can't deny Life's call. I long for its warmth and past memories flood me, drag me down to face my inner demons. To preserve my memories, my mental integrity, I walk among the living, follow them, observe all their moves, feed on an illusory bliss as a heroine addict quests for artificial joy. Yes, most of the dead cannot abide to be parted from the living, especially the ones we lived with or cared for in that brief sparkle of light known as existence. We crave too much for the gentle touch of soft, warm skin. We lust for the fleeting rush of heated air exhaled from pumping lungs. We thirst for the elusory comfort of being home.

And yet, we are parted. We can simply watch. But can we stand to face what we once were? Look in the faces of those we called "love"? Maybe not, but I can't help to return, with regret, to the place I used to consider home.

However, it stands like a burlesque, this reflection of my old abode. Paint is peeling away, and wood is rotten, eaten by maggots and greenish mold. The front porch has no light bulb, and evil-looking spider webs, dripping obscene fluids, fill its darkened vault, barring my passage. But it's just an illusion, as my will and need to bask again in the familiarity of my beloved house is too strong to be hampered by such a weak mirage.

There is no need to force my way through the heavy paneled door, as it stands ajar in the Mirror World, because ghosts have no uses for mortal barriers. My mind conjures in a darting instant the image of a sturdy and carved affair; an expensive, if unnecessary, piece of vanity for an otherwise simple dwelling.

Chains whip out of the dark, shattering away the engraved glass memories of my mind window. With rusted hooks they pierce my phantom flesh, tugging at it as hungry stray dogs would do to a carcass. I twist, pulled in all directions at once. The ambush is well planned, but I won't give up. Already dead, I feel no fear.

Loathing, despair, and sorrow. Those are my companions in the cold embrace. Fear, love, and joy are flickering candles in a raging storm. Alas, I belong to Death, and Death belongs to me.

Suddenly, the tormenting strands end their pull, as a shadowy figure emerges from the threshold. Silent as the fish of the deepest reaches, the form motions for me to hurry and get inside. I obey and, with stupor, find myself facing yet another alien challenge.

A thin film, wet and sticky, hampers my passage. It looks an awful grayish white, and it stinks far worse. Like adipocere, the wax-like organic substance molded out of body fats in putrefying corpses, it's crumbly and putrid, so I poke through it with ease. It's just another trick of this land of sorrow.

"Finally, we meet, pardner," exclaims the stranger once I step inside what remains of a once beautiful and sunbathed house. Now dust and cobwebs decorate, disrespectfully, the vacant living room; the name an evil joke, for no living creature mulls here. The stench of Death is even stronger and a taint of corruption and waste permeates my surroundings.

Who is this stranger? And what does he seek from me?

SHADES

"It's not angst that drives you here, but passion."

The dark stranger seems to coalesce while he talks, his shadowy forms gaining new features, slowly, like in one of those old movies when Lon Chaney Jr. got stuck by silver and reverted to human form. It is a stop-motion trick running wild in front of my phantasmal eyes.

"D'ya want to hear a ghost story, darlin'?" the shadow man asks, as a bright and toothy smile pierces the blackness of his face, soon followed by a pair of all-too-white eyes lacking pupils. "We've been tellin' 'em by yonder times. Except, this time, you're into it."

His voice sounds familiar, yet there's this mocking tone, this hateful laugh ringing below it. It makes me angry. I feel my body stir, and everything gains a reddish hue. I try to rebuke, but it has been so long since I uttered a single word that only a low moan escapes my flimsy lips, sounding alien and distant to my ghostly ears.

The stranger busts into laughs at my attempt. "So alone, pardner. So much time alone..."

And now I see him for what he is. He's my twin, yet in life I had none. Same face, same features. Same size, same scars. A dark reflection made into spectral flesh.

"Do not be afraid, darlin'. Ya had to face this, now or then. Ya wandered yander n' yonder in these Deadlands, but never came back to face your failures, your passions, and what keeps ya here."

He comes closer and I see worms crawling under his pallid skin—living waves rippling through a sea of dead flesh. Molds and warts mar his features and spasms agitate his muscles.

"Who are you?" I utter, my voice still hoarse and feeble.

Again he laughs. "Me?" He shows contempt in his unseeing eyes. "I'm the one who knows your secrets. I'm the one who loves you best. I'm the thirteenth at the banquet. I'm the uninvited guest. I'm the whisperer in the dark. I'm the voice of all your malice. I'm something ya'll never part with."

And I recognize him for what he is. He... *It* is my Shade, that part of my soul that feeds on angst and regret, not my Ego, which longs for emotion, yet finds none. My worst enemy doesn't live out in this unearthly mirror world, but back inside my head. For Man is not truly one, but two beings. My existence is fueled by emotional energy; it craves for suffering and anxiety. A deadly combination of Id and playground bully. My implacable and inescapable foe. The one who led me to the wrong path—one made of thorns and rusty nails. It is all my hate, greed, and darkness distilled into being, so selfish and dumb that it has no concern for our common destiny.

"What do you want from me, hateful tempter?" I rebuke with scorn in my voice.

The Dark One closes distance and rotates his hateful eyes inside sunken orbits, showing me the dark splotches of alien fungus that is slowly eating them away. Or perhaps, they are just a display of his own pain.

"Ya have to face your demise, pardner! Ya have to face it all."

As hate-filled words spill from his decaying mouth, chains surge out of his black figure and coil on me thrice, like a spider spinning its deadly web on a hapless insect. Again I'm bound by these detestable restraints, yet, this time, no crooked implement pierces my unearthly flesh. They just bond me to my hateful twin; he pulls at the strands as a farmer does to a stubborn mule.

Suddenly, the rotting wooden planks creak and splinter downward, and we both fall into the inky crevice. Wailings and screams of long-gone specters surround us as we fall deeper, squeezed in an unwanted embrace of loathing and hate. The further we plunge, the darker it gets, and even my *deathsight* can't see the bottom of it. An ill wind made of tortured voices twists and plays on us as we drop down, and madmen's laughs fill my still heart with fragments of poisonous angst.

It is a gallery of horrors weighing me down. Brightened by an eerie fluorescence, this carnival of freaks parades on both sides as ancient statues in an infernal wax museum.

In deep shadow, a feminine figure stands impossibly tall, her limbs spidery and wretched. From needlelike fingers, flashy strands like a puppeteer's strings, she pulls on a smaller creature while her inexpressive face stares at me with empty orbits. The captured thing writhes and tugs to get free from the deadly grasp, yet, having no limbs, it can just wriggle, like an earthly worm screaming a silent wail of agony.

On my left, a scraggy humanoid—I'm unable to discern its gender—rests chained on the rocky floor. The manacles, holding it prone, bite deep into its skinless wrists and ankles, and a greenish fluid bleeds out, pools down in foul puddles that reek of vomit and rotting fish. It's screaming, this poor creature, as a clockwork-looking insect starts to peel off its face with the buzzing sound of a thousand tiny chainsaws. Then, on membranous wings, it flies, carrying away its ill-gotten booty; a living mask of flesh and blood perennially frozen in a voiceless cry.

On my right, a plump child, his distended abdomen crawling with subcutaneous maggots, dangles from a lattice of fishing hooks, the skin on his back pulled beyond belief—and his shape deformed in a twisted parody of clothes left to dry in the backyard. Yet, his face seems painless. He keeps typing on a machine's keyboard an endless series of incomprehensible words.

A living jack-in-a-box, made of vertebrae and wires springs out of a container decorated with darting eyes. Warped faces, with impossibly large smiles running from chin to ear, glare at me from dark recesses, their bloodshot eyes filled with malevolence. A hellish bard, dressed in leathers, is playing a wet tune with strands of his own innards, each dull note producing more blood than sound. A woman whose face is made of cracked porcelain. A brawny warrior bristling with an armor of tiny blades, each single dagger growing out of his flesh. And skeletal figures sporting dead fish eyes, living dolls stitched together by wriggling sinew. Monstrosities more apt for a charnel house or an anatomy session than to walk as living beings.

"Who are these people?" I ask my captor as he drags me through this labyrinth of freaks. "And what have they done to suffer such a cruel fate?"

My warped reflection turns to me, yet, now its face looks different: a leathery mask studded with metal clasps covers its repulsive lineaments and a zippered opening allows its mocking voice to reach my ears.

"Don't ya really know who the poor fucks are? Do not fret, my darlin', cause as soon as ya can say 'pain' ya goin' to remember 'em all!"

The cavern's walls appear to contract, as though it's a living, breathing creature. It tightens as we advance, and soon we face a dead end.

No, it is not. For what appears to be a darkened wall in truth reveals itself as liquid blackness. My twisted captor jerks at my bounds, and with a sudden thrust we both plunge in this watery oblivion.

* * *

I find myself in a dark place, yet a yellowish artificial light plays with its shadows, not the greenish cast of what I'm used to. No trace of my impious tormentor. Apparently, I'm free.

My eyes scan the surroundings and something different catches my sight. No warping, no decay; all things appear as in the land of the living. I'm inside a lightless, rusting hulk of a building, crisscrossed with half-rotten catwalks and splintered supports. The scarce illumination provided by feeble streetlights stands outside like a succession of uncaring sentinels. This huge, defunct manufacturing floor is covered in an inch-deep layer of dust, broken glass, and rat droppings. Rusting remains of cannibalized assembly lines remain in place, slowly crumbling, while frayed conveyor belts sag on skeletal tracks. A row of empty offices overlook the floor from above, the only access by way of a dangerously ruined, rust-shot staircase. Pieces of the roof have collapsed, leaving wide patches of the floor exposed to the sky. The pavement is cracked and stained with decades-old oil drippings. The scrabbling and squeaking of rats is magnified by uncovered metal surfaces, but what attracts my attention is a sound of a different nature.

Muffled, a woman's whining reaches my ears, and I move forward, more affected by curiosity than piety. And I see two shadowy figures silhouetted by the weak lampion's halo. One is lying on the rubble-strewn floor, her white eyes gleaming in tears and chilled in terror, her legs and arms crossed protectively. The other is a larger male, his broad shoulders outlined by the heavy leather surcoat, thick arms outstretched to grasp at the struggling girl. There's something wicked in his right hand, something familiar.

A blade.

Instinctively, I rush onward, forgetting I'm just a ghost, unable to affect the physical. I'm like a frame in a movie reel. I exist, yet I'm not real in this world of flesh.

The blade rushes down and, in a swift and cruel motion, cleaves across the woman's throat, severing veins and arteries. She chokes on her own blood, the hapless creature, as it spurts with every heartbeat from her mangled neck; a curtain of blood descending her body, while a caul of darkness fades in her sight. I know too well that last gleam in the dead girl's eyes, for I'm part of it, or at least I lived it once.

The brute stands up and tilts his head, regarding his act like a work of art. He seems pleased by what he has done, and shakes and thrives in the afterglow, much like a satisfied lover basks in orgasmic throbs after intercourse.

I come closer, half-expecting this poor victim's soul to coalesce into my unearthly world. However, nothing happens; she just stands still, warm blood pooling under her lifeless body. I turn my head to face the assailant as red rage fills my whole essence. I want to rend to shreds this cold-blooded killer. I want for him to pay.

But I can't.

My rage dissolves as fast as morning mist when his too-familiar face comes into view. He's me, this wretched monster, this foulest of murderous beings. He bears the same visage, yet shares none of my piety. I hate him, but mysteriously, I find myself unable to act. And what is worse, a part of me seems to cheer at his evil deed.

"Seen? Remember what ya did, my pathetic mate?"

Again my Shade's odious voice shrills somewhere in empty air. I turn to look for the offensive tormentor, but it is just its disembodied mouth mocking me from unseen reaches.

At last, I remember. Yes, I was this monster: a killer of innocents, an unjust reaper of early seeds of life. I remember all victims, each one of them, and I fall on imaginary knees as the Shade's laughter vibrates in the now vacant lot.

"Yes, ya were a monster. Yes, ya were me! Accept it as it is and ya'll be allowed to leave this land of sorrow, made of regret and fragmented memories. Nothing binds you here, except your self-reproach. Embrace your nature and follow me to Hell."

A raging river of blood and blades, cuts and stitches, faces wracked by pain runs before my ghostly eyes. Pleading women, more warm blood, hooks and skins... faster.

The chubby face of a sweet kid, his eyes wet by burning tears... until I gouge them out...

Faster.

Hamstrings and innards, gory trophies, my hand on my penis as I jerk off to pleasant memories of my last hunt...

Faster.

Arianna's face. Her disbelief turning to disgust as cops carry me out in chains... away from our house. A jail full of madmen... a preacher praying for my lost soul... the long walk to my final seat...

Faster.

A date on a calendar: July the 13th, 1964. Huntsville, Texas...

Me seated on 'Old Sparky'... a lightning bolt.

Nothingness.

My eyes return to the grinning Shade. "I don't believe in Hell... or Heaven. What could be worse than this? Alas, I dismiss you with all my will, for something pure still calls at my soul."

That said, I fade away, looking for the only person I hold dear. The only person who can give me hope.

ANCHORS

I look for her at the gravesite, yet Arianna isn't there.

She has never been there. My beloved wife left the living world in

1977, when fate, in the shape of thunderstorm and slippery road, caused her car to skid off into a waiting ditch. I'd waited patiently, trusting her to show up soon or later, but that never happened. For thirty-five years I visited her tomb, in vain.

I also visited the hospital in which she drew her last breath. And her family's home, vacant and demolished. Guthrie Café, place of our chance meeting. And a large shopping mall, once the site of Alamo Drive-In, where I took her virginity on the Impala's backseat. Green Huntington Hill is no more, now covered by magma of concrete and low-rent condos, where an ounce of grass—more thistle than Mary-Jane—costs less than a hundred bucks. A rusted car stands on blocks out in someone's yard, and malnourished dogs snarl behind fences at my passage.

I drift southward, to First Precinct. This is the place I was brought to in chains. And the place where I last spoke to her. Funny. This place has never changed. Its antiseptic-smelling rooms still look out of the Sixties, with cheap wood paneling and suspect sketches tacked to the walls. Outside, a larger fleet of dented Chevrolet cruisers fills a dilapidated parking lot.

Still no sign of her; not even her smell lingers here.

Again I return to Marlowe Cemetery, then back to Guthrie Café. Until I remember the place I ought to go, and like a windblown leaf I waft to our old house.

She isn't home, but this time it's different. As I hover in the living room, I see it as it really appears. The place is alive with modern furniture, and strange pictures line the walls. There stands a TV set the equal of which I'd never seen. Flat and hanging from a wall, as masterwork's pride, its charcoal screen reflects the dying sun. Weird knickknacks and other memorabilia fill shelves and shelves, while acid-colored cushions clash with a striped couch, and a bubbling aquarium defiantly challenges my faded memories. Only the walls I recognize; still, they are painted in a different color. Someone else lives in this house.

And now I understand the Shade's riddle. I have been living in the past, for years anchored to a world which is no more. I linger there, having no place to go.

She comes home at 7 pm, laden with bags. I'm startled by her voice.

Is she talking to me?

The girl throws her key inside a bowl, then passes straight through me, shivering at the contact. No, she doesn't see me. Talking to a portable phone, she laments those weird cold spots inside her house—*my house*.

Abruptly, something pierces my left arm; I feel ghostly flesh being

torn by burning steel, and I turn in terror to face this new, unearthly assailant. I'm wrong, for what I see chills imaginary blood in my exsan-
guinous body. Out of my wrist, rusted steel is steadily growing from a
ghastly hole, wriggling out like a metallic woodworm. It runs out of the
wound, pulled by invisible hands or by its own inner life, then straightens
down and phases through the floor. I'm shocked, yet I feel no pain. I'm
just restrained by this surreal construct, so I yank at it and test its effect-
tiveness. It seems to yield, as I can freely move, so I roam from room to
room trying out its limits.

Bathroom, study, and kitchen, downstairs.

Attic and bedroom, upstairs.

The chain just follows me, a brand-new appendage issuing from my
wrist, yet going nowhere. It fades a few inches short of the floor, the
damn thing, and I wonder about its purpose.

Meanwhile, my home's new dweller has reached me in the cozy bedroom. She's undressing, hastily taking off garment after garment. There a
shoe flies, uncaringly kicked off. A pair of jeans hurtles through my form,
passing harmlessly and striking the pinkish-colored wall. I'm awestruck as
this young creature discloses her beauty to my unliving eyes. She's slim
and toned up, with slender legs and creamy skin. Her short, blond hair
crowns a face more akin to angels than to lowly mortals. And an angel she
is, as her comeliness projects a halo inside the Mirrorlands, the equal of
which I also have never seen since my demise. I'm charmed.

I feel myself lusting for her; something new in my dreary existence.

Again!

A second chain worms out from the mangled hole and flies through
ethereal air until it plunges, ghostly, inside the girl's back. Panic becomes
my master, as I watch in horror the rusty shackle slide toward her beating
heart. What have I done!

Withal, she seems unaffected. She keeps removing her underwear as
if nothing happened. Then, she passes through me and runs downstairs. I
expect the linking bond to pull me along, considering the guilt I feel for a
deed I did not commit. Yet, the expected tug never comes and I'm
amazed by this inexplicable trick.

Relieved, I follow her down, finding her talking again to the damned
wireless phone. She's talking to a man, for I can clearly hear his masculine
tone pouring out of the goddamned device. A black spot, darker than ink,
forms inside my bleary conscience, growing inch by inch like malevolent
cancer, the more I hear from the unseen boyfriend. Is it jealousy... or
maybe envy, this impious sensation invading my essence? How come?

Loathing, despair, and sorrow were my only companions in this abominable afterlife. Love, passion, and joy I never knew.

Scared by this novelty, I storm through the front door, unwilling to stand more, and prepare myself to return to my forlorn existence.

Impossible!

The chains yank at me, impeding my progressions, and a chilling pain wracks my whole being. I try again, but it still hurts. I twist, writhe, and wriggle, but they don't yield. Enraged, I bite at my wrist, going, as we say in Texas, *coyote ugly*, ready to chew off my offending hand. But my phantom teeth are worthless in the effort; they simply munch through thin air.

I howl my rage in frustration, and then I jerk again, fruitlessly, at my demonic bonds. Nonetheless, they don't give up on their dull purpose, but I do not surrender, for time I have in quantity.

* * *

Later.

Bored by my futile efforts, I stand inside my new prison. Half-heartedly, my eyes scan the boundaries of this unexpected confinement. My forlorn world has shrunk; all that's left of it is just this accursed house. And my rage grows at my vanished tormentor, for I'm sure this is another of its depraved pranks and it is enjoying it deep inside my soul.

Something new distracts me. Her boyfriend has arrived and is making love to her. Envy and lust fill my blazing psyche, and I rush to the appalling sight of the man on her candid body, attracted by the warm, comforting sensation that sexual activity dispenses. Nonetheless, my Shade takes hold of me and I lunge toward the source of my painful jealousy.

The tingle of her fingers seems electric, crackling on my newly found skin. Through another man's lips I moan, as I eagerly bury my face in her neck's fragrance.

God, I'm inside her man!

Incredulous, I trace her jaw's outline with borrowed, nervous fingers, savoring the warmth of living skin. It had been so long since I felt this way. I abandon myself to this unfair embrace as dizziness of possession mingles with my host's arousal and mine. Like a euphoric cat, I purr, and that grumble feels good in this alien throat. She runs her hands, slowly, from back to buttocks, squeezing at the fleshy pulp with heightened ardor.

"Please, slow down, don't be too eager," she whispers.

I feel remorse for this shameful act, yet I can't refrain from indulging in this taste of life. I kiss her lightly, and her soft shiver sends waves of ecstasy through my stolen body.

Finally, I understand the meaning of those awful chains.

They're anchors, fastening my essence to this place. Love for my old house is the first. And lust for this woman, the second. I'm bound to this place for eternity, chained down by base want and material greed. I'll haunt this place like the ghosts of legends, my fetters forged out of craving and possessiveness.

This place is my haunt, and I will never leave.

"Please," she repeats, "I want to take my time."

Somewhere deep inside of me, the Shade emits a ghastly and wicked laughter, as I hear myself answering with purloined lips.

"I'm not going anywhere."

FOURTH GABLE FROM THE RIGHT

ROBERT W. WALKER

When he entered the front door, it had not been easy; it was as if the house did not wish him to enter her empty rooms. As if no human had a right to be here. The key seemed unable to work at all, and to be honest, he stood in the foyer now wondering when and how he'd gotten inside. For days now he'd been light headed and in a strange daze.

The house chided Charles; it told him in no uncertain terms that he was not the man everyone believed him to be. The room he stood in now, the master bedroom, said he wasn't even the man *he* believed himself to be. He was in such a fog that he did not recall coming upstairs to this room, but he understood why he had come here first.

This fog and the struggle with his own home had begun days earlier, since the funeral, and it persisted. It proved most unctuous and disturbing. In addition, the room *chilled* him straight to the bone. The old manse certainly had its drafts and was given to cold in the past, but nothing as frosty as now.

Charles had written about so many houses in so many of his tales; houses with porches and gables and bay windows and spiraling stairways. He stared out over London now from the fourth gable from the right, the one overlooking the street, but the glass was so in need of cleaning that the view was impossible. Charles had also written of London hovels along the Thames—that ribbon of life and death that ran through the city, pumping commerce like blood. He had also created so many characters, stitched together from the whole cloth of pen and imagination. Characters developed from the voices in his head. The voices, he told his wife and children, and anyone who asked, that had indeed come from his head, which in essence proved the lie he told himself.

In point of fact, it was the greatest lie of all the myriad of lies that crafting fiction led to. Still, all the fabrications coming from the voices, all went in to prove time and again the truths that dwelled between heaven and hell; truths lurking just beneath the surface of Charles' brain. Truths dealing with the human psyche and soul and how one must cherish soul over material matters.

Few understood that the voices he relied on to produce his stories did not come from his head the way they did with other authors; no, his voices came from the *house* and its various rooms. Each room had its own voice and its own collection of characters lurking there. They came from the fabric of the house; from the flooring, the ceilings, the walls, the stone of each fireplace in each and every room. But how does one confess such things to other people, even those most intimate of relations? Fear of the asylum kept Charles from ever divulging the secret of the rooms in his manse.

He made his way from the now silent master bedroom and bath to wander the second floor hallway, his destination the stairs and his office afterward. It was a ritual. Wake up and rush to the study to hear the voices and to settle on one dominant insistent voice to move his pen again.

The voices often came with images of twisted, roiling, smoke-like disembodied creatures from the Invisible World here. They poured forth from the lines, spirals, and shapes in the oaken doors. They seeped from the mahogany balconies and stairwells, settling over him like a shroud and whispering in his ear each plaintive story.

He stood at the top of the stairwell and glanced at the ceiling. All remained silent on the third floor. Not so much as a thump in the night. He looked down to the bottom of the stairwell, hopeful he might hear something, anything, coming from the wooden steps. But nothing came back; no report. "Where are you!" he demanded to know. "All my human contact has abandoned me to death! Not you, too!"

Full-blown stories always came from the voices that rose from the rosewood, the pine, the cypress. Every bedroom, every great room, every closet, and even Charles' office. The house exuded stories told by a plethora of voices that only he could hear. It was as if the house had chosen him alone. It might whisper the occasional wisp to one of the children when they were toddlers, but they'd all gone now. Unlike the children in those early years, Charles had copious amounts whispered to him, whole bloody novels in fact! The rooms here had produced numerous novels, many hundreds of thousands, nay millions of words.

Home they say is where the heart is, Charles thought as he surveyed the empty manse from which so many parts of him had fled. For Charles, home is, now and always had been, where the stories reside. The voices that came from his proper Victorian home were often filled with a rich power, like the voice he imagined of a Shakespeare or a Bacon or a Marlowe, but not always. Some rooms in the house were filled with strident, ear-wrenching cries—the grief-stricken sound of banshees, revenants, and the *ill-at-ease* in death's grip. Still other rooms sounded the edginess of a liar, a cheat, a thief, a killer even, while others proved the soft voices of children at distracted play.

Charles began step by step down the spiraling staircase. As he did so, his left hand played along the bannister, trying to coax out a sound, a voice, a story. Halfway down the staircase and still nothing came of his desire to hear its latest story. Only silence returned, an unbearable silence.

The voices dictated each story, setting and place, established circumstance and chose whether gentle or ghoulish behavior was warranted. They dictated pleasure, passion, pain, indeed every emotion known to Charles.

With a pipe that had long died out in his mouth, Charles, famed author known the world over for his episodic tales published in the *London Times*, now wandered from room to room, alone in the house. The children had all made lives of their own, in other homes, in other places about London, and his wife had passed on, as had all his intimate friends. After his wife's death, he had secretly held séances in an attempt to reach her, to find out if she was safe and in a good place, but the house only mocked such efforts, laughing at him until he finally gave up any hope. Upon discovering the chicanery of séance operators, he stopped altogether.

The house had known what a sham the séance conductor was long before Charles had come to the conclusion he was being bamboozled. All the same, Charles had forgiven himself for becoming a mark for a con man. It was as Shakespeare had said, "Love doth make fools of us all." In fact, that voice stating this had come from his bookshelf. Charles had come to the realization that the level of his remorse, coupled with regrets, had constructed a horrible grief and depression, which in essence was the beginning of the end of the voices in the rooms until soon his pen was altogether silenced.

At the bottom of the stairs, Charles attempted to get some words from a wooden sculpture of Poseidon trying to tame a seahorse, a replica of the brass original by Claus of Innsbruck. He'd been unable to write, and writing for Dickens was life itself. Massaging the statue felt like an act of desperation, and in fact, he allowed that it was just that. He'd never gotten a voice from that dead wood. He wanted to shout at the staircase and the foyer before him. His normal life had disappeared; his life had become a long nightmare of a horrid case of writer's block. The pain of being unable to carry on as a creator of characters now caused Charles to analyze why he could no longer write.

He erupted in a cursing of the house over his head. He wanted to curse and shout further still, but it seemed useless and no one, certainly not the phantoms, were having any of it. It was as if they could not, or would not, hear his pleas. He wanted to throw open a window then and shout it to the street below in the manner of Ebenezer Scrooge in *A Christmas Carol*. He wanted to shout his pain and for someone to tell him the reason why! But what was the true reason? Some said there was no such thing as writer's block; that it was just an excuse for getting nothing accomplished, a form of *malaise*, another word for procrastination... But this was somehow different. Somehow larger than any so-called block, for the house, his sweet home, no longer spoke to him as he moved from room to room.

The voices had abandoned him here in the hearth, the long hall, and the kitchen.

His nerves were rattled and he figured he could hear them rattling inside his frame like chains forged in life, a life sacrificed to his work, his fiction. This while at the same instant hoping against hope the rattling was coming from one of the rooms. Of course it must be his imagination, that and this ridiculous writer's block.

Then he thought he heard a whisper reverberate through the walls.

It was coming from the room at the end of the hall, his study. This room, aside from his bedroom, had always spoken the loudest and the most often. He tried to rush now toward his study, anxious, excited, but Charles found his movement restricted by an unfamiliar force that he'd encountered a few times now in the house. It felt like a wall of cold that pushed back at him, a force that seemed bent on keeping him from advancing, as if this entity did not wish him to enter the now-whispering study.

Finally reaching his study, he placed his hands together in prayer, begging to hear the whispers that seemed to be racing from him. *I want to understand; speak to me,* came his plea to the house, a silent prayer that the room must hear! Why had it gone silent? What had it whispered down the hall to him just then? *Speak to me*, he silently pleaded. *Damn it, I am Charles Dickens! Speak to me.*

But even his own voice in his head was not making a sound. He wondered if he could even form words any longer, when he heard his oaken desk whisper, "Charles... You no longer *belong* here."

Dickens gasped and silently dropped into his old chair. He found that even his leather chair no longer spoke. Not so much as a squeak or the old familiar squeal. Realizing he had no substance, the reason for the house's silence dawned on him.

The house was in search of a new man, a new hand, and a new pen; Charles' had gone silent. The house needed a new voice; it needed to concern itself with its own life. Thus, it needed a sentient being known popularly as a storyteller.

This realization washed over Dickens as his ghost form began to lose its cohesiveness and to seep into and become one with his beautiful old, oaken desk. There was an audible sigh throughout the house, but no one to hear it. Days before, the study had been emptied of all of Charles' books and notes, and now the office was empty of the man's spirit.

Years later, the house was reopened as a memorial and a museum, everything replaced and retouched; everything but the people who once resided within had been *returned*. Some who visit say that they feel Dickens in the very walls and the staircase. Others say they *hear* a Dickensian voice that they attribute to the ghost in the desk *trying to get out*. Then there is the story of the night watchman.

The night man secretively began writing while seated at Dickens' desk. The museum watchman had taken the job as a temporary arrangement as he wanted to travel and write. His name was Oscar... Oscar Wilde.

SPIRITUS EX MACHINA
NELSON W. PYLES

1

Travis Byron walked carefully through the dimly lit hallway as he followed the man in grease-stained coveralls. It was only a little after 10 pm, but it felt much later. He wasn't as nervous as he was apprehensive. What he was about to see had been hidden from the public for the last 70 years; only a handful of people had been allowed to view it. He felt mildly rankled and maybe just a little intimidated by that bit of knowledge.

Earlier, his girlfriend Penny had told him he needed to relax. "It's just a car, love," she had said sweetly, holding his face in her hands and kissing him lightly. "A stupid, old car."

He had smiled back at her and returned her kiss. But he was still not convinced that it was just a stupid, old car. For one thing, it wasn't *just* a stupid, old car.

It was a murderer.

"Only a bit further, mate," said the man.

"Thanks," Travis said back, adding, "I'm sorry, what's your name?"

The man looked over his shoulder briefly and smiled a broken-toothed grin. "Name's Tim, sir. Thanks for askin'."

Travis smiled a little. "Thanks for bringing me back here. Sorry it's so late."

"Don't think nothin' of it," Tim said. The way he said think "nothing" with his thick accent made it sound like "fink nofin". "Not many geysers get to see the Jag."

"I've heard it hasn't had a lot of... visitors."

Tim laughed. "Yeah, you could say that. Not many would want to, though."

"I'm hoping you're wrong," Travis said. "My employer is counting on the novelty of this car to make good on his investment."

Tim slowed down and stopped. He turned around and looked at Travis. "You seem like a good bloke. Not a tosser like your boss, so I'll give you a bit of free advice. Yeah?"

Travis was taken aback by this abrupt stop, but he raised his head to show he was interested in what Tim had to say. The man leaned in close.

"Once your boss has this car moved, get as *far away* from it as possible. Quit if you has to, but get away from it."

Travis opened his mouth to speak, but Tim continued. "I know it sounds right barmy, it does, but I speak the truth. That car is flat out *bad*."

Travis looked somewhat mortified as he grinned. "Look at you, taking the piss!" Travis said, laughing. "You started to worry me a bit there, mate."

Tim smiled, but not because he was happy. "Sir, you may think it's funny, but you won't for long. I absolutely guarantee."

Travis kept his smile, but again, he felt mildly rankled not only by what Tim said, but how he said it. *I absolutely guarantee...*

Tim turned and continued to walk. It took Travis some effort to follow the man.

In less than twenty-five seconds, they both arrived at a door marked, **Storage Garage 481**. Under the faded green marker was another handwritten sign that looked just as old declaring: **Absolutely No Entry**.

"Don't worry 'bout the sign," said Tim, answering Travis' unspoken question. "That's just to keep wandering folks out of here."

"Do you get many wandering folks?" Travis asked. "I mean, this garage couldn't be farther away if it were bloody Penkridge."

"You a Penkridge bloke? I *knew* you was a small town geyser." Tim's genuine smile returned. "From Wolverhampton meself. Practically family, we are."

Travis was getting weary of all of this stalling. The night was getting longer and he was losing some patience. He looked at Tim, who was still smiling like an idiot and not making any attempt to unlock the garage.

"If it's all the same Tim, we can talk about footie later. I do have a job to do here, as do you."

"Ready to be on with it then, are you?"

"Yes."

"Right. Wait right here."

Tim grabbed the keys from his belt, found the right one, and unlocked the door. He opened it, but did not allow Travis to enter. "Right back," Tim said as the door closed slowly behind him. There was a dragging sound and the door reopened with Tim holding two folding chairs. Travis suddenly had a sinking feeling the moment he saw the chairs.

"Here you are. Take a seat, sir."

He held the chair out to Travis, who refused it.

"What is this?" Travis asked loudly. "You take your sweet time dragging me across this warehouse and we finally get here, you bring me a fucking folding chair?"

Tim didn't flinch and continued holding out the chair. "Right. There's a few things needed to be discussed, sir, and *now* is when we do it. Take the chair, and with all due respect, don't talk to me like I fucking well work for you."

The tone of Tim's voice was colder and more direct. It didn't have any of the "local boy" charm anymore. When he said *things* it didn't come out sounding like *fings*. Tim was serious.

Without a word, Travis took the chair, opened it, and sat down. Tim nodded and did the same. He fished out a soft pack of cigarettes from his coverall breast pocket with two fingers. He offered one to Travis. "Fag?"

Travis shook his head.

Tim took one from the pack and returned the rest to his pocket. He reached into his pants pocket and grabbed a cheap lighter to light up. He inhaled deeply, and when he exhaled, there was just a very thin stream of smoke. Travis waited impatiently for the man's explanation.

"In 1955, there were this accident at Le Mans,' Tim began. "Killed, when all were said and done, eighty-eight people. Flippin' tragedy if there ever were one, right?" Tim took a deep drag and continued, allowing the smoke to drift slowly from his nostrils. "That car was never driven again. Packed up and locked away, quite like this one here. Sold last year for over a million, American anyways. Nice little tidy pile of cash for the owner, init? Nowhere near what your tosser of a boss is paying for this, yeah?"

Travis had to agree. He'd heard about the Le Mans tragedy and the huge payout last year, which is what had ignited his employer's interest in the first place. He thought he was getting a steal with this car at eighty thousand pounds, and Travis had gladly offered his services to make sure it was worth it.

"Well, true, but the morbid fact of the body count has a lot to do with it I'm sure," Travis said.

Tim took time to look at his smoke before speaking. "Is that what you really think? Cos I'll tell you something for nothing, mate. I'd rather have about ten of the other car than this one in there."

"I'm not following you. This car here carries a considerably lower body count than the Le Mans," Travis said. "And by considerably, I mean *very* considerably. Only twenty people, if I'm correct."

Tim gave a short bark of a laugh.

"Listen to yourself, mate. '*Only* twenty people?' Are you fucking daft? *Twenty people*, man. So, it isn't eighty-eight, but there's still blood, ain't there? Broken homes and families."

"Eighty-eight is a hell of a lot more death than twenty, so yeah, as bad as twenty is, it's a damn sight better than eighty-eight. Not much really to change that little fact."

"Except, for the one detail you're forgetting," Tim shot back. "The Austin Healy 100 Special that killed eighty-eight people and ruined or injured at least one-hundred and twenty more did it all in *one shot*."

Travis opened his mouth to say, "So what?" but found that he couldn't utter a word.

"Let it sink in there, boy-o. The eighty-eight people killed all got killed at once. The little Jaguar on the other side of this wall killed 20 people *one at a time*."

"Bollocks," Travis said. "Total bollocks. You're starting to waste my time here. If you're done taking the piss out of me, I'll be having a look at my employer's property."

Travis was furious now and stood up. Tim remained calm and refused to look up at Travis. He just fixed on some stain on the floor and looked almost sadly resigned. He let smoke out as he exhaled.

"You're gonna want to hear this, mate. Not kidding," was all Tim said.

"I suppose you're going to tell me a car that's damn close to being a century old and hasn't had a working motor in it for the bulk of that time just rolls off all by itself and kills someone once in a while. Yes?"

"That car ain't moved in about two decades," Tim replied. "It don't roll around on its own. Never has, but I will assure you that car is a fucking spook if there ever was one."

Tim took one last drag from his smoke before dropping the butt on the floor. Travis looked and saw a pattern of similar burn marks in the floor. Tim finally looked up at Travis, not smiling.

"When you're in there alone, you're gonna want to ask me some questions. I may or may not be here to answer them on your way out, as I don't like to go in there if I don't have to."

Travis softened slightly. "Wait, you aren't going in?"

"No. So if you got any questions, ask 'em now."

"Well, I haven't even seen it yet, have I?" Travis said. "Look, I'm sorry, but this is all really——"

"I'm telling you, sir, that car is fucking *dangerous*. If you were smart, you'd go tell your employer that everything is fine and let him deal with it, but you should just turn around and go home."

Travis looked at Tim and saw he was shaking slightly. The man was terrified. Tim looked as if he were going to say something, but didn't. "Tim, I'll be fine, but wait out here, alright? I won't be too long."

Tim looked like he wanted to run.

Travis held up a hand. "Give me five minutes and then pound on that door. Is that a little safer?"

Tim seemed to ponder this and then he nodded. "Five minutes, no more. Maybe only four, but don't get too close to it, and for fuck's sake, don't touch it."

Travis smiled and walked to the door. Tim grabbed his shoulder. "And whatever it shows you isn't real," Tim said, nearly whispering. "It's all a lie."

Travis frowned and then smiled, if only to reassure Tim. "Five minutes, maybe four. Don't touch it. Got it."

Tim released his shoulder and Travis opened the door. As the door closed, Tim stood trembling and stared at the door. He began to count slowly to three hundred. He debated counting to two hundred forty, but he hoped that Travis would be okay.

He really didn't seem stupid.

2

Travis closed the door, locked it, and reached out to his left, feeling the wall for the light switch. He found it and switched it on, hearing the heavy light overhead click. They were the newer, non-incandescent lights that would take a minute or two to light up bright. There, not two feet in front of him, was the car.

After listening to Tim go on about it, he expected it to growl at him, but it stayed put, good little car that it was, and did nothing close to growling. Travis stared at the car as he took a heavy step forward, closer to it. "I'm not supposed to get close to you," Travis said quietly to the car. "You're some sort of spook as I am to understand."

The car did nothing.

101

Travis walked slowly around it. It was a beautiful car. A 1954 Jaguar XK120. A sleek, black convertible, and absolutely gorgeous. It was a dream car, really. A total race car—one seat for the driver—that just screamed to be driven. This was a car that was built for racing and designed for winning. And win this car did; it won all three of the races it ran until it was considered a jinx by Walter Carmichael, the car's original owner, driver, and eventual third victim.

Travis looked intently at the car, and although a thin layer of dust covered it, it still looked shiny and beautiful. Tempting even.

"You're a beautiful spook, that's for sure," Travis said quietly to the car.

Circling it one more time, he decided to get to work. He took off his messenger bag and set it down on a workbench situated along the wall on the opposite side of the car. He opened the bag and took out three things, one of which was a camera.

He turned around and started taking pictures of the car. As he did so, he began to talk as he walked quickly around the car.

"Julian Fitzgerald, died 1956, leapt from his third-floor flat six hours after repairing a faulty hose," Travis said. "Spencer McDaniels, died, also 1956, about four hours after rotating all four tires. Massive heart failure. He was twenty-three years old and healthy as an ox."

The car simply sat there as Travis circled it, taking pictures and talking. He was rattling off the name of every person who had died and was linked to the car.

"Carmichael, of course. Took a straight razor to his own bloody neck and nearly decapitated himself after retiring you. Not less than one hour after the fact."

He made his way back to the workbench and put down the camera. He then stepped forward and touched the hood of the car. The moment he made contact, he felt something akin to a static electric shock jump into his arm, but he kept the fingers on the hood. He walked around the car again, running his fingers along the sleek surface, all the while reciting the names of the victims.

"Sean Radcliffe, 1961, the first buyer post Carmichael. Died from a self-inflicted gunshot wound to the head. Right in the driver's seat."

As he walked around to the back of the car, he looked into the empty driver's seat. He blinked, thought he saw a dark shadow behind the wheel. He didn't stop walking, but he did keep looking.

The shadow seemed to take shape until he saw a man sitting in the driver's seat, looking right at him.

"Hello, boy," said the man. "I imagine you know who I am."

Travis stopped and nodded. He stood at the right side of the car. "Hello, Sean."

Sean Radcliffe smiled a rotten-looking smile. Travis could see a black hole on the left side of Sean's head.

"What is it you hope to accomplish here, boy?" Sean asked, still smiling.

"If it's all the same, Sean, I got some more names to go over, but I was wondering who was going to be the first to show up."

Sean laughed. "Are you trying to piss something off today? Cos, this is about the right way to do it I'd reckon."

"Yeah," Travis said, starting to walk around the car again. "I kind of figured it would be. Would you like to hear more names?"

"I know 'em all already, but why not?" Sean said as he faded away.

Travis cleared his throat and began again. "Alex Karras, died 1969 after rebuilding the engine. Exactly *47 seconds* after rebuilding the engine. The garage caught fire and burned everything except the car."

A man appeared in the driver's seat. He was horribly burned and charred. A blackened arm casually hung out of the car as Travis walked toward the front.

"That was a fun one," the Alex-thing said.

It spoke with a slight accent. Travis thought it might be Greek. Blocking out the thought, he continued reciting his list of names. He went through the names of every person on the list of the deceased, and for each one, a spectral form appeared in the driver's seat. The last name he recited was Fenwick Byars, a mechanical engineer who, in 1998, had simply gone into the garage where the car had been stored.

The form of Fenwick Byars appeared in the seat, grinning at Travis, who had decided to stop. "You've rattled all of them off, boy." Fenwick said as Travis returned to the work bench. "Or have you?"

Travis didn't turn around. "No. There's one more. Just one."

The Fenwick-thing laughed. Because he died of asphyxiation, the laugh had a hoarse quality. "Oh yeah? You wouldn't be countin' yourself in the list yet, would ya? Cos, make no mistake. You are next."

Travis still didn't turn around. "Can you tell me what you are first?"

The Fenwick-thing laughed again. "I think you know."

"I do, I just want to hear it," Travis said flatly.

"I am not at liberty to say," the Fenwick-thing said after a moment.

Travis finally turned around and looked at Fenwick. He was holding a black book covered with symbols and a small silk bag that had on it a picture of a tree with three white flowers. The Fenwick-thing lost its ashen look and its jaw loosened.

"You're a *Yurei*," Travis said. "And I'm kicking you the hell out of this car."

The Fenwick-thing vanished and the lights began to dim. Travis threw the small bag on the hood of the car. One of the light fixtures exploded.

"Hamilton Byron, died 1995 by his own hand in front of his grandchildren," Travis said, his voice shaking. "All he had done was deliver a package to the garage where this car was being kept."

Suddenly, as if on cue, Hamilton Byron appeared in the car's seat. His wrists were sliced and there were blood stains on his palms. Unlike the other spirits, this one looked frightened.

"You ought not to toy with this, Travis," the Hamilton-thing said. "Take that bloody hex thing off the car."

"You aren't my grandfather," Travis said. "But I did want you in this form when I removed you."

There was a sudden pounding on the door.

"A few more minutes, Tim!" Travis shouted as he opened the book.

"Bollocks!" Tim responded. "Time to get out, sir!"

"Yes, time to get out," the thing that looked like his grandfather said. "And take that... *thing* off of the hood. You might live if you do it now."

"You end here, *Yurei*. That *ofuda* will make sure you're gone for good. Of course, you know that already." Travis found the page he was looking for and began to recite from the book. The thing that looked like his grandfather began to contort and writhe as the words became louder and seemed to carry an actual weight. Travis kept repeating the words, even as the memory of his grandfather's death began to explode in his head.

Travis and his sister had been kids, but old enough to know something was wrong when their grandfather had come home, crying in agony. He went into their parent's kitchen and sliced open his wrists. He staggered back into the living room, blooding flowing steadily from both wrists. His sister screamed hysterically until his mother came downstairs and began screaming. The old man didn't allow anyone near him to help. He still held the large knife he'd used to cut himself.

He said one thing before collapsing. He looked at Travis, all of ten years old, and said simply, "Yurei." And then he died. His sister and mum forgot the word almost instantly and regarded it as a crazy person's last thought. Nonsense, in other words.

But the word haunted Travis and he never forgot it. He spent years trying to find out what it meant. With the advent of the internet he discovered what it was, and even then he hadn't been sure of its meaning. It wasn't until he became friends with a guy at university named Kenada Odaka, or Kenny as he was called, that he discovered he'd been making a mistake.

"You sure that's what he said?" Kenny had asked over a pint. "Cos that's... well, fucked."

Half drunk, Travis nodded. "Yeah, that's what he said. Yuri. Some stupid Russian thing, but I can't make anything out from it. Is it a name or what?" Travis drained the rest of his pint.

"No, mate. I think you're pronouncing it wrong. I think he meant, *Yu-rei*. Like *you ray*."

Travis swallowed hard and said, "Fuck, that's *it*. I was pronouncing it wrong, but that's what it was."

It was Kenny's turn to finish off his pint. He downed it and raised a hand for two more. He leaned in close to Travis. "Trav, a Yurei is a spirit. A vengeful ghost that haunts something. Usually like a house, or something. I don't see why it wouldn't go to a car."

"What, you mean an angry ghost is haunting a fucking *race car*? That's stupid." Travis tried to laugh.

"Yeah? You're the one who's been looking for an answer all this time, and I just gave you one. This stuff is no joke, mate."

Travis looked at Kenny.

"And no," Kenny said, paying the waitress when she brought over the next round. "I'm not taking the piss. Tomorrow, we'll go see my granddad. He only speaks Japanese, but he'll lay it all out for you."

"But this is England, Kenny. You're the first and only Japanese anyone I've ever seen. How does a Japanese evil spirit wind up in an English race car?"

Kenny shook his head. "You don't get it. It doesn't matter. I'm sure it's called other things everywhere else, but it's not like one thing is stuck in just one place. Bad stuff happens everywhere. I'm Japanese, but I'm fucking just about as English as you, yeah?"

Travis let that sink in as he clinked his pint with Kenny.

The following year, he managed to find someone, on Kenny's grandfather's suggestion, who could help. He had spent three months in Japan, learning from a Buddhist priest named Master Inshiro. He had learned enough of the language for the ritual and had memorized the words, but Master Inshiro said that the book with the *ofuda* was more powerful.

"The *Yurei* is a powerful spirit," Master Inshiro had told him. "And it matters little how or why it is in this object. It only matters that it be removed. The incantation will drive it out and the *ofuda* will keep it out, but be careful."

And here was Travis, years later, in front of a car he was convinced was possessed by a vengeful spirit. And he had been right.

He heard Tim outside trying, and failing, to open the door.

"You weren't supposed to lock the fucking door!" Tim yelled, pounding on it furiously. "You have got to come out of there!"

Travis drove Tim—and his grandfather's death—out of his head. He kept reading the incantation from the book of Shinto writings Master Inshiro had given him. The Hamiliton-thing was still writhing in the seat and beginning to fade.

"You can't do this!" the thing screamed.

Travis closed the book. "I *have* done it. Now, get out and leave this car."

A second and a third light bulb exploded over head, leaving only one to illuminate the garage. A loud wail rose from the car, but Travis sensed it went deeper than the car. It nearly deafened him, but then it went quiet.

After a moment, Travis reached out and touched the hood of the car.

He felt nothing but the hood, which was a little warm, but cooling. Tim continued to hammer on the door. Satisfied, Travis walked to the door and unlocked it.

Tim burst in, not knowing quite what to expect. He looked at Travis and what he was holding before shifting his gaze to the car and then back to Travis. He blinked a few times. "Sir? What did you—"

"It's over, Tim," Travis said. "This car is just a car now. It's done."

Tim rubbed his jaw and looked at the bag on the hood of the car. "What's that then?"

Travis smiled and started to gather his things. "Let me tell you all about it. Fancy a pint?"

3

One week later, Travis sat down at his computer in his home office in Penkridge. His girlfriend had gone out to dinner with her friends.

"I wish you'd come out with us," she'd said somewhat sadly. He'd been in an odd mood since coming back from his trip to view the car. "Are you sure you won't come out?"

Travis smiled and shook his head. "I've got a few more things to do and I think I'm going to turn in early, love. You have fun. Bring a curry back for me?"

She kissed him on his head. "Sure thing." And off she went.

He grabbed his messenger bag from the floor and pulled out the camera. He hadn't looked at it since he shoved it in the bag at the garage, was almost afraid to look at it. He turned it over in his hands and pulled out the memory card. He put the camera next to the keyboard and inserted the card into the hard-drive port to see the pictures.

As it loaded, the lights flickered slightly. The menu appeared on his screen.

It was thirty pictures of the car at different angles. Travis felt his heart begin to pound in his chest. He clicked on the first one and there was nothing out of the ordinary. He clicked the arrow to see the next one.

Nothing.

And then the next one.

Nothing. And yet…

He clicked the next one and saw that something was there, faint, but definitely there.

He clicked the next one, and it looked like something was beginning to take form behind the car's steering wheel.

He clicked the next one and the next one.

Something solid was showing up in the picture. His heart began to pound harder and faster.

With each click, a thing, shadowlike in appearance, was indeed taking shape in the driver's seat, and he was expecting to see a version of the first apparition behind the wheel. He clicked ahead faster now, and then he stopped.

It was not the first apparition.

It was… him.

It was blurry, but it was most definitely him, looking directly at the camera. His face was expressionless and dead. His eyes were black and drool was dripping out of his mouth.

He raised a hand to his own mouth and noticed he was drooling. He jerked his hand away and the next picture clicked on its own.

There was no car.

It was a picture of him, in front of his computer, as if taken from behind.

He looked behind him and saw nothing. When he turned back around, the next picture was him again, except looking for what was behind him. His expression was one of sheer terror.

He looked at the camera next to the keyboard and he knew.

He knew right away where the *Yurei* had gone.

The next picture on the computer was a closer picture of Travis, slumped dead on his keyboard and Travis screamed—for the very last time.

ADVERSE POSSESSION
MARIANNE HALBERT

Willard pulled his hat further down over his ears as snowflakes swirled around his face, biting his cheeks.

Between coughs, Tommy was droning on about the land, pointing out the various headstones and who they belonged to. You'd think the guy was making introductions at a dinner party. Willard looked past his old poker buddy and saw the glow of the fading fire through the window in the house up the hill.

"Now the Burtons here," Tommy said, "they were the ones who put the reinforcements in the bridge that crosses the crick. God bless'm for that." The wind picked up even more, howling through the trees. From behind them, in the direction of the denser woods, Willard heard the cracking of brittle limbs and the sudden shriek of an animal. The sound cut off almost as soon as it had begun, but Tommy snapped to attention, frozen for a moment, only his eyes moving as they searched the forest. He choked out another cough, then moved in the direction of the house.

Finally.

They stepped onto the bridge and Tommy pointed out some rotted planks.

"Meant to fix those last spring. The new planks're in the shed." He looked around again, his eyes lost and haunted. Willard thought Tommy might actually be considering going to get the planks and fixing the bridge right now. Below them, the water's surface was frozen, decaying leaves trapped in its icy grip. Beneath the brittle surface, something dark flowed back and forth.

"I'll take care of it, Tommy. You're leaving her in good hands." *Numb hands at this point.*

Tommy nodded. He towered over Willard and weighed at least twice as much, but once they'd stepped off the bridge on the other side, he seemed to deflate a little.

They walked up the hill toward the house. With his large, gloved hands, Tommy grabbed a couple of logs from a snow-dusted wood pile. He nudged the door open with his boot and went straight to the hearth. The fire had mostly died down, and when he tossed the first log in, weak flames licked at it from the ashes.

Willard moved toward the stove—*My stove as soon as the papers are signed*—and put on a kettle. He pulled two blue speckled mugs from a cupboard and set them on the kitchen table.

As the fire cracked and sputtered, Tommy pulled off his gloves and hat, and unbuttoned his coat, sending a shower of snowflakes onto the linoleum floor. What was left of Tommy's white hair looked matted to his head in some places, stuck out wildly in others. Willard scooped some instant coffee into the mugs, already having decided a real coffee pot would be one of the first additions to his new home.

Tommy pulled open a desk drawer and grabbed some pens. The paperwork was already on the kitchen table, being guarded by a ceramic rooster and a wide-eyed, owl-faced napkin holder.

The kettle whistled, its shrill cry cutting through the otherwise silent house. Willard filled the cups, watching the steam rise. Both men took a seat at the table.

"Well," Tommy said, "I guess this is it. Most folks don't want to buy land that includes a cemetery, even though I dropped the price to rock bottom. The thought of it scares most, and the duty to maintain the easement scares off the rest." He took a sip of his coffee. His words were slow, deliberate. He looked Willard in the eye. "You do understand, that's part of the sale. You buy the property, you must maintain the easement."

Willard shifted in his seat. "Well, sure, Tommy. But you said no one's visited that graveyard in over thirty years. How hard can it be?"

Tommy's jaw clenched. "It don't matter. Whatever, whoever needs access to or from, you gotta respect that. You won't just own this land now. You're responsible for it. And for everything on it." He'd worked himself up and fell into a coughing fit. He pounded one fist into his chest a few times. Willard moved to get out of his chair to assist, but Tommy scowled and waved him back down.

Tommy reached for a pen and scribbled his name, Thomas Fitting, on the land sale form. Willard reached across the table, pulling paper and pen closer. He signed it as well, Willard Cowell.

"I'll leave you to it then," Tommy said. He slipped back into his coat, clomped across the linoleum floor, and took his key ring from a hook near the door. "One last thing, in the cellar, there's a—" He looked out the window in the direction of the graveyard. Distracted, he repeated, "There's a—," then he got a queer look on his face, strange enough that Willard followed his gaze to see what had caught his attention. A swirl of snow, darkened by dirt, skirted the far side of the creek. Willard heard a loud thump and turned back to see Tommy prone on the floor, his face a twisted grimace.

"Tommy?" he said, dropping to his knees. Willard gripped his hand, and for a moment he was certain his fingers were about to snap under the pressure. Tommy's bluish lips moved, but only a wheezing sound escaped, as his eyes glazed over.

Willard stood, grateful that the old bastard's ticker had held on long enough for them to complete the sale. He used the old pea-green wall phone, its cord twisted and tangled, to make a pointless call to 911. He sipped his coffee, letting the warmth of it move down his throat as he watched the dark cloud of snow dancing along his creek.

Willard woke up on the couch to the sound of animals screeching in flight. Over the past month, he'd grown accustomed to the black silhouettes of bear and moose sewn into the cushions. To the stuffed trout hanging on the wall. He'd even gotten used to the shadows that seemed to pass outside his window at night. But he still couldn't abide that brief, yet piercing bestial screeching.

Blinding mid-morning sunlight now shone on the large icicles hanging from the eave. He listened to the *drip drip drip* as the drops fell into the slush beneath the window. He swung open the lock on the sill and tried to lift the window. At first it didn't budge, but then the winter-long seal released and he slid the window up. The fresh breeze he'd anticipated was quickly overpowered by a terrible stench. The word *carcass* crossed his mind. Something had died out there. Willard slammed the window shut, causing an icicle to plunge and shatter. He went to the kitchen and made scrambled eggs for breakfast. Halfway through, fork midway to his lips, he caught himself staring at the portion of the floor where Tommy had taken his last breath.

About an hour later, he slid on his boots and coat and headed out the back door. He saw the axe leaning up against the wood pile, and again thought of Tommy, who'd probably chopped all the wood himself.

As Willard walked down the hill, the smell of death grew even stronger. He was almost across the bridge when he heard a wet splintering sound; his foot shot out from under him. He flung his hands out to his sides to grab the railing, then looked at the hole he'd just made in the rotten plank. He took a wide step over the missing area, noticing the dark swirling of the water below. *Friggin' Tommy*. He could've had the decency to fix that damn thing before he kicked it.

Willard moved through the graveyard.

"Missus Pritchard, you're looking lovely today," he said. "Don't suppose you'd be so kind as to point me in the direction of the dead body?" He hadn't really paid much attention to these stones during Tommy's tour, but he looked closer now. Eleanor Pritchard. Beloved Wife Mother, 1748–1810. Steward 1810–.

A winged skull was etched into the stone. Its empty, round eyes reminded him of the owl that still sat on his kitchen table. He looked at the next headstone. Jonathon Pritchard. Faithful Husband Father, 1739–1814. Steward 1814–.

An identical winged skull was also at the top center of his stone. He continued looking at the other graves. Other families. All had a name, year of birth and death. Although the design of the winged skull varied slightly over the years, the image appeared on every stone. And all had that curious "Steward" designation, with a year and a dash beside it. Willard shook his head and went back to looking for the source of the putrid stench.

As he moved deeper into the woods, he was surprised to still see the occasional grave. Some were just a flat stone slab, the words so worn away he couldn't make them out. Then he came to a mound. Surely not, he thought. *A burial mound?*

Something crunched under his boots and he scuffed at the melting snow. At first, Willard thought it was just a tree branch. He knelt and lifted it in his bare hand. He ran one finger up and down the slender curve and recognized it for what it was.

A bone.

He got up and walked around the mound, saw a pyramidal structure made of weathered stone slabs. He guessed the base to be six by six. His gaze moved up the steps of the altar, where more bones, jaws, teeth, and antlers lay scattered. But it was seeing what was draped *across* the altar that caused a cold spike to race down his spine. A coyote carcass, tongue hung slack, one eye glazed over, the other missing. The same sunlight that had started the slow process of melting his icicles had begun its work here, too. A gaping hole in the animal's side revealed ribs and flesh. But not enough flesh. *Something's been feeding.* And were those claw marks ripped into the stone?

Willard looked around and realized that there were hundreds of animal bones, but no tracks. In fact, he couldn't remember seeing any animals, or tracks, anywhere on the property. Searching the ground, all he could make out were long drag marks in the melting snow and in the dirt. He remembered the look on Tommy's face when he'd heard that animal shrieking from the depths of the forest. That animal's death cry had put Tommy on guard. But against what? Willard's heart started pounding, and he broke for the house then, racing through the woods, around the headstones. Out of breath, he paused, gripping a stone for support. He was trembling, or at least he thought he was. A knot began to form in the pit of his stomach when he realized it was the stone that was vibrating.

"What the—?"

He stepped back. Same winged skull. Thomas Fitting. 1935–2013. Steward 2013–.

"Tommy?" Willard asked. His voice cracked as he said it, and he realized he was on the verge of hysterics. Now he *was* trembling. He reached out toward the stone, sunlight glinting off something in it that sparkled. The moment he touched it, he felt the vibration and jumped back as though he'd been bitten. "No, no you did not!"

Willard raced across the bridge and scrambled up the hill. He slipped and began sliding down toward the creek. He clawed at the ground, gripping roots until his descent was halted. Lying on his side, panting, he focused on his task.

Calm the fuck down.

He slowed his breathing, then stood and made his way up the hill. Cold mud soaked through the knees of his jeans from when he'd fallen, and he shivered.

He walked into the house, oblivious to the mud he was tracking in. *Screw it.* It's not my house. Not my floor. It's Tommy's. And the Burton's. And the Pritchard's. And whoever the hell was buried in that mound. He felt a rage welling inside him. He stormed toward the table, grabbed the ceramic rooster by the neck, and hurled it at the wall. It shattered, and its head bounced back toward him, coming to rest at his feet. He kicked it; it skittered away, disappearing around the corner. Willard looked toward the owl napkin holder.

"You're next." But he went straight to the fridge and grabbed a can of beer. He gulped half of it before approaching the kitchen window. Tommy's window. He stood back a little, wanting to see out, but not wanting to be seen. He slugged down the rest of the brew. He grabbed what was left of the six pack by its plastic ring and pulled a chair up to the window, little white, red, and black shards peppering the floor around him. As he drank, Tommy's words came back to him.

"You must maintain the easement. Whatever, whoever needs access to or from, you gotta respect that. You won't just own this land now. You're responsible for it. And for everything on it."

Willard finished his fourth beer, and then shuffled through the desk, ransacking papers and slamming drawers until he found what he wanted. The deed to the house.

He scanned it, his vision a bit blurry. Taxes *blah blah*. Easement to the cemetery. Adverse Possession Clause. *Failure of the landowner to defend his property may result in the property permanently reverting to a previous dweller.*

The windows were shut, but Willard could swear the stench of that rotting coyote had found its way into the house. What else had Tommy been trying to tell him? He started in on another beer and began to doze off. The can slipped from his hand, dropping to the floor and toppling over. Beer began to gurgle and stream out of the opening. Willard watched as little piss-colored streams carried bits of shattered rooster across the floor.

The cellar.

It was the last thing Tommy was talking about, right before he dropped. Willard stood and walked across the hardwood floor of the family room. He stumbled, knocking the stuffed trout on the wall askew. He moved to the back of the hallway and stood in front of a doorway. Layers of paint peeled from its surface. Eggshell white, underneath that, robin's egg blue.

Willard swayed a little, but reached for the dark handle and opened the door. He made his way down the steps, his knees and the warped wood beneath him creaking with each step. The walls were old cement block. He stood in a single shaft of light shining from the hallway above. He moved his arm around until he felt a chain, and pulled; the room was illuminated by a single bulb suspended from the ceiling. The cellar had a dirt floor. A pile of arrowheads and a crumpled, rusty musket lay discarded in one corner. An unfinished brick wall jutted out from the south side of the room. He moved around it and saw a stone leaning against the brick. *It's not just a stone*, his mind insisted, *but a tombstone*. The side facing him was blank. He had to know.

Willard leaned down, the effects of the beer causing his head to swim. He put his hands on the headstone and tugged until it leaned away from the wall. The bulb above him was swinging in a dizzy frenzy, causing the letters and the shadows from the etching to stretch and shrink.

Willard Cowell.

Upon seeing his own name, he snatched his hands away from the stone. It dropped toward him, scraping along the front of his shin and smashing his foot. Willard howled and yanked his leg until his foot was free. Blood began to seep through his jeans, along the area where his shin now burned.

He'd only seen it for a moment, but it was definitely his name etched into the headstone. And that same, haunting winged skull. Had Tommy done that?

He lurched up the stairs and made his way through the house to the back door. He stood in the open doorway, breathing deep. Squinting, he looked across the creek, beyond the graves. He couldn't see the altar, but he knew it was there. And whatever had been feeding on that wild dog was there, too.

Tommy had been trying to tell him something. To explain. About the stewards. He was so damned insistent about maintaining the bridge. So that whoever, *whatever* needed access could pass. How long had that been going on here? From the looks of the cemetery, and the burial mound, hundreds of years at least. But Willard didn't sign up for that. He just wanted some cheap land and privacy. The land this side of the creek would have to do. Not only was he not going to repair the bridge. He now planned to destroy it.

The axe, dull and silent, beckoned him. He grabbed it and limped down the hill toward the creek. He slipped and went down on his injured leg. When he stood again, blood stained the snow. Willard took a tenuous step up to the bridge. He thought of the parade of shadows he'd seen outside his window. The screeching of the animals in flight. The claw marks scratched into the altar.

Why hadn't the others thought of this? Half drunk, and half crazed, he laughed at his own ingeniousness. Giddy, he swung the axe high and felt the jolt run up his arm as the axe bit into the wood. He swung again. And again. The sun was setting, hiding behind the trees. Something dark swirled in the water below him. As he made more progress, the thing's movements became more frantic.

"Good, you son of a bitch. Without the bridge, you can't come up my way anymore, can you?" Willard cackled and kicked out a plank. His foot went through the hole, and he could swear that blackness swirled and raised up with the water, hungry, reaching for him, just before he pulled his leg back up.

Panting, he looked to the graveyard. The shadows of the headstones grew long in the sunset. Then they began to move.

"No," he whispered. He could taste stale beer on his breath, and a hint of bile made its way up his throat. His head was pounding. Willard looked to the water and screamed. "No!"

He swung the axe in a fury now. He heard moaning coming from across the creek. He heard the wood splinter under the force of his blows. He glanced up to see the shadows moving toward him. He realized with a deafening certainty that these were the shadows that passed outside his window. Tears were pooling in his eyes, spilling down his cheeks. His entire body was shaking. At last he chopped through the last remaining log holding up the bridge. It collapsed into the creek. A wave of elation swept over him as he cried and laughed at the same time.

"Ha, take that!"

One of the shadows approached the far side of the creek bed. It was moaning. But then it said a word. It said his name.

"W... i... l... l... a... r... d..."

Somehow, he knew it was Tommy.

"You shoulda warned me, Tommy. You did me wrong."

The apparition moved closer, groaning, clearing its throat until he could understand it. It sounded gravelly as it spoke. Every word was an effort.

"The animals know this is a hunting ground. They flee until we herd them here. The bridge lets us pass, so we can seek its nourishment. We can't cross over water. Without the bridge, we are trapped here. But *it* is not. And without a feeding, it grows hungry." The Tommy-Thing sounded forlorn with its next words. "It will be hunting soon."

The darkness rose up out of the water. Willard stumbled backward and slammed into the ground. The inky liquid licked the ground, his boot, the blood from his shin, like a tongue. The decayed leaves, the earth itself, drew forward, a chaotic ravenous mass. Willard flipped to his stomach and clawed his way up the hill. A growl echoed behind him just before something sharp raked his back. He screamed, but a huge earthy claw clamped down across his mouth, muffling his shrieks. He instantly understood, as horrifying as the animal screams were, why they never lasted long. The axe lay nearby and he swiped for it, but another claw gripped his ankle and began dragging him down the hill. The icy water chilled him as he was sloshed through the creek. His lungs were burning as he tried to scream, but still the beast pressed down on his mouth. At one point his head struck a rock and he blacked out from the pain.

When he awoke, he saw the starlit sky above him. He tried to sit up, but found that his wrists and ankles were bound. His eyes opened wide as he swung his head back and forth, frantic. Roots. Roots held him fast. He was on the temple, but something seemed different. Something was missing.

The burial mound.

He heard a sniffing and sensed something behind him. Then he realized where the mound had gone. It was circling him, that dark tongue licking his cheek, moving down his neck. It went lower and he stiffened. It moved past his waist to his leg. It slid up and down his shin, salivating over the taste of his blood. Then the mouth of the beast opened further, revealing rows and rows of teeth, just before they sunk into his flesh and ripped out a chunk of his leg. The graveyard shadows stood back, silent witnesses to the slaughter.

Willard thrashed against the agonizing torrents of pain that unrelentingly racked his body. The roots, sprouting thorns, tightened, digging into his wrists and ankles. He tried to scream, but a new tendril snaked around and constricted his throat, rendering him utterly helpless. He squeezed his eyes shut, but opened them when he felt a familiar hand grip his.

Tommy.

Out of the tear-blurred corner of his eye, Willard could see what remained of the coyote. Every bone was picked clean. He thought of his headstone and knew it wouldn't stay in the cellar much longer. He hoped he'd make a better steward than he had a landowner. And as he squeezed Tommy's hand in a death grip, he hoped the coyote hadn't suffered long.

OUT OF THE CORNER OF HIS EYE
GORDON ANTHONY BEAN

I opened the front door to find my buddy Mitch standing there. I was taken aback by his appearance. He stood there looking completely disheveled, hair a mess, unshaven, and smelling as if he hadn't bathed in days. His eyes were wide open and glazed over, as if he were drunk. I wondered if there was a trace of madness there as well. Something was very wrong with my friend.

Mitch grabbed my collar and pushed me back into the apartment. "I'm scared, Gary," he screamed, his face close to mine. I could feel his spittle and smelled the sourness of his breath. "They're everywhere. No matter where I go, they're there."

"Mitch, calm down," I said, trying to be as soothing as possible. At six foot four, Mitch was a tank of a man and the last person you wanted to ever see get violent. "I'm not following you. Can you go back to the beginning?" I gestured to the couch. "Have a seat and let's talk, okay?"

Mitch paused for a second, as if weighing his options, and then sat down on the couch. "You won't believe me. Even I don't believe it, and I'm right in the middle of it."

"You're my best friend. You can talk to me. I'm here for you."

Mitch looked around the room and wiped the perspiration from his brow. "All right. I'll go back to the beginning and tell you what happened. But understand this. Once you start down this road, there is no turning back. This is some seriously fucked up shit that I got involved in, and because of that, I'm going to die. There are things we were not meant to know, and sometimes we should just leave things alone. Are you sure you want to get involved?" He paused to glance nervously at the front door before continuing. "I'm giving you a chance to steer clear of this, man. Tell me you don't want to get involved and I'll leave and never bother you again. Your life will depend on this."

I paused. Mitch was my best friend, but something about his grim demeanor made me nervous. I walked to the kitchen and came back with two beers. I handed one to Mitch. "Okay, I've decided. I'm in. Tell me everything."

Mitch took the beer and drained it in one long swallow. His hands shook as he handed the empty back to me. "Got another?"

I got up and went back to the kitchen and came back with the rest of the case. I had a feeling that we were going to need them.

Mitch looked around the room again. I could tell he was terrified. He took a long pull from the bottle and wiped the back of his hand across his mouth. "It began about six days ago. No, let me change that. It began a bit over a week ago. My grandfather was in the hospital. He had leukemia and the doctors were giving him perhaps a day or two at best. They had moved him to hospice care to try and make him as comfortable as possible during his final hours. Well, it was pretty late and most of the family had gone downstairs to the coffee shop. I was alone with my grandfather, sitting by his bed when the room began to feel cold. It was like the temperature dropped ten or fifteen degrees in a matter of minutes. Suddenly he sat up and grabbed my arm. He looked at me, his eyes wide and panic stricken. He screamed out that they were waiting and for me to not let them get any closer. I couldn't understand what he was saying. There wasn't anyone there. I tried telling him this, but he wasn't listening and was clearly getting more and more agitated. I tried to get him to calm down, but he kept screaming that they were there to take him away and that he wanted me to help him. I didn't know what to do. Then his eyes rolled back in his head and he fell back on the bed. He was dead, and while I didn't want to admit it at the time, the moment he died, the room started to get warmer.

"Six days ago, I was back at work, staying late trying to catch up on the work that had built up while I took my bereavement leave. I was trying to wrap up the brief I was working on when I swear I saw someone moving out of the corner of my eye, just behind me on the peripheral edge of my vision. Now understand that this was a Tuesday evening around eleven. The office had been empty for hours. Even the cleaning crew had come and gone, so I knew I was alone in there. Naturally I turned around and saw there wasn't anyone there. I peered out my office door and looked both ways. The office was dark and empty. Like anyone would in such a situation, I called out, asking if anyone was there. Of course, there was no answer, but for the life of me I felt as if I was being watched. Have you ever had that feeling where you were sure you're alone and yet you feel as if someone was right there with you?"

I nodded. I've spent many a late night at the office and know that every sound the building makes is enough to make someone feel unsettled.

"Anyways, I walked around the office. First thing I did was check the front door. It was locked, of course. I also checked every cubical and office and saw that I was indeed alone. But I know what I had seen. I was sure that there had been someone moving behind me. I just couldn't believe my mind was playing tricks on me. Still, I felt foolish, so I returned to my office, hoping to finish up and get home. Here I was, a grown man in his thirties, and I was jumping at shadows.

"I sat back down and went back to the work on my brief. Not even ten minutes later I saw movement again out of the corner of my eye. I jumped up and looked around, but no one was there. Unless the person could simply blend in with the shadows, I was alone in the office. I kept telling myself that, yet I felt a cold tightness around my heart because, even though I couldn't see anyone, I felt that someone was indeed there with me."

Mitch paused and finished his beer in two more gulps. He opened his third and slouched back against the back of the couch.

"Did you ever consider," I asked, trying to be as sympathetic as possible since Mitch was clearly under a lot of strain, "that maybe all you saw were shadows shifting in the low light."

"Yeah, I did."

I saw the anger beginning to build in him. I also saw something else I had never seen before from my friend, and that was fear. Mitch, who would never back down from anything, was terrified.

"Anyway," Mitch continued, "I couldn't work after that. I packed up my laptop and paperwork and headed home. The next day I went to work at my client's office to review some paperwork. They had me set up in their conference room, which, I need to add, was very well lit. In fact, the entire conference room had three glass walls that allowed people to look over the office. The back wall was floor-to-ceiling windows that gave you a great view of downtown Manchester."

Mitch paused again and took three more swallows of beer. "As I was saying, the conference room was very brightly lit. There were no shadows in any part of the room. I was glad for this because I was still shaken from the night before. So, I was pretty calm and going about my work when it seemed as if someone moved by me in the conference room. Someone had moved on the periphery of my vision, moving around in the shadows. There was no denying it that time. I jumped up and looked around. Again, there wasn't anyone there. The conference room was empty and the door leading out to the main office was closed. Whatever was there had moved by too quickly to get a real visual. I asked the receptionist, whose desk was directly across from the conference room, who had just come by to see me, as I was too lost in my work to notice. She looked at me as if I had two heads and replied that I had been alone in the room all morning. I asked if she was sure, and she replied that anyone would have to get by her to go to the conference room and that she had been at her desk all morning.

"That was enough for me. I packed my things and made an excuse to the client that an urgent matter had suddenly come up. At that point, all I wanted to do was get home."

Mitch reached for another beer. As he drank, he looked around my apartment as if he were expecting someone to come out of the shadows and take him away into the darkness.

I asked him if he wanted me to order a pizza. I was definitely hungry and the beers were giving me a decent buzz. I had to admit, Mitch's story had captured my interest. I always enjoyed a good ghost story, and I suspected there was a lot more to the tale. Mitch agreed to the pizza, so I called and placed the order. "So what happened next?" I finally asked. I sat back down and opened another beer while I waited for Mitch to continue.

"After the incident at my client's office, I headed straight home. I turned on all the lights in the den and made myself comfortable in front of the television. I couldn't focus on any show because just as I started to relax, I would see movement off to the side that would cause me to get up and look for the source. Even though I could sense someone there with me, I couldn't clearly see who it was. It was as if I could get a glimpse, but nothing more. This went on for the rest of the day. I finally took a sleeping pill to knock me out so I could get some rest.

"The next day things got worse. I began to see movement on the periphery of my vision with a greater frequency. I began to get a better sense of who they were. They appeared to be dressed all in black, with long black trench coats and black fedora hats. I still couldn't make out any features, but I got a sense that their skin was a neutral shade of grey. And while it seemed as if their very essence was getting clearer, my sense of discomfort was growing as well. They seemed to be watching me. They also seemed to be waiting for something. As to what their purpose was, at the time, I still did not know."

The doorbell rang and I nearly jumped out of my seat. It seemed as if Mitch's story was getting to me. I don't know why I looked over my shoulder as I went to get the door, but I was suddenly feeling very paranoid, as if I were being watched as well. I opened the door a crack and to my relief noted that it was the pizza delivery guy. I paid for the order and brought the pizza and paper plates back to the living room and set everything on the coffee table. Mitch was looking pretty pale and I asked him if he was okay. He simply nodded and reached for a slice of pizza.

After we ate, Mitch continued. "By the fourth day I was so shaken, I called in sick to work. I just couldn't face being around people. I wasn't sure if I was hallucinating or seeing apparitions. Either way, my nerves were shot and I wanted to spend some time online to see if anyone else ever had these symptoms. You see, by this point, I was able to see the people in my peripheral vision with much greater clarity. I saw their faces, or at least what passed for their faces. You see, their skin was indeed a pale grey, but they had no other features. They did not have eyes, noses, mouths, or even ears. Their heads were simply smooth and featureless under their black hats. The odd thing was, they kept looking at me, and while I still did not know what they wanted, it was clear that they were waiting for something and it involved me.

"Trying to ignore their presence, I went online. I googled everything I could think of relating to the grey men in black who appeared to me but no one else. I spent most of the day going from one website to another and felt that the search was truly a waste of time. I was about ready to give up for the day when I hit upon a link that looked promising. It was a blog written by some teenage kid a year ago who talked about seeing the Grey Men. He provided links to online libraries and other websites that gave documented accounts of sightings of these men going back as far as recorded history.

"The similarities between each documented case were quite frightening. In each instance, a person had reported having either visions or hallucinations of movement in the shadows from the periphery of their vision. And while they tried to get others to believe what they saw, no one else did as they were the only ones who had the visions. With each case, the individual mentioned that they saw the shadowy figures more vividly with each passing day until they finally reached the seventh day."

Mitch helped himself to some more pizza and another beer. I was pretty drunk by this time and had already started nursing my beer. I had work the next day and I knew that it was not going to be a good one. "So what happened after seven days," I finally asked, getting impatient at my friend's extended silence.

Mitch looked at me. His eyes were red and even more glazed over than they had been. He glanced over his shoulder and continued. "Well, in each case, people claimed to have seen the Grey Men for a full week, starting as nothing but vague shadows but gradually evolving into clear figures with no faces dressed all in black. As with me, no matter how hard they tried, they could never see the Grey Men head on. It was always off to the side, just out of reach. And like me, each person's visions were personal. No one ever had anyone else see what they saw. So that led to the seventh and final day." Mitch turned quickly and his vision seemed to linger in a spot near the corner of the room. I followed his line of vision but didn't see anything.

"Did you see something?"

Mitch nodded. "They're here. I can't escape them, Gary. They're everywhere. It's already too late, you see. Tomorrow makes the seventh and final day. Are you sure you don't see anyone against the wall?"

I shook my head. "Something is different, isn't it?"

Mitch looked at me. "They are slowly moving out of the periphery. I can almost see them head on. Want to know what I see?"

I didn't want to. I swear to God I wish I never answered my door tonight because, while I couldn't see anyone, Mitch's story was getting to me. I actually felt as if there was someone in the room with us. "Yes," I replied, my voice low and raspy.

"Very well," he continued. His voice was low and somber. "I see three men in the room with us. At least I assume that they are men. They are walking around the room, but they seem to be focusing on me. They move as if they're images in stop motion photography. As if they're still frames shifting slightly with each successive image. As I said before, they are dressed in black from head to toe. Their clothing is unique in that there are no lines or seams or any distinguishing designs. It's simply black and fluid-like, as if it is part of them rather than clothing. The darkness is so deep, it almost appears as if their forms are nothing more than outlines of nothingness where one could get lost in the dark void of their bodies. They all look to be the same height, about six feet tall. At first they all appeared to wear black gloves, but now I see that their hands are nothing more than extensions of their coats. The most horrific thing is their faces. As I said, while they have no features, their grey skin seems to be liquid and seems to flow into the darkness that makes their hats and coats. While they move and appear to be following me, there is nothing to indicate life in any of their faces. Just before, they all turned to face each other and appeared to be speaking to each other, although they did not make a sound. Then they all turned in unison and pointed to me. I knew then and there that whatever they were, they were sentient."

"That's horrible," I said, hugging myself to suppress a chill. "What do you think they want?"

"There's more, Gary," Mitch said as he stood up. He began pacing back and forth. "You see, on the seventh day, everyone who has seen the Grey Men dies. In each case, the death was horrible and violent."

"Surely you don't believe that. It's clearly nothing more than an urban myth that someone blogged about."

"Listen to me," Mitch screamed. "It's all real."

"How can you be sure?" I protested.

"The kid's blog had all kinds of personal information online, including his school. It didn't take much searching to find out where he lived and who he was. You see, I checked online for the local papers from his hometown for deaths of a fifteen-year-old kid around the time of his last blog entry. Sure enough, the *Akron Beacon Journal* had an online piece a year ago about Jimmy Barnes, a fifteen-year-old kid who was tragically killed by a commuter train as he crossed the tracks. Apparently the train hit him and then dragged him for a full quarter mile as the conductor tried in vain to stop the train. There wasn't even enough left of the kid to even have an open casket."

"That doesn't prove anything, Mitch. It could simply be a coincidence."

"Let me finish. The article also interviewed some of his classmates. What was most disturbing was how Jimmy's best friend claimed that Jimmy had been acting very strangely the week before he was killed, and he even claimed that Jimmy was worried about some guys in black suits who had been following him."

"That's a hell of a ghost story," I said to Mitch. "What are you going to do?"

Mitch stood and slowly walked to the front door. "I had better be going. Thanks, Gary, for being such a good friend."

"Are you okay to drive?" I asked.

"Does it really matter," he replied sadly. "They are here with me, Gary. It's only a matter of time now."

"Wait," I cried out as he tried to leave. "Who are they? Why do some people see them and not others? Was there anything on the website?"

Mitch sighed. "They're death. We are not supposed to see them until it's our time to die. Sometimes a person sees them by accident. The best way to describe it is like peeling back the curtain to see the workings of the universe. The Grey Men gather the dead. Where they take them I don't know. No one who ever witnessed the Grey Men lived long enough to confirm this, but it seems to make the most sense. There are things we are not meant to see or know. I got a glimpse of what lies beyond, and now they are coming to collect. I guess there are things we simply are not meant to know."

Mitch turned then, whispered that he was sorry, and left without another word. I stood there alone in my apartment, and no matter how much I turned up the thermostat, I could not shake the chill that ran down my spine.

* * *

Mitch is dead. The whole idea of him dying seems like a bad dream, but it happened. I would say I was shocked, but somehow I knew that when he left my apartment that would be the last time I would ever see him. His sister called me the day it happened. It seems he was on his way to visit his grandmother at the nursing home in Concord when he lost control of his car on Route 93. He plowed into a flatbed truck in front of him doing at least 70 miles per hour. The bed of the truck sheared off the roof of his Lexus and the top of Mitch's head. He was killed instantly.

Mitch's funeral was a few days later; I paid my respects to his family and watched as they lowered his coffin into the ground. I was numb as it hit me that I'd never see my best friend again.

Just as I was about to leave, I felt a chill and swore I was being watched. I turned around but there was no one behind me. I turned back to the service, but then, out of the corner of my eye, I saw some movement in the shadows of my peripheral vision. My mouth went dry as I realized that, thanks to Mitch's tale, the fabric of reality had been exposed for me as well, and that one could never really get the genie back in the bottle. I wondered how I would spend the next seven days—and whether I would tell anyone.

A STITCH IN TIME SAVES NINE
EDWARD J. MCFADDEN III

Sunlight streamed through the octagonal attic window, casting dancing shadows across the old wood floor. The small window was open a crack, and the smell of smoke from winter fires and the faint scent of rain carried on the breeze. Shannon wept as she carried a cardboard box up rickety steps, her stomach boiling with pain. Scars of wood lath could be seen along the stairway walls, the old plaster falling away like dried skin.

The stairs ended in the center of a room with a gable roof, and one could only stand under its peak. Several boxes, an old bike, and bags of old clothes sat between ceiling joists and along the far wall. Across from the Christmas decorations, there was a small pile of boxes that represented all that remained of what her father had owned when he died. The box she carried was the last of it, and now that she had moved everything, she felt better, like she had put her father's memory in its proper place.

He had died when she was a teenager, and her grandmother had stored the boxes for her since her mother wanted nothing to do with them. She had never really gotten over the divorce, had even refused to go to Ray's funeral. Shannon's mother wouldn't tell her what he had done, or why it was so bad that she couldn't forgive him even in death, and Shannon didn't push. She had learned from her father to let the past be the past.

"Only you can make the past the present," he would often say when Shannon was sad.

When her grandmother passed and the old family house was being sold, Shannon had stored her father's belongings in a public storage center—that, at least, her mother could do. And not for him, but for

Shannon. And now, since her new apartment was the top floor of an old Victorian and she had access to the attic, she had decided to move the boxes so she could go through her dad's stuff, something she had been unable to do upon his death.

She had been thirteen when Ray Allen Gregory caused a tragic car wreck that left him and two of his friends dead. Shannon had escaped the wreck unscathed physically, but the trauma of the event and the loss of her father had taken her many years to recover from mentally.

The old steps creaked under Shannon's weight as she stepped into the small attic. She sneezed from the dust tickling her nose and throat. She was twenty-four now, in law school. She tried not to think about her dead father, but his memory always seemed to be right there in front her, waiting to be acknowledged in some way. Some days she would almost feel him walking with her, sitting in class, like a shadow. She felt like that at that moment, and paused, closing her eyes and trying to master her feelings.

Stepping forward, she tripped, and the box she was carrying crashed to the floor, the top splitting open and dumping a myriad of items onto the aged wood planks. Shannon looked at her feet, all about the floor, but nothing could be seen as the culprit responsible for her fall. Rising, she dusted off her jeans and blue blouse, pushed her long, brown hair from her face, and started to retrieve the fallen items.

The very first thing she saw was the tape. It rested on end, its title clearly visible in the sunlight streaming in through the attic window. The spine of the tape read:

A Message to My Daughter
Ray Allen Gregory

Shannon reached for the tape, but as her fingers went to wrap themselves around it, she paused, a chill running through her. She felt nauseated, and her head began pounding in rhythm with her heart. Her mind staggered at the thought that her father had made her a tape, left her the ultimate message in a bottle, but she doubted she would have the strength to watch it. She wasn't sure she could handle seeing his face and hearing his voice.

The tape was old-school VHS, but she had a triple player that played VHS, discs, and video cards. With an effort of will, she snapped up the tape and made her way back down the attic steps to her living room. She popped the old tape into the machine. It squealed at first, its gears and rubber belts not having moved in several years. She flipped on the TV, and her father's image stared back at her.

Shannon fell backward onto her couch, her shock and horror propelling her as if she had been pushed by an unseen phantom. The image of her father was aged: he was gray, and his face was pocked with liver spots and sagging skin. He looked years older than when he had died.

She frantically squeezed the remote; the tape sputtered to a stop and the TV filled with white static. Shannon's breaths came in ragged gasps now, her heart pounding in her chest. Had she seen what she thought she had seen?

Not possible, she thought, and squeezed the rewind button.

As the tape loped through the rewind process, her mind ran back to her father's funeral, and how she had felt like he was watching her the entire time. Ray had been a young-looking forty, his blond hairline receding a bit, but revealing very little of its gray. He had been of medium build, and his face had no specific markings or distinctive features. But what Shannon remembered most were his eyes. In life, her father had piercing blue eyes that looked through you like an MRI, but they could also be comforting. In death, she felt his eyes gleaming with defiance from beneath their closed lids. At the wake, she thought she had even seen him blink once or twice.

Yet she knew that was crazy. Her mother had identified his body, and signed the authorization to release his undamaged organs to the donor network as he had wished.

The tape slammed to a stop as it finished rewinding and Shannon jumped, her nerves frayed, stomach twisted, and the idea of what she was about to see—what she might see—was pulling her apart like a loved one's betrayal.

She hit play.

The static formed into a face before giving way to blue screen, and Shannon blinked. Then an image of her father standing in front of his workbench in the basement filled the frame. He was young again, his bright blue eyes, full of life, were staring into the camera. Shannon smiled. She had not known him then. He wore a blue sweater, with jeans, and she could see that he had large dark patches beneath his eyes.

"Hello, testing 1... 2... 3... That's what I'm supposed to say, right?" said her father into the camera. He leaned casually against the workbench and looked at something off camera that she couldn't see. When his gaze returned forward, he had his words together. "I'm not good at saying things, Shannon, I think you know that. And I'm certainly no movie maker… but I thought it might be a good idea if I left you a little advice just in case I'm not around when you're old enough to need it." He paused again, looking down.

"You were born today, May sixth, nineteen ninety-nine. You're so tiny, Shannon, no bigger than my forearm, but I can tell you are gonna be a smart one. How? Just by the way you watch me with those cool black eyes. Anyway, I may update the tape in the coming years, but I've broken down the Ray's meaning of life speech into three main ideas."

Shannon hit pause, the tears coming like a storm and slashing jagged scars across her heart. Her mascara ran down her face, making her eye sockets almost black, like her father's on screen. His face stared back at her, and she thought she could see a frown beneath his mask of joy. She hit pause again, and her dead father's picture jerked into motion.

"One thing that took me my entire life to learn is that time is limited. Most people, me included, spend the majority of their lives looking forward, waiting for something special to happen or for some event that will pass and leave them looking forward again. Then there are those who constantly look back, reevaluating every bad decision, rehashing old fights and old victories. But you can't change the past, so it's best to just let it go and focus on the future, and the way you do that is to live in the present. Don't put off until tomorrow what you can do today, don't spend your time foolishly holding grudges or being hateful. We get very little time in this life, Shannon, and each second counts. Every damn one."

He paused, a tear sliding down his cheek. Shannon remembered that piece of advice well, as he had preached it to her many times when she was growing up. When she complained about doing school work, he would tell her he wished he could go back to school. When she said she was tired, he would say listen to your language tapes while you nap. If she cried, he would tell her to get it out, and after a few minutes he would make her stop and pull herself together. "Self-pity," he often said, "was the death of man."

When he continued, he looked a little embarrassed, like someone telling another person not to smoke while blowing smoke in their face. "You know your mom and I… Well, we both love you very much, more than anything, and we want you to have a great life. But to do that you need to understand that people who aren't your family, and some who are, will try to take what is yours, make you play by their rules. Your family, Shannon, they are the ones with whom you should place your trust.

"And finally, last but not least, I'll go with a cliché. Follow your heart. There are going to be times in your life when you'll be asked to do things you know aren't right. You are my daughter, so I know you'll understand what I mean when the time comes. You'll get a tiny burning feeling in the pit of your stomach as guilt starts its war against your brain, which might be telling you the benefits of doing what you are told are greater than doing what is right. Do what is right, Shannon."

He paused again, wiping his teary eyes with the sleeve of his sweater. "Well, as I said, I'll probably update this as I think of more pearls of wisdom." He stepped forward to turn off the camera and stopped, his eyes and face filling the entire frame. "If you are listening to this, and I'm gone, don't spend a lot of time mourning me, Shannon. Live. Make my life worth something by making something of yours."

The screen turned blue for a few seconds, then filled with the father she knew. He seemed happier than in the first chapter, the black patches beneath his eyes almost gone, his face tanned, eyes bright. It was the day of Shannon's graduation from elementary school, and the pride was so clear in him that she smiled through her grief. He went on for over half an hour, talking about the award she had won, how beautiful she looked. Before he shut down the camera, he told her she was making him proud, and she no longer even needed his tape. "The tape is more for my sanity at this point than yours," he said, and the TV screen went blue.

There was another short message two days after her graduation from middle school, and it was basically a reiteration of the prior update. Her father looked like she remembered him, yet she couldn't help but see him in his coffin. The update ended and the screen cut to blue. Shannon held her breath, waiting for the tape to continue. After a few seconds, she breathed deep, letting the air out of her mouth with an exasperated sigh. The room was silent save for a tree branch scraping against the side of the house. She hit pause after a minute or so, wiping her brow with the back of her hand. Leaning back, she stared at the blue TV screen.

Shannon went into the kitchen to grab a beer. Twisting off the cap, she downed half the contents with one long pull, her nerves a jumbled mass of relief and despair. Then the sound of static made her eyes grow wide, and she dropped the bottle, which shattered on the ceramic floor with a loud *pop!* She ran from the kitchen, and as she entered the living room she froze, her eyes transfixed on the TV screen that now displayed white crackling snow. Then her father was there, an older version of what she had just seen, but definitely her father.

His hair had grayed, and his eyes had lost some of their luster. He wore a strange shirt that had stripes going in a million directions, and his skin seemed dry, like he had been baking in the sun. When he spoke, she couldn't take it any longer.

"How is this possible?" she shrieked, as she picked up the remote and stopped the tape.

She fell sideways and lay prone on the couch, wondering if she had cracked, gone over the proverbial edge. *How could my dead father make a tape?* She rose and hit eject, and the tape came clear of the player. She studied it closely, but there was nothing unusual about it.

That's when the little voice in her head told her to smash the thing to oblivion. It wasn't supposed to be here, its existence wasn't possible, and therefore it wasn't real. *Destroy it!* But she couldn't. Human curiosity clutched her, pulling her free of rational thought and scattering the seeds of fantastic and unusual ideas. *Is the tape of another place? Another time? Maybe there is an important message for me here? One so important that if I ignore it my life might be changed in some irrevocable way?*

She loaded the tape into the player and hit play.

Her father looked into the camera like a man condemned to death, and the motions of his body seemed slow, as if he was in great pain. He was in a room Shannon knew well. It was her new apartment. The one she currently sat in. Her father had the camera resting on top of the TV cabinet. Shannon squinted, pain filling her head.

When her father spoke, it was with a voice she hadn't known, but that clearly was her father's.

"Shannon, I love you, sweetie," was all he said, over and over again, like he had gone insane. His eyes welled with tears as he stared into the camera, not sure what to do or say next. Then he said, "It's not my fault. Something slipped when we had the accident, Shannon. Realities blending, rewriting each other and splitting time. Since the accident I can see things. You, but so many of you. I can't save you all. It's not my fault." He paused, looking away from the camera, and rocking back and forth on the same couch she sat on.

It is your fault, thought Shannon. "What did you do?" she yelled at the empty room.

Then her father was screeching, "I can fix it—but reality always finds a way to correct itself. There's nothing I can do about that!" Her father rose and walked behind the couch, tripped on the rug, and the upper portion of his body was lost from the camera's view.

Shannon looked behind her, expecting to see her dead father standing there, smiling at her, arms outstretched. She had imagined that scene often enough, hadn't she? But there was no one standing there.

"What's happening!" She pleaded with the image on the screen, but her father had turned off the camera, plunging the TV screen to its familiar silent blue.

There was a crackle of static, then Shannon heard the words "unfortunate timing," followed by, "love her."

Then her father's image appeared, the one she had seen when she had first inserted the tape. He was half bald, his old eyes tired and lost. Brown freckles dotted his face and head, his skin sagging slightly, like her father's skull had shrunk. He was frail looking, and the bleakness with which he looked into the camera made her cry again, her mind on the verge of snapping. Her index finger hovered over the stop button on the remote, and every bone in her body echoed in unison with her brain: *Stop watching. Destroy it!*

But she couldn't, and when her father spoke, the bile that filled her stomach rose in her throat and she wretched.

"I don't know why I'm updating this, maybe so if you see it your fate might change somehow. But I doubt it will. I remember your funeral like it was yesterday, Shannon. Seeing your young pale face in that coffin made my heart want to burst. And not a day goes by that I don't remind myself that I was supposed to be the one to die. Me. I was supposed to die in that car crash. Not you Shannon." The screen turned blue, and the tape stopped, filling the screen with static.

Pop!

A bulb in the overhead lamp had blown and Shannon jumped. She gawked at the TV screen, and the video player shrieked. Shannon stepped backward, tripped on the rug, and fell backward. The base of her skull connected with the corner of the coffee table. Her neck broke with an audible, bone-rattling *snap!*

No time left.

LUCK IS NO LONGER A LADY
JEFFREY C. PETTENGILL

Anticipating winning big in the casino reinvigorated Antonio's failing energy levels. Until he walked past the slot machines beyond the registration desk, his focus had been on crashing after the long flight from Boston via Los Angeles. His plan on the shuttle from the airport to the Riviera had been to get in a short nap before grabbing dinner and a show. Now, as the elevator rose to the fifty-seventh floor of the Monaco Tower, he no longer wanted to sleep. His palms itched. The desire to try his hand at craps, or roulette, grew. For the first time since learning he'd be in Las Vegas for a convention, he believed he'd actually leave here a winner.

* * *

Stepping through Room 5727's doorway, Antonio Gianelli shuddered. It felt as if he had just stepped into a walk-in freezer. "You've got to be kidding me," he muttered. Irritation laced his voice as he tossed his carry-on bag onto the king-size bed. "What the hell have they got the thermostat set to? Thirty-two degrees?"

He strode to the air conditioning/heating unit. It didn't sound like it was on, but he supposed it could have just stopped moments before he opened the door. Placing his palm against the metal vent, his brow furrowed in puzzlement. It was not cold to the touch, at least no colder than any metal would be against his skin. He turned the knob to HEAT. It didn't move. The crinkling of his forehead deepened. He then twisted in the opposite direction. It spun easily.

"That makes absolutely no sense at all," he said as he took a step back. He rubbed the back of his neck with his hand. His mouth contorted into a sour pucker that moved from side to side. He returned the dial to its original position. The little arrow on it pointed to the word HEAT once more. Looking more closely at the control panel, Tony saw the button beside the word OFF was depressed. The unit's motor instantly kicked on as he pushed down the ON button.

"There, that'll be better." He nodded, placing his palm over the vent and feeling the warm air caress his chilled skin.

Satisfied the room's temperature would be more to his liking soon, Tony set about claiming the room as his own. He hung his business suits in the closet, placed his toiletries in the bathroom, and even put his underwear in the dresser drawer. He was only going to be in the room for a couple of nights, but he refused to live out of his luggage like a vagabond living out of a stolen grocery cart.

As he closed his bag and bent over to pull the zipper, a soft, cold zephyr caressed his ear. "Gino?"

"Huh?" Tony looked to his left and right. He couldn't have heard anyone; he was the only one in the room. His brow furrowed once more. He tilted his head first to one side, then the other, straining to hear something beyond the heating unit.

There was no one else in the room.

He shook his head and finished zipping up his bag. "Must have been somebody passing by outside in the hallway. If the walls are as thin as the door appears to be, I hope I don't have any honeymooning couples to either side of me. I don't need to hear them going at it in the middle of the night."

* * *

So much for breaking the bank, Tony thought, slipping his seventh twenty dollar bill into the slot machine. He pressed the Max Bet button and watched the symbols spin around. *Come on*, he prayed, *let me win at least one spin.*

The tumblers stopped. His heart sank. Once more they failed to line up for him.

Without waiting, he pressed the button again. He wanted the losing combination to disappear.

It was replaced by another non-winning display.

"Stupid machine." He slapped the modern one-armed bandit. The woman at the machine two down from his gave him a reproachful look.

Keep it to yourself, you old bat, he mentally spat at her.

"Can I get you another drink, sir?"

A look at the scantily clad red-haired waitress who'd appeared next to him mellowed Tony's temper some. "Sure," he slurred in response. "Gimme another bourbon."

Without taking his eyes off her, he pressed the Max Bet button again.

"Did you say something to me, young man?" The question came from the other side of him, from the old biddy.

"No," he responded, turning to look at the woman who had given him the distasteful glare seconds ago. "I was talking to the waitress."

"What waitress?"

"What? Are you blind as well as being a buttinski? The one standing right here." He turned to point at the hot little redhead.

She was no longer there.

He spun around in the seat, looking in all directions. She was nowhere to be seen. She couldn't have gone and placed the order that quickly.

"Where'd she go?"

"Where'd who go?"

"The redheaded waitress I just gave my order to."

"I didn't see any waitress."

Tony continued to scan the casino floor. She had to be around here somewhere. She couldn't have disappeared without his seeing her. This part of the casino was fairly open as this bank of machines was next to the gaming tables.

"I don't know how you could have missed her. You were looking straight at me while she was standing right here asking me if she could get me anything."

The woman shrugged. In a matter-of-fact tone she said, "Don't know, but I didn't see anyone other than you beating up that slot machine."

Tony scowled at her. "Well, just mind your own business, lady."

The woman's eyes widened. She huffed and put another five into her computerized money vacuum.

Turning back to his machine, Tony smiled. Three red bars lined up across the wheels.

* * *

Pressing the Bet One button once more, Antonio Gianelli watched the last of his credits disappear. His irritation at the non-winning displays progressed to something stronger. He had gone through everything he had won on that one spin, plus another forty dollars afterward. To top it off, the waitress never returned with his drink. So, what had once been mild annoyance, and disappointment at his inability to step away from the electronic bandit, was now an urge to make the waitress pay for not taking care of his order.

A buxom brunette waitress came around the corner and he called, "Miss." With a struggle, he managed to keep his annoyance from his voice.

"What can I get for you, sir?" she responded in a cheery tone.

"Yeah. I ordered a drink some time ago and I haven't gotten it yet."

"Oh? I'm sorry to hear that, sir. Can I get it for you?"

After a moment's thought Tony shook his head. "No, I'm going to head back to my room now."

"I assure you, sir, it is not our habit to let our customers be treated in such a way. You don't by any chance know who took your order?"

"No, I didn't get her name."

"Can you possibly point her out to me?"

Shaking his head, he said, "Nope. I've been looking for her, but I haven't seen her since I gave her my order."

"What did she look like? Maybe I can figure out who it was." She gave him a hopeful smile. Tony could see in her face she really wanted to make him feel better.

"Well, first, she had red hair."

"Red? Are you sure, sir?"

"Positive."

"Could it have possibly been auburn? That can sometimes look red if the light hits it just right."

"No. It was red. Bright red. I know the difference between auburn and red. It was so red she could have been Carrot Top's sister."

The woman paused. It was obvious he was positive about this. The puzzlement on her face showed she wasn't quite sure how he was going to react to what she was about to say. After taking a deep breath, she said, "Sir, there are no cocktail waitresses working at the Riviera with red hair."

* * *

Tony's mind was still wrestling with what the waitress had told him as he opened the door to his room. He turned on the small light in the doorway. It barely illuminated the room. Sitting on the bed's edge, he tried to make sense of what had happened. He had talked with the redhead, and she had responded to him.

No, that wasn't right. She had spoken to him first, asked him if he wanted another drink, and he had given her his order. Why would he have responded to someone who wasn't there in the first place?

Reaching over he pressed the button turning on the bedside lamp. The room brightened. Pulling his hand back, it brushed against something on the nightstand next to the lamp. Turning to look, Tony's right eyebrow arched. There, inches from the lamp's base, was a tumbler half filled with an amber liquid.

What the hell is that? he wondered. *Where'd it come from?* He hadn't had anything to drink in the room. He hadn't been in the room long enough since he arrived to have done anything except stow his clothes and pee.

He picked up the glass. It was cold. He brought it to his nose and sniffed.

Bourbon?

It couldn't be real. He hadn't poured it.

Despite feeling the glass's weight in his hand, and the liquid's familiar pungent aroma wafting into his nostrils, he still didn't quite believe it was real. With his heart tripping like a hummingbird's wings, Tony sipped.

The whiskey's familiar burn ran down his throat. Realization struck him like his grandmother's wooden spoon when he tried to sneak a sample of her Sunday sauce. It was real, which meant someone had been in his room.

Setting the glass back down, he frantically sprang from the bed. Like a dervish he checked his stuff. It didn't take him long to confirm nothing was missing. In fact, nothing was disturbed. Nothing, that is, other than him.

* * *

"Are you sure you didn't pour the drink yourself and then go out, forgetting all about it?"

Tony let out an exasperated sigh. It was the fifth time the hotel security officer had asked him the same question. "I'm positive."

The uniformed man looked around the room. "And nothing is missing?"

"No." He struggled to keep the irritation out of his voice.

The annoying rent-a-cop opened the door to the minibar. "Hmmm.

It looks as if you haven't taken anything from here."

"No kidding. I told you that five times already."

"Mm-hmm. Take it easy, Mister Gianelli. I'm just trying to do my job and investigate your claim."

Tony didn't like the man's reaction to any of his responses. It was clear he didn't believe anything he was saying.

"And where did you get the glass tumbler with Riviera imprinted on it?"

"I told you, Barney Fife," his frustration with this line of questioning seeping through, "I found it sitting on the nightstand filled with bourbon when I came back."

"So you said," the man said, ignoring the tone and the put down. "But where did the glass come from? The hotel doesn't use glasses like that."

"I don't kno... what?" Tony looked at the security officer. He remained silent for a moment as his brain registered the implication. Then he said, "They must use them someplace."

"I assure you, sir, they don't. The rooms are all filled with plastic cups for customers to use. And none of the ones used anywhere else bear any sort of imprint on them." He paused, giving Tony a skeptical glare over the tops of his heavy, horn-rimmed glasses. "So, where did the glass come from?"

* * *

"Gino?"

Tony grumbled as he rolled over, away from the chilly current of air kissing his ear.

"Gino?"

He drew the blankets tighter around his head to keep the other ear defended against the frostiness nipping at it.

"Gino? Where have you been?"

Suddenly he felt like he was lying under sheets of ice.

Groaning his irritation, he forced his eyes open, got out of bed, and staggered across the room to the heating/air-conditioning unit. Somehow he made it without stubbing his toes. Fingers clumsy with sleep fumbled over the controls. He turned the knobs completely one way and then the other. The thermostat kicked on and warm air started blowing from the vents.

"If the room doesn't warm up and stay warm," he grumbled, heading to the bathroom to relieve his suddenly full bladder, "I'm calling the front desk to have them send someone up to work on it."

He squinted his sleep-heavy eyelids against the soft-white bathroom light as it came on.

"Have you forgotten me, Gino?"

Tony's forearm suddenly felt as if it were being touched by five narrow popsicles. The shock of it caused an involuntary relaxation of his bladder muscle and he urinated all over the floor as he turned to locate the source of not only the touch, but also the ethereal feminine voice he had just heard so clearly.

It wasn't possible for anyone else to be in his room. He had flipped the door's thumb latch, which prevented the door from opening fully, *and* secured the dead bolt. There was no way anybody could have gotten inside.

And yet... he had heard the voice. Hadn't he?

It was distinctly a woman's voice. But where was it coming from? And who was Gino?

His eyes passed over the huge wall mirror, not fully taking in what it was showing, though some part of his mind registered something out of the ordinary. At first he wasn't sure what it was exactly, but he had seen something. Bringing his gaze back to the mirror, he stared at his reflection. His breath caught in his chest. His eyebrows arched.

There, in the mirror, just behind his right shoulder, was the red-haired cocktail waitress. She looked at him hopefully, her eyes almost begging him to say he hadn't forgotten her. Part of him wanted to reassure her that was the case, but he knew he couldn't lie to her, because the lie would be so much worse.

"Who are you?" he stammered. "What are you?"

The look of hope on her face melted. Her eyes grew large, round, and began to glisten with moisture. "You don't remember your Lucky Lady, Gino?"

The woman's voice was now much clearer than it had been earlier, though it was barely a whisper. It trembled a little as she spoke, filled with the hurt his response inflicted.

"My name's not Gino. It's Tony." He continued to stare at her reflection in the mirror. He didn't dare turn around for fear he might actually see someone standing behind him. So long as he only saw her in the mirror, he could convince himself later it was only a dream, that this whole experience tonight was a figment of his imagination. Something brought on by his exhausting flight.

"Tony? You're not Gino Gianelli?" There was a hint of disbelief in her voice. It was more like a refusal to believe.

Hearing his last name connected with the first name turned on a 100-watt bulb inside his brain. "Uncle Gino?"

Gino Gianelli was his father's oldest brother. Nana Gianelli had frequently commented on how much he had looked like his Uncle Gino and not like his father. Tony didn't know very much about the man. His uncle had died just before he was born. There had been a rift between the brothers, which no one in the family would talk about. The few times he could remember his father talking about him, his old man always had a look of disgust on his face.

"How do you know Uncle Gino?"

There was a pause, then the redhead said, "I was his Lucky Lady whenever he was here." A bemused smile lit her eyes. "Last time he was here he walked away from the tables with twenty-five thousand dollars."

Tony exhaled, his warm breath turning into a cloud in the bathroom's cold air. "Twenty-five grand?"

"Yeah. It wasn't his biggest haul, but it was the most memorable."

"Why's that?"

"Because as he turned over his last hand and cleaned out Little Frankie Raposo, Gino turned to me and said, 'You're too lucky for me, baby. What say we get married so I never lose that luck?' I nearly died right there as I screamed. It was every cocktail waitress's dream at the time. That some big spender would take them away from the life of schlepping watered-down booze to compulsive losers. And it was going to happen to me." Her pallid face brightened with the crimson of a blush. "Gino told me to go get myself ready and to meet him in his room. Then we'd go get married.

"I remember I felt like I was walking on clouds as I went to clock out and get my purse. I giggled as I told every girl I saw I was going to marry Gino. A couple of them tried to talk me out of it, saying how I was being foolish and he was just reacting to the gambler's high of winning such a huge pot. 'He couldn't be serious,' the jealous ones said."

She paused, eyes slightly vacant as she lingered on the joyful memories. The bliss she was caught up in faded though.

"What's wrong?"

She shrugged. "I don't know. The last thing I really remember is knocking on Gino's door. It opened and I don't recall anything else. Just fragments of images of many people coming in and out of this room. Attempts to talk to them, to find Gino, with no success. Until now. Until you showed up in this room looking just as dashing. You're a dead ringer for my Gino."

It was Tony's turn to blush. Against his better judgment, he steeled himself and turned to look directly at the woman. He wasn't sure what he'd actually find standing behind him, but someone had to be there. He wasn't imagining this conversation. He had to look her directly in the eyes, to see for himself if she was real.

All that was behind Tony Gianelli when he turned around was the bathroom. Spinning in a complete circle, he stared at the mirror. The only reflection there was his own.

* * *

Light from the laptop's screen illuminated Tony's face in the darkness. Wide eyes looked at the pictures he had pulled up from the online archives of the *Las Vegas Sun*. They were of a hotel room with two dead bodies, a man and a woman. The woman, wearing the cocktail waitress uniform of the Riviera, was on the floor propping the door open. The man was splayed out across the king-size bed. He was bound as if he were about to be drawn and quartered. Blood soaked into the coverlet, darkened it in the grisly black and white image. The headline read, "Lady Luck Leaves Riviera Regular."

Tony read the story out loud, hoping the sound of the spoken words would make it possible to accept the facts.

> The Riviera Hotel was stunned by the brutal murder of longtime regular customer Gino Gianelli and cocktail hostess Mary Anne Barstow. The two were found brutally slain in Room 5727 by another guest at the hotel at 2:30 am.
>
> The reason for Miss Barstow's murder is not known at this time, though one source speculated it was a case of being at the wrong place at the wrong time. However, the possible motive for Mr. Gianelli's demise is a bit clearer. Witnesses confirmed that earlier in the evening Gianelli was a big winner in a poker game with Francis "Little Frankie" Raposo. Raposo is reputedly connected to Salvatore Giancana. This connection, however, has never been proven.
>
> What has been verified, though, is that Raposo is a sore loser. There are numerous police reports filed against "Little

Frankie" for assault and battery against individuals who won money from him in the casino. To date, Raposo has never been charged for any of these allegations.

Tony sat back in his chair, combing his fingers through his still bed-tousled hair. "Holy crap!"

He looked at the clock. A shiver ran down his spine as he noted the time, it was 2:30 am. Which meant it was 5:30 am back in Lockwood, Massachusetts. Definitely too early to call his father to talk about this. Why hadn't his father ever told him? Why didn't anyone in the family talk about how Uncle Gino died?

Without really thinking about it, he reached over and picked up the mysterious glass of bourbon and downed it in one gulp. Liquid fire scorched his throat on its way to his empty stomach. He knew he'd probably pay for that later with indigestion, but at the moment he wanted the alcohol to give him the courage to talk with his father.

Picking up his cell phone, he called.

* * *

"I don't want to talk about it, Tonio." The voice on the other end of the phone was old, gruff, and had a thick Sicilian accent. The anger came through his father's sleepiness quite clearly in his refusal to discuss Gino's murder.

"Come on, Pops," Tony pleaded. "We've got to talk about this. It's two-thirty in the morning here in Vegas and I'm sitting in the same room on the same day Uncle Gino was killed some forty years ago. Not to mention I've had a personal tête-à-tête with the bimbo Uncle Gino was supposed to marry. I think I deserve to have a few questions answered."

Silence.

"I knew your going to Vegas was a bad idea," his father finally said.

"So you've said for weeks, ever since I said I had to come out here. Now tell me why it's a bad idea."

His father sighed heavily some 2,400 miles away. "Because Las Vegas has never been lucky for our family. Gino was only one of many to fall victim to the Vegas Curse on our family."

"Vegas curse?" The incredulity in Tony's voice was not lost on his father. "Come on, Pops. We're living in the twenty-first century. Nobody believes in curses anymore."

"Scoff all you want, Tonio, but it is true. Ever since your Great Uncle

Lorenzo was sent there to try and keep Bugsy Siegel from building the Flamingo. They found pieces of him in four different construction sites around the city." The tone in Guiseppe Gianelli's voice was flat. He sounded like a man reciting something he could care less about. "My cousin Marco was killed in a plane crash on his way there for vacation. Aunt Adele tripped coming out of the Golden Nugget and split her head open like a cantaloupe. I can go on if you want."

"No need, Pops." He let out a big, sorrowful sigh.

"When are you coming home, Tonio?" The question was filled with desperation and concern. The intensity of it pulled on the younger Gianelli's heart. For the first time in his life he got a true sense of just how much his father loved him.

"I'm flying out tomorrow... make that tonight at 8:25. I should be back in Boston by 8:47 am."

"Okay." There was a pause. Tony thought about saying something re-assuring, but nothing came to mind. "Take extra good care of yourself, Tonio. I love you, son."

Tears instantly welled up in Antonio Gianelli's eyes and a lump formed in his throat. His father had never in his life told him he loved him. For his father to say that meant he was terrified he'd never see his son again.

"I love you too, Pops." Struggling to keep back the intense emotions, Tony continued, "Don't worry. Everything is going to be all right. I'm not about to do anything stupid or get into it with any mobsters while I'm here. I've just got a couple more seminars to attend. I'll call you as soon as I land in L.A. for my connection."

* * *

Standing in the shower, Tony let the steaming water stream over him. He had attempted to get back to sleep, but had failed to drift off. He hadn't been able to get the newspaper photos out of his mind. Nor could he get away from the fear his father had expressed. Then there was the so-called Vegas Curse on the Gianelli family. That was the most absurd thing he ever heard, but his father believed it. And if his father believed it, so did others in the family.

Considering that fact made a small, irrational part of his brain consider the possibility the "curse" was real.

Standing there, he fought the niggling mental voice, arguing with it, trying to chalk the family deaths up to mere coincidence and not to any curse.

"Bah! Humbug," he finally sputtered, turning the water off. He grabbed a towel and stepped out of the tub.

As he put his foot down on the frigid ceramic tiles, he slid, losing his balance. Tony flailed his arms, trying to grab on to something solid. His hands grasped the shower curtain, pulling it taut as he cantered backward over the bathtub. Several Italian expletives exploded from him as he saw the stuccoed ceiling directly above.

Before he fell back into the tub and cracked his skull, Tony felt two spots of intense cold on his back. It was like someone placing their hands under his shoulder blades. It was like being temporarily suspended in mid-air, as if he were poised between life and death. It was a moment that seemed like an eternity as he wondered when he would finally fall.

Then the pressure against his back increased. The coldness spread deeper into his shoulders and down his back; slowly his body righted itself without any effort from him. Standing on the bathroom floor, his legs trembled. He gripped the sink's basin to steady himself so he wouldn't fall to the floor.

"Thank you, Mary Anne."

"You're welcome, Tony," came the familiar voice behind him. "Thank you for calling me by my name."

Tony looked in the mirror, but the condensation on it obscured the lovely redheaded spirit from view. He turned his head around and saw the translucent apparition "standing" in the bathtub. He smiled his appreciation.

"Well, now that I know it, I figure it's only proper for me to use it." His heart continued to hammer in his chest.

She smiled back. Her eyes traveled the length of his body, pausing at his groin. A wicked smile formed playfully on her lips. "Are you sure you're not Gino? You do look incredibly like him, in so many ways."

Tony's face flushed. "Well, we are family after all."

Mary Anne giggled; she sounded so alive and truly joyous.

"And it looks like you are my lucky lady as well. I'm so lucky you were here to prevent my falling. I thought for sure I was going to crack my skull on the tub."

"Well, not a lady anymore," she responded, "but I couldn't let any harm come to Gino's nephew." She paused a moment, looked down at the floor, and then asked, "When you found out my name, you didn't by any chance find out what happened to Gino and me?"

It was a brief internal debate whether or not he should tell her what

144

he had learned. He really had no choice. She deserved to know the truth. Perhaps, if all the movies and legends about ghosts haunting where they died had any shred of truth in them, she would be able to move on to a better place.

"Yes."

Tony related everything he had learned about their murders. When he was done, the ghost nodded. "Thank you," she said.

"You're welcome." To his surprise, her face remained calm. Part of him had anticipated a very emotional reaction. He'd imagined both outrage and vehement denial. What he got was complacent acceptance.

"It actually feels comforting to know the truth. Not knowing what happened to either of us has been the most hellish part of my existence."

"I can imagine," Tony said. "I hope now you can cross over to wherever you go when you're dead."

"We'll see, though I do think there could be a pretty good reason to linger around, especially if there's a chance I can leave this room." Her eyes were bright with hope and possibilities.

"Oh really? Like what?"

Mary Anne didn't respond. Instead she floated across the floor, though she moved as if she were actually walking, and out through the bathroom door. She hovered in front of the room's exit for a moment, looking like she was bracing her courage. Then she thrust her cloudlike hand out and into the door. She inched forward, sliding her arm further into the door until it was past her elbow.

"Oh, I haven't been able to do that before." Excitement filled her voice. In one quick movement she plunged her head through the door as if she were dunking it into a bucket of water.

From the other side of the door came a joyful cry, excitement and freedom.

Within the blink of an eye, the rest of Mary Anne Barstow's spirit disappeared.

* * *

With the last of the conference's seminars over, a weary Tony Gianelli sat at the roulette table looking at his remaining fifty dollars in chips. He had some time to kill before he needed to leave for the airport, so he hoped he might be able to make back some of what he had lost the day before. But so far, no such luck.

As he contemplated cashing the chips in, a soft, cold wind caressed his ear.

"Nine red."

"Huh?" Tony's eyes widened. He recognized the voice, though he hadn't expected to ever hear it again.

"Put everything on nine red. It's my birthday. It's what Gino would always bet when he played roulette."

"Really?" he said under his breath.

"Trust me."

With excitement and nervousness mixing inside him, Tony placed all the chips on nine red and sat back.

The wheel spun. The little ball traveled around the outside in the opposite direction. His eyes followed it as it descended down to the wheel itself, bouncing jauntily from one number to the next. It threatened to come to a stop several times, and others around the table bounced along with it between joy and frustration. But not Tony.

With one final hop, the little sphere came to rest.

"Nine, red," called the croupier. He placed the dolly atop Tony's chips to indicate it was the winner. "Looks like Lady Luck has finally arrived at your side, sir."

In that instant Tony knew the "Vegas Curse", for him at least, was not real. A smile so broad it hurt his cheeks spread across his face and said, "Well, luck is definitely at my side, but she's no longer a lady."

A soft feminine giggle from invisible lips tickled his ear.

IN A LONELY PLACE

CYNTHIA WARD

She comes to herself in an elegant room she has never seen before. Yet—she feels a sudden clutching sensation, like a muscle knotting at her breastbone—the room seems familiar. The high ceiling, the cut-crystal chandelier, the closed drapes of deepest red velvet, the grand fireplace of carved white marble, the hardwood floor beneath her body—every detail of the room feels as familiar as the hands she raises, suddenly trembling, to her head. How can the room seem so familiar, when she has no memory of what has happened to her?

She might be someone with a word on the tip of her tongue, who cannot speak it—knowing the meaning, and knowing there is a word for the meaning, yet struggling to find the word that has been lost in the depths of her mind. But, however much she struggles, she cannot remember how or why she recognizes this room. Why can she not remember the place—house? apartment? mansion? She simply cannot remember—

The knot in her breast tightens as she realizes, she cannot remember anywhere.

Then she realizes something else, something far more devastating. Her anxiety grows. She cannot even remember her own name.

She begins to shake and fears she might collapse and sink back into darkness.

Be calm, she tells herself. *Explore this place. Sight can prompt memory. See more of this place, and something might come back. Memory* will *come back.*

She makes herself get up and sees that she is naked.

Her trembling escalates.

Don't worry about that now, she tells herself harshly. *Get moving. You'll find*

147

something to wear.

She forces herself to take a step. She does not fall. She takes another step, and another. She is moving. She must keep going if she is to have any hope of regaining her memory of this place, of discovering who and where she is. And so—despite her nudity, despite the shaky limbs and terrible lightheadedness that threaten to topple her with every step—she keeps walking.

She explores the room and the rooms she finds around it—cavernous, high-ceilinged rooms with glowing chandeliers and beautiful, but cold, fire-places—and finally recognizes the place. This is the house she has always wanted, the house of her dreams.

The glorious house where she hoped to dwell one day, with her true love.

The rooms are enormous and totally empty, the windows hidden behind elegant velvet drapes the color of blood.

She is alone.

She raises a heavy fold of drape. Her fingers tighten convulsively, crushing the dense nap, for through the soaring window she sees only darkness. It is not the spilled ink of stormy midnight, nor the starry sky that would limn other houses, nor the totality of a deep and lightless cave. Not a natural blackness, but rather an utter and impossible blankness that makes her eyes ache and her mind reel with dizziness. Her trembling fingers fling the velvet across the pane so she will no longer see the impossible.

Unhindered by velvet or glass, the blankness flows over her. It seems to fill her eyes and throat, as solid as mercury; it chokes her. It fills every fiber of her being. But in the fraction of time before the blankness overwhelms her mind, she realizes she has choked before; and she never got back her breath.

Awakening, she sits convulsively upright. She can see again. She can feel again.

What she feels is terror.

Be calm, she tells herself. *You fainted. That's all. It was night, and you were already upset—you were scared before you ever looked out that window—and it was so dark outside, you worked yourself into a faint. Calm down. Look around. You've figured out where you are*, she tells herself, and carefully does not ask herself how she came to find herself in a house that exists only in her dreams. *You've figured out where you are, and if you keep looking around, you'll find out who you are. You'll be fine*, she assures herself, ignoring the tension that holds her in its fist.

As she grows calmer, she realizes that she is lying on the white cover-let of a broad bed, although she saw no furniture in her explorations. She is naked no longer, but dressed in a long, white gown. Her hands are folded upon her breast, and stiff, intricate lace scrapes her palm. Across the room is a pale woman, all in black, save for the white shirt and the white rosebud in the lapel. The tension against her breastbone grows tighter, for there was no bed or wedding gown or other person in this place before—and it seems that she should recognize this pale young woman. She begins to shake, realizing with marrow-deep certainty that this woman should not be here.

What am I thinking? I must *keep calm,* she tells herself. *I don't know if this woman should be here or not. I don't know anything about her—maybe she lives here, and has just come home. She must be someone I know,* she thinks, *if I'm in her house. I must examine her—calmly, carefully—if I'm to have any hope of remembering who she is.*

The pale woman is very young, very tall, very thin. Her stance is solemn, with hands clasped at her belly. Her hair is almost colorless, shoulder-length, lank, and her eyes are blue. So blue. They are that perfect shade oceans seek to emulate. And those eyes, bluer than the most pris-tine ocean, look upon her with an intensity that makes her shiver and ache. She rises up from the bed, intending to cross the vast room to the pale woman.

The pale woman is suddenly beside her on the bed, and the woman's tuxedo is gone, every inch of her pallid flesh exposed; and her own wedding gown is gone, as suddenly, and her skin presses against the pale woman's cold skin, as cold as her own. But the coldness does nothing to extinguish her sudden, furious ardor for the pale woman, or the ardor of the pale woman for her.

And when at length she lies exhausted, the pale woman rises on an elbow to look at her, and ferocious emotion twists those white features. A red mark appears high on the white throat, a line that slants to the left ear. Staring, shivering, disbelieving, she watches the pale woman's face grow paler, then darken to blue, to purple.

Lips gone swollen as blackberries part, and the pale woman speaks for the first time:

> "When once you stood beside me,
> "I saw a false constancy;
> "Tell me now who you might be."

She opens her mouth to reply, but terror has stolen her voice, though she does not know what the pale woman's words mean. Or who the pale woman is. Or who *she* is.

Then, suddenly, the pale woman is gone.

The blankness returns in a rush, filling her, but before it fills her entirely, she has a vision of falling from gold to blue. It is a terrifying vision. It is a terrifying sensation, this plunge toward a restless, moving blue that cannot match the blue of the pale woman's eyes.

Before she strikes the blue vastness, everything turns black.

As the blackness fades, she finds herself lying, naked, on the bed. She glances to either side, wild jerks of her head.

She is alone again.

The pale woman is gone.

She begins shaking with relief that the nightmare (*surely it was only a nightmare!*) is over.

She sits up. She goes still. She is no longer alone.

There is a woman across the room.

The woman stands, facing away from her; but she knows this is not the pale woman. This woman has black hair that flows, straight as night-spun silk, down her back, to a waist of delicate narrowness, and hips of a lyre's graceful breadth; below the short, sun-colored dress, the woman's strong legs are as bare and brown and smooth as her arms, as if sculpted from stone.

She feels a chill, as if she has seen this sight before, this very sight, but she pushes the thought away—she must not think of it. She must not pursue the knowledge, must not even *think* of pursuing it. She might not like that knowledge, for it might be—

No! She will not think of the strange, frightening words of the pale woman, or of how the pale woman's face turned purple; she will not think of the pale woman at all! *This is not the time for memory*, she tells herself. She can worry about regaining her memories later. Not now, when she is rising from the bed, compelled by the black-haired woman's beauty. She must see this woman's face. She must see this woman.

She approaches the black-haired woman, helplessly drawn and utterly willing.

The woman's head turns, looking back with black, guarded eyes. She cannot bear the terrible, vulnerable beauty of the woman's face. Yet she cannot look away.

Nor can she stop her advance.

She wants this woman. Nothing else matters. *It is always this way*, she thinks suddenly, and wonders at the thought. *The thought is not important,* she tells herself immediately. *Only this woman is important.*

She reaches for the black-haired woman, her fingers closing on firm muscle, pulling the woman's shoulder back. Her eyes meet the watchful, wary gaze. Her mouth finds the full lips, cold as stone, and as still. Her hands stroke the smoothness of brown arms, curve against the heaviness of full breasts, flatten on muscled stomach. She touches everywhere with a patience that, she realizes, is as uncharacteristic as it is necessary.

Finally, the black-haired woman is as naked as she, the silken sundress suddenly vanishing; and the woman is turning to her. She presses the woman against the wall, bracing one hand against ash-pale wood. She straddles the woman's leg and her fingers slide up the bare thigh. They slide up, and inside; and inside is wet, and so very cold.

She goes still as midwinter ice. The knot gripping her breastbone clenches tighter, but she wants this woman. Neither the terrible knot nor the dreadful cold matter.

Nothing matters, except getting what she wants.

It was always like this, she thinks. *Always, nothing mattered when I wanted a woman, except getting the woman I wanted. But that is as it should be,* she assures herself. And she takes care not to ask herself why she put the thought in the past tense. *It was always like this* and *nothing mattered when I wanted a woman, except getting the woman I wanted.*

She feels the woman tremble at her touch, and the trembling makes her realize that she has been with this woman before.

A second memory comes hard upon the first: the black-haired woman is shy with the pain of an old, hidden wound, as old as childhood, and so must be seduced as if against her will with every encounter. *How do I know this about the black-haired woman? It doesn't matter; nothing matters, except getting the black-haired woman.* Suddenly she remembers that she had wooed the black-haired woman with declarations of desire, of passion, of love greater than she had ever felt—greater than anyone had ever felt—and with those declarations, she'd won the black-haired woman.

The black-haired woman raises her head. Their eyes meet and she cannot move; it is as if she has been struck to ice by the black-haired woman's expression. It is a stone mask of pure hatred. As she stares, the knot at her breastbone dreadfully aching, the black, silken hair goes coarse and brittle. The smooth, brown skin shrivels and cracks on the bones, and keeps cracking, until it falls like powder onto the bed. A skeletal hand raises a small prescription vial that has appeared from nowhere; and the vial in the black-haired woman's fleshless grip is empty.

The lipless mouth opens, the knife-edge teeth part.

"She and she and you and me,
"All trapp'd as if by the sea.
"Free we are not, 'til you be."

Then bone and hair crumble to ash and blow away on a breeze she does not feel.

She flees the room, terrified, screaming, "Who am I?"

There is a long sheet of glass hanging on the wall. She has not seen it before. It is not a window. It reflects the room.

Trembling, she approaches the hanging sheet.

In the glass—a mirror, she realizes; it's a mirror—she sees a young, fair face and a firm-muscled, fair-skinned body.

She recognizes herself, and jerking with the recognition, she remembers her name.

Phyllis.

She clutches at the name as if it were a stone pillar, a source of strength and support.

I am Phyllis.

But the name means nothing—offers nothing.

"I am Phyllis!" she cries, insistent.

But no matter how she speaks her name, or how often, Phyllis still does not know who she is.

She jerks again, pulling convulsively away from the mirror, for in the mirror she sees the pale woman again, the white woman wearing the black tuxedo, the white woman whose face turned darkest purple. She cries out at the sight.

In the mirror, the pale woman's face is white once more, and her formal garments cover her pallid body again. And Phyllis is in the mirror beside her.

But it is not a reflection Phyllis sees.

In the mirror, both women are very young. They face each other, holding hands. Watching them in the mirror, Phyllis can hear their voices as they speak vows.

Wedding vows. The young women are swearing to love one another until death do they part.

Phyllis feels the emotions and knows the thoughts of the Phyllis in the mirror.

The mirror-Phyllis thinks it is love, at first, for she can think only of Fiona (finally, the Phyllis who watches the mirror learns the pale woman's name). But now that the newlyweds live together, it seems whenever they are not loving, Fiona and Phyllis are fighting. Even something as simple as whose turn it is to wipe the kitchen counter must be disputed for hours. Soon, Phyllis finds herself avoiding their tiny apartment, and she realizes that what she and Fiona have cannot be love. Fiona is not the one she loves, but—she understands it in a rush that makes her mind swirl drunkenly—the gorgeous red-haired woman she met in the university library. She loves the red-haired woman, for she cannot stop thinking of the red-haired woman; and they do not fight, only talk, laugh, and make love in the high, resinous grass of a field near the campus. And so Phyllis moves in with her new love, her true love, the red-haired woman, and it is so *right* that even the news that her wife, Fiona, has killed herself does not shake Phyllis's sense of rightness.

But the red-haired woman is so busy with her pre-med studies and her job at the campus clinic, she cannot spend much time with Phyllis. And Phyllis comes to realize that the red-haired woman must not love Phyllis. Nor, Phyllis realizes, does she love the red-haired woman. Phyllis has discovered that she loves the brown-eyed, black-skinned woman she met at the natural foods store; the woman who always has time for her, the woman she can't stop thinking about.

Phyllis watches herself in the mirror and feels an ache grow deep in her chest as she witnesses her mirror-self—her earlier self—living with a succession of women, each her greatest and only love. When her earlier self leaves, a few of her lovers are not surprised, but all are grief-stricken. And some are devastated.

Her first lover, her pale wife, Fiona, who hanged herself.

The black-haired woman, Isabella, who swallowed barbiturates.

And the golden-haired woman, Jacqui, her last lover, who did not kill herself—no. Jacqui did something else.

Something equally dreadful.

But Phyllis, struggling for the revelation, cannot remember what it was that Jacqui *did*—

Damn them! Phyllis' hands close into fists. Whatever Jacqui did, it was wrong. And Isabella and Fiona, killing themselves—*that* was wrong, too. They overreacted. Why? Why did they respond so irrevocably—so *stupidly*—when Phyllis realized she was wrong?

It was a simple mistake anyone could have made. Phyllis didn't mean to hurt them. She never meant to hurt anyone. So—she has to be honest—they had no reason to get so upset with her.

In the mirror, Phyllis sees herself on a remote shore. Her mirror-self is older than she was when she married pale Fiona. Her mirror-self leaps, sure-footed as a goat, across barnacled, gray rocks, her breathing quickening with the effort, her lungs filling with chill, salty air, though her progress is slow. Watching her approach, Jacqui smiles. Above, the sun is bright as the crimson leaves of a sugar maple, bright as Jacqui's golden hair. The lovers are taking their first vacation together. But Phyllis has met a woman in the island town, a lovely local girl named Stephanie, and on a granite boulder above an autumn tide as blue and hard as the sky, Phyllis confesses to Jacqui that she loves Stephanie.

Jacqui's face transforms; it seems almost to shatter, like glass.

Then she shoves Phyllis.

Golden sunlight floods Phyllis' eyes as her world is upended. A plunge, a splash, then the blue tide is closing over her, stunningly cold and surprisingly deep. Her eyes close tight at the fiery touch of the salt water.

Phyllis does not know how to swim. She grew up in a paper-mill town more than two hours from the coast. Slowed by surprise, hindered by the water, Phyllis reaches for the rocks, her mind filled with images of herself climbing them, escaping the ocean.

But her blindly flailing hands find only water.

She forces her eyes open despite the terrible salt burn. The boulders are hazily visible, but she is too far away, a body's length and more from the nearest one, and then she is caught in the current. It is taking her out to sea. She thrashes wildly reaching for the surface, terrified and desperate, unable to swim.

Her heavy jeans, cotton shirt, and wool jacket drag her deeper, ever farther from the sun-lit surface—ever farther from Jacqui's dark shadow, rippling on the waves.

Phyllis' lungs ache and strain. Despite herself, she breathes. She chokes. Salt water sears her lungs.

The shadow spreads, covering the water.

The world darkens.

She killed me!

Phyllis jerks, remembering she is not in the mirror. She half-turns away, pressing her hands against her chest. She leans forward, as if she has taken a punch deep in the gut. Her mouth is open, a scream in her throat. But emotion chokes her. No scream—no sound—can emerge.

And as she stands, screaming silently, she regains all the memories—all the flashbacks—that had filled her mind as she died.

Phyllis remembers everything she had forgotten, even elements of her life that she never saw in flashback as she was drowning, and had never thought important when they happened:

Pale Fiona making the black tea Phyllis drank by the quart during finals week; Fiona carrying her to bed when she fell asleep over a textbook.

Black-haired Isabella turning up outside her last class of the day, though Isabella's courses met clear across campus; Isabella giving away her cat, knowing Phyllis hated the whole selfish species.

Golden-haired Jacqui showing her how to dress and act like an urbanite, when they moved to the big city after graduation, and never making her feel awkward in the process; Jacqui suffering when she gave up cigarettes because the smoke made Phyllis cough.

Wait! Phyllis thinks. *Why am I feeling bad, like I treated them badly? They were the ones who were inconsiderate. Jacqui listened to country-western music, even though I kept reminding her that she was born and raised in the north and ought to despise that crap. Isabella insisted on collecting toy cats, even though I always told her how childish and undignified it was. Fiona devoured romance novels, even though I kept pointing out what a silly habit it was for a woman who'd never wanted a man.*

Phyllis shakes her head. *I should not be feeling this way! A partner meeting your needs—that proves her love. But a partner insisting on doing things you don't like—that means she never loved you. I was right when I realized I didn't love them, either*, Phyllis told herself. *I was just waking up from the illusion of infatuation.*

Movement in the mirror catches Phyllis' eye.

She turns to the mirror and sees Jacqui.

Jacqui steps off the boulder from which she'd pushed Phyllis. Jacqui is wrapped in a blanket, crying and shuddering, her clothes dripping water, her cell phone in her hand. She is being helped across the barnacle-scabbed rocks by paramedics and a sheriff's deputy, and she is telling them that her friend fell in the ocean. Other deputies walk the barren shore, talking on cell phones as they look out to sea.

"Phyllis couldn't swim," Jacqui tells the deputy and paramedics helping her walk to the waiting ambulance. "I jumped in after my friend," Jacqui says. "I tried to reach her! But I couldn't save her. The current—" She sobs. "I couldn't save Phyllis!"

There are no witnesses; Phyllis and Jacqui were alone on the rocks, alone on that stretch of shore that cold autumn day. Phyllis watches in disbelief and rage as paramedics and deputies believe Jacqui, taken in by her passionate weeping and her wet clothing (for she immersed herself, Phyllis has realized, to aid her deception). Jacqui seems to be grieving.

Perhaps she is grieving.

But mostly, Phyllis tells herself, *Jacqui must be glad. Exultant. Rejoicing in the knowledge that she got away with murder.* Phyllis realizes that Jacqui must hate her for finding another woman.

The image in the mirror changes, and changes again. The mirror is skipping across Jacqui's life after the murder of her lover. Jacqui returns to the city. She does not return to work or go to the grocery. She stays in her apartment and calls in sick. She takes to her bed. When a friend calls, she says she is fine. She can get away with the lie because she has no close friends or family in the city where she'd moved with Phyllis—she is from another state, halfway across the country—and she is not so close to her coworkers that any will drop in unannounced. She has told no one that Phyllis is dead. No one has reason to come by and check on her. No one will see that she stays in bed, her face twisted with emotion.

Jacqui hates me, Phyllis realizes, *and she won't let go of her hatred of me.*

She won't let go of her memory of me.

She won't let go of me.

Jacqui holds me here, Phyllis realizes, *in this place that should not exist—*

Does not exist.

With a cry, Phyllis flees the mirror and Jacqui's emotion-torn face in the mirror.

Phyllis runs through the empty house, screaming her rage at the one who killed her and trapped her here, in a place that is no place.

The beautiful, empty rooms are seventeen in number. Phyllis, wearying, slows down and counts them. Seventeen. It is, she realizes, the number of lovers to whom she swore everlasting and exclusive love.

Exhausted, Phyllis stumbles. Her knees strike honey-hued oak. She is before the mirror again, or the mirror is before her.

In the mirror, Jacqui lies in the bed she shared with Phyllis. Jacqui's face is twisted, her eyes sunken, her body gaunt and motionless. She is wasting away.

Phyllis understands suddenly.

Jacqui is *dying*.

Phyllis never meant to hurt Jacqui. She never meant to hurt anyone. How could Jacqui hate her? How could Jacqui kill her?

How can Jacqui kill *herself*?

And how is it that the sight of Jacqui dying makes Phyllis feel like she is suddenly tearing apart from the inside?

Phyllis touches her breastbone, a light contact of fingertip to skin.

This terrible, rending pain, deep inside—

Is this what Jacqui is feeling?

Is this what all Phyllis' lovers felt when she left them?

Her memories fix on Fiona and Isabella, who killed themselves.

Immediately the tearing pain worsens, sharpens, like a great blade cutting furiously inside.

Phyllis cries out. "I never intended any harm!"

But the pain grows worse, the blade sawing more fiercely, with rough and splintered edges. Phyllis sprawls writhing on the floor. It is so unbelievably intense that she can hardly make a sound. She cannot speak the questions that are like another blade cutting her mind:

What is this pain?

What is this emotion?

How can I bear it?

How can anyone?

Is this what Fiona and Isabella felt? she wonders suddenly. *Is this why they killed themselves?*

Though the pain is unbearable, Phyllis makes herself look at Jacqui in the mirror.

Is this what Jacqui feels?

Is this what Fiona and Isabella felt, a pain so terrible, they took their own lives?

No, Phyllis thinks. *Fiona and Isabella did not kill themselves because they felt what I feel. They felt something else. They felt something much worse.*

They felt despair.

But Jacqui—

Jacqui feels what I'm feeling now.

And it's killing her.

I can't stop her from dying, Phyllis understands. *I'm dead. I'm helpless. My intentions are useless here, in this place that is no place. My intentions don't matter—*

Phyllis presses her hands to her head. Driving the heels of her palms into her temples with agonizing, punishing force, she realizes…

My intentions didn't matter when I was alive.

Intentions don't matter. Intentions never mattered.

Only actions matter.

And my actions—

Phyllis' head tilts with the force of the cry that tears from her throat. She claws at the oakwood. She scratches until splinters drive, like needles, into the soft flesh beneath her fingernails.

I killed Fiona. I killed Isabella. Killed them as surely as if I'd blasted them with a shotgun.

I want to die, to escape the pain of this.

I cannot die. I cannot escape. I'm already dead.

And the same pain is killing Jacqui.

What will happen to her?

Will she also be trapped in a place like this that holds me—a place that is no place?

"No," Phyllis whispers, though Jacqui killed her, and sent her to this place that is no place. "Not again. Please, Jacqui," she says, raising her voice despite the pain. "Not you, too."

Phyllis swore love so many times, but she never felt it. If she had, surely she would have felt pain as terrible as this at the slightest thought of losing her lover. No, she'd never felt love.

What she'd felt was want. Only want. And she lied to everyone she wanted to get what she wanted.

Lied to everyone.

Including herself.

"I'm a shell," Phyllis whispers to the mirror. "I'm hollow. Empty. I'm worth less than a grain of sand. I'm not worth dying over. I'm not worth hating. Jacqui, please. I don't even deserve your contempt. Don't kill yourself over me."

The pain that cuts and tears inside Phyllis is worse than the fiery burn of salt water in her eyes. Worse than the strangling, scalding agony of drowning. *But this cannot be how my lovers felt*, Phyllis thinks. *When I left my lovers, my wife, they felt far worse than this.*

Someone as faithless and selfish as I could never understand how they suffered.

Forgive me, Jacqui. Forgive me, Isabella. Forgive me, Fiona. Forgive me—

Phyllis begs forgiveness of everyone she has wronged.

She knows they have no reason to forgive her.

But she asks.

She jerks, startled. Astounded.

They have appeared, the two women who killed themselves when she left. And they are not in the mirror. Black-haired Isabella and pale Fiona stand before Phyllis, mere inches away. They seem to tower over Phyllis where she kneels, the splinters driven bloodlessly beneath her fingernails. And they look upon Phyllis, Isabella with her black eyes and Fiona with her blue.

Phyllis cannot meet their gaze. She looks down, her face burning with shame, her heart tearing apart at the knowledge of what she has done.

"Forgive me," she whispers, knowing that forgiveness is undeserved, forgiveness is impossible. But she cannot say or think or hope for anything else in the crushing grip of her revelation.

They are silent.

Phyllis cannot help herself. She looks up.

She speaks, her voice soft as a feather's drift. "Please."

They look upon her, silent as sunlight.

Then their lips move, pale Fiona's and black-haired Isabella's; and Phyllis hears a whisper, two whispers, the familiar voices, speaking as one. "I forgive you."

Phyllis looks down, emotion filling her throat like seawater, scalding, choking.

When she finally looks up, she sees no one.

Fiona and Isabella are gone from this place that is no place.

They're free, Phyllis thinks.

I am not.

Phyllis looks in the mirror.

She sees her murderer, Jacqui, lying motionless on their bed, her eyes closed and her face as hard and bitter as iron.

Phyllis fears Jacqui will never be able to forgive her before she dies.

Then Phyllis stiffens as understanding strikes her, sudden and consuming as lightning:

Jacqui's death will trap me in this place that is no place.

And Phyllis realizes something else.

When Jacqui dies, she won't be free, either.

Jacqui's emotion will trap her in a place like this—a place that is no place.

Jacqui, the woman who murdered me.

Jacqui, whom I should hate.

Jacqui, whose death I should vengefully desire.

But Phyllis feels no desire for Jacqui's death. She feels only the terrible blade cutting and tearing everywhere inside, and a ferocious wish to keep Jacqui out of a place like the one in which she is trapped—a place that is no place.

"Jacqui," Phyllis whispers. "Let go. I don't deserve your forgiveness, I know. But if you don't let go, you'll die."

In the mirror, Jacqui's eyes open. She does not raise her head, with its temples and cheeks hollowed by dehydration. But she glances around, as if she has heard someone, and her sunken eyes move in their sockets, searching her room.

Her eyes go still. Her head seems to relax against the pillow. The distortion of extreme emotion leaves her face. Her expression calm, she closes a hand on her cell phone, which lies nearby. A shaking finger finds a number and presses it, and a second number, and a third.

Phyllis hears the first ring, cut off immediately by a voice.

"Nine-one-one, what is your location?"

"Jacqui!"

159

Jacqui looks up, sharply, as if she has heard Phyllis' voice.

Jacqui seems to be looking through the mirror. Looking straight at Phyllis.

Jacqui's dry, cracked lips move. She does not speak aloud. But Phyllis can read her lips. It is a short, clear sentence. Three words.

I'm sorry, Phyllis.

"Please state your emergency," says the voice of the Emergency Services Dispatcher.

Jacqui bends her head to the cell phone and begins speaking.

The image of Jacqui vanishes, and the mirror disappears from the wall.

Phyllis looks around.

The house of her dreams—the house of her damnation—is dissolving.

Phyllis closes her eyes and waits.

THE SUITCASE
MICHAEL THOMAS-KNIGHT

After endless miles of dark featureless driving, something caught Jason's eye. The parkway, lined with trees and shrubbery was not a friendly place for pedestrians; however, someone had made their way to the shoulder up ahead, attracting attention of any passing car, of which his was the only one.

It was late on a Wednesday night, in the middle of June, when fog and mist enveloped the land like a soft white glove and crickets peeped through the shroud, letting drivers know that the earth was still there. Jason's whole world was comprised of what could be seen through the windshield, what the high beams of his Honda Civic could illuminate. Looking out the side windows caused disorientation, the dark, fog, and blurred movement yielding nothing for the eyes, as if he were traveling through space to a distant galaxy.

He let up on the pedal for a better look, not that he would have stopped; as a rule, he didn't pick up hitchhikers. Just a peek, harmless amusement, a diversion from the boring drive he'd made every night since taking the job at the diner. A college graduate, he had worked for a major insurance company for the better of ten years until the downsize and layoffs. With the job market dismal at best, he secured a job with the diner working from 3 pm until midnight. He'd been working there since.

As he got closer, the beams of his headlights illuminated the figure. She was young, but not a lady by any means, with her denim cut-off short-shorts, T-shirt tied off on one side to expose her belly, and spiked heels. She had long, fawn-like legs, glossy radiant skin, and brown-blonde feathered hair that became animated with each of her awkward steps. She had her thumb out and carried an old, hard-shelled, yellow suitcase.

To stop would be tempting, just to get a closer look at the young woman's glossy thighs, sexy mid-riff and wanton neckline, but Jason reminded himself that he was a sensible and practical man. She looked like trouble with a capital "T" and her story of how she wound up abandoned on the parkway… He definitely did not want to get mixed up with that. Women like her were best regarded from a distance.

Jason stepped on the gas pedal and his car pulled away from the two-legged headache. After a few moments, he glanced in the rearview mirror to take another quick peek. He moved his head to get the full range of the mirror's view, but she was gone. Behind him was empty road, dismal fog and darkness, same as the road ahead of him.

Jason assumed that would be the end of the story.

Thursday Night

Jason drove home, same as any other night, 12:30 am. He came upon the spot where he had seen the flashy hitchhiker on the previous night. He renamed the straight length of road in that area *Hitchhiker's Stretch,* for his own annotation. He had told his tale of the late night hitchhiker to the guys at work, how he slowed down to take a look and how it provided a cheap thrill. It was an even split in opinion, some of the guys saying he should have stopped and others saying it was best he had kept going.

He passed the exact spot where the hitchhiker had been standing. He followed the spot with his eyes just to help him recall the titillating excitement of seeing her flash her thumb at the roadside. There was no hitchhiker tonight. However, as his vehicle passed the area and he turned his attention forward to continue on his way, he noticed something in his peripheral vision. Out of the corner of his eye, in the high-speed blur, beneath the canopy of bushes—yellow. That was it. Yellow. He disregarded this visual entry to his mind and continued home.

Friday Night

It was a clear night with better visibility than there had been in days. Jason drove home, the roads somewhat more busy than other nights—the summer bustle heating up and the weekend warriors out in full force.

When he came upon Hitchhiker's Stretch, he turned his attention to the side of the road, hoping to catch sight of the yellow object again. He had to get a better look to satisfy his own tenacious curiosity. There was one set of headlights behind him, but they were a great distance back. Jason assumed it would be safe to slow down and he did, to thirty-five miles per hour. He craned his neck to see out the passenger's side window, searching the shadows of the untamed brush about ten feet from the roadside.

Just when he was going to chalk everything up to his own hyperactive imagination and continue on his way, he saw it. The corner of the yellow suitcase that the woman had been hauling stuck out from under the shrubs. Mingled with other garbage and litter, it was barely noticeable, but because he knew it was there somewhere, it grabbed his attention. Jason quickly glanced in his rearview mirror and saw the pair of headlights behind him growing considerably larger. He sped up, getting the car up to the speed limit within seconds so as not to call attention to himself. He thought about going back after the car passed, but decided it was none of his business and he should just leave well enough alone.

At home Jason watched some television and listened to the messages on his answering machine. He tried to relax from his workday and forget about what he saw on the road. However, the suitcase engaged his mind with curious scenarios and untold tales concerning the dark expanse of Hitchhiker's Stretch. He recalled the sight of that woman and it reminded him of something he could not quite identify. Yes, he remembered a girl, the one he and his friends had picked up last year during one of those boys'-night-out excursions. It could not be the same woman; he knew that, so he pushed the memory back into the darkest unlit corner of his mind, where rarely visited memories hid, locked away from conscious daylight.

It took time for Jason to fall asleep, for his mind to let go of its persistent inquisitiveness. Eventually, he did, but his dreams where haunted by misty hypnotic visions of the hitchhiker and the yellow suitcase.

Saturday

Saturday arrived as a clear day with blue skies. It was his only day off, but he didn't mind. He was happy to work as many days as he could. He spent the day cleaning his apartment, washing his car, and writing checks for overdue bills. The normalcy of menial tasks wiped his mind clean of any preoccupation over Hitchhiker's Stretch.

On Saturday night he had dinner with his friends, Cameron and Elisa. Newly engaged, they asked Jason to be in the wedding party. He told them there was no way he would miss out on being part of their wedding, and he would be there to share their joy.

Jason wanted to ask Cameron about an incident with a girl that he could not quite recall through the haze of time and the fog of a drunken memory. He could not recollect any details of the event and was sure Cameron could help, but the opportunity never seemed right to ask him. A drunken liaison with some floozy was not a topic to bring up during a couple's engagement announcement. So, he let it go. They toasted the engagement with wine, shared some old memories, and Jason returned home with brightened spirits.

Jason's sleep was nuanced with disturbing visions and disjointed memories. *He saw flashes of himself, Cameron, Shaun, Brian, and someone else—a girl—in a car off the parkway; they were passing a bottle of Jack Daniels. He saw the girl trying to refuse the bottle as Brian shoved it in her mouth, pouring the fiery liquid down her throat. He saw hands groping her, touching and squeezing. She pushed them away, protesting, getting louder, and then finally, she screamed.* Jason woke with a start, sweating and nervous. The dream slipped away from him, receding quickly into labyrinthine obscurity.

Sunday Night

Jason had been ill since morning; his body felt run down, his muscles were aching, and he was feeling a bit queer in the stomach. At first he attributed it to the overindulgence of the previous night. It became clear, however, that something more was happening. He struggled to get though his shift at work, pushing himself to keep a smile on his face for customers. Gia, the diner's hostess/cashier, asked how he was feeling.

"Not so great," Jason said.

"You look pale, your face is pasty white," she said.

By late evening he grew hot with fever, but he finished his shift without incident. The midnight manager happened to come in a little early. Upon seeing Jason, he told him he would cover the last half hour of the shift and that Jason should head on home. Jason thanked him, grateful to be relieved from duty.

Jason exited the diner at 11:30, feeling a bit queasy. He was on the parkway in minutes. The Sunday traffic had already diminished to a slow trickle and the empty roads enabled him to push the speed limit. He turned on the radio to get his mind off of his deepening nausea. The hard rock show that he often listened to on his Sunday night drive, *Finger's Metal Shop,* was playing on WBAB. Alice Cooper's *Sick Things* reverberated through the car. *Sick Things,* Jason thought, *really sums up the night for me.* A fine mist had settled over the parkway, common fare for South-Shore Long Island during the early summer months. He raced through the mist and the umbrella-like trees crowding the road, giving the illusion of streaming through a tunnel.

Jason began to swallow hard, repeatedly, as excess saliva collected in his mouth. He thought about what he had eaten during the day, trying to pinpoint a suspect for his sickening gut. Perhaps it was the Chinese food he had eaten for lunch that was left over from Friday. Perhaps it was the Chicken Francoise he had eaten tonight at the diner. Either way, his body wanted whatever was sitting in his gut out of him. He could feel that his digestive system had shut down, the undigested food sitting idle, his innards in submission screaming *no mas*, and poised on the threshold of revolt.

A deep-seated belch rose from Jason's gut and he tasted bile in his mouth. It stung the back of his throat. He felt the first convulsion of his abdomen and it became clear that he was not going to make it home without incident. This surge was coming on and increasing in strength with each passing second. Seeing a clearing off the side of the parkway, Jason pulled the car to the right and stepped on the brakes, needing to stop immediately. The strangling brush and shrubbery receded back from the road in this area, leaving ten feet of crab grass—enough to park his car and have room to settle this matter with his stomach. With his judgment compromised by illness, Jason jammed on the brakes too hard. The car skidded onto the grassy clearing and lurched to a stop, kicking up pebbles and patches of weeds in rounded clumps.

Jason jumped from the driver's seat and ran to the passenger side of the car so he would be less noticeable to other drivers. He bent at the waist and rested his hands upon his knees. He opened his mouth and a hot stream of saliva poured out. He spit in the grass several times, and suddenly the feeling started to recede. He didn't want that. He wanted whatever was in him causing such misery to be gone.

Jason didn't even realize the familiarity of the area where he had stopped. He tilted his head up a bit to see his surroundings. Yes, it was— he was at Hitchhiker's Stretch, within close proximity to where he had originally seen the woman thumbing a ride only days ago. With his stomach momentarily settled, though the battle in no way over, Jason straightened up for a better look around. His eyes were drawn to the thick briar and greenery further back from the road. He looked over and there it was. The yellow suitcase. Peeking out from under the brush and fallen foliage.

Testing his steadiness, he stood and took a few tentative steps. He was alright for the moment, but he knew it wouldn't last. A churning whirlpool rumbled within his gut, but he was able to function. He turned his attention to the suitcase.

The brush was thick, thorny and full of spiders, crickets, and who knew what else. Jason opened the passenger-side door of his car and depressed the button that popped the trunk. He removed a crowbar, one end of which had a sharp curve, like a giant fishhook.

Jason hooked the handle of the suitcase with the crowbar and dragged it out into the clearing. He looked at it lying flat on the crabgrass, begging to have its latches clicked and opened. Other than being yellow, there was nothing special about it. Jason wondered why it had garnered so much thought and consideration from him. He threw the crowbar back into the trunk of his car and then slammed it shut.

He had come this far and knew he had no choice but to do it; he would open the suitcase. Walking back to the yellow luggage, Jason winced at a sudden tug in his gut. Another step and a painful spasm wrenched his mid-section, bringing him to his knees. Involuntarily, his throat opened and emitted a low vocalization that would lead the way for the half-digested food to soon follow. A tidal wave of hot bile soup gushed from his body. Small, firm chunks of food whacked the inside of his gums and teeth as they passed out of him. He fell to all fours, careful not to drop his palms in the steamy discharge. The wave ended with a guttural growl and gasps for breath while he tried not to inhale the smell of vomit.

Before he could get his lungs replenished with air and oxygen, another spasm squeezed his gut, emptying more liquid fire from his insides. This wave came from deep within him. Near the end of the expulsion, Jason felt something hard and unnatural pass from him. It scratched the back of his burning throat and clicked against his teeth. It flew out and landed in the grass before him, small, shiny, and metallic. It was a key; a very small key like the kind that would open... a suitcase. He barely had time to register this thought when he saw movement out of the corner of his eye. He gasped for air and tried to douse the flames in his throat by swallowing.

A surge of vomit came upon him for a third time. Footfalls stamped across the crabgrass toward him as he emptied his gut and gasped for air. Jason looked over in time to see those long bare legs capped with spiked shoes taking giant strides, purposefully and determinedly, toward him. A line of viscous fluid hung from Jason's lip and nose like a stalactite. He spit into the grass several times, eventually dislodging the slime, before looking at the hitchhiker. He saw her right leg swinging back out of sight, and before he could react, it came rocketing forward, the spiked-heeled

166

shoe colliding squarely with his dribbling chin.

His head jerked backward and then fell forward, dangling between his shoulders. His chin stung as if a swarm of angry bees had attacked him. Not understanding why any of this was happening, Jason mustered up some energy to look at the hitchhiker. He did not like what he saw.

All the anger of earth's violent history resided within her, the fury of the eons collected and focused in one entity that now had Jason in its sites. He was reminded of a catchphrase his mother used to voice, *heaven beside her*, which meant *hell within her*. Her eyes flared up in a vehement red glow, molten lava from this rage-filled she-demon, piercing heat, scorching the very air within her field of vision.

Still on all fours, feeling another surge of vomit grow to inevitability, Jason scampered back and tried to pivot away from her direct onslaught. She swung her right leg back like a pendulum and brought it forth, the top of her ankle hooking under Jason's armpit and the top of her shoe crashing into his jawbone. If not broken, it was at very least dislocated. A fire-hose stream of fresh vomit exited his mouth at an angle to the left, rather than straight out in front of him.

He was helpless, defenseless. There was no more worry or concern and no more fear—just the notion that he had to go with the flow, let it happen, and trust in the mercy of God.

Then he heard the song, reinforcing his mother's words. Clear as day... *Alice in Chains*, Lane Staley, from beyond the grave, singing, "... *like the coldest winter chill, heaven beside her, hell within.*" He prayed it was not coming from his car radio, that he was hearing it in his head. If it were actually playing on the radio at this moment in time, it meant *The Powers That Be* had already abandoned him, that fate was stacked against him and all was lost.

On the third kick Jason heard a ringing in his ears, saw a squiggly ribbon of blood jettison from his lips—dancing in mid-air before his eyes before falling to the ground. Mercifully, the world went away and his consciousness succumbed to blackness.

When Jason came to, two faces were staring down at him. Flashing red and white lights filled the air and squashed electronic voices barked through various police radios. One of the officers wiped blood from Jason's face with a rolled-up bunch of paper towels.

"Sir, you're going to be alright. We called for paramedics."

The other officer chimed in, "Were you struck by another vehicle?"

"No," Jason managed to say. "It was the girl, a woman. Did you see a woman?"

Both officers looked in the same direction, off to Jason's right. Apparently, there was another person on the scene that both officers now looked to for an answer to Jason's question. Jason heard the man's voice, but he could not see him.

"I didn't see no girl. When I rolled up here, this guy was flailing all about like he was having some kinda seizure," the man said.

One officer—Jason realized was a woman—continued to question him. The other officer, whose voice was definitely male, stood and walked away.

"Sir, do you have epilepsy or some other condition that would cause convulsions?" the female officer asked.

"No, I don't. It was the woman, I tell you. The woman with the yellow suitcase. She did this to me," Jason insisted.

"You mean this yellow suitcase?" The voice drifted across the grass from a short distance away.

Jason turned his head as much as he could toward the sound of the voice. He saw the male officer crouched down in front of the yellow suitcase, prepared to open it. It was difficult to keep his head turned, so he looked back to the female officer.

"It's locked," the officer said.

"There's a key around somewhere, I think," Jason said, not sure if he was correct after he had said it.

"Can you tell me your full name, sir?" the female officer asked.

"Jason Mackey," he grumbled.

"I think I found it. Could this be it?"

It was the other man's voice, the Good Samaritan who called the police after finding Jason lying, all beaten and bloody, at the side of the road.

"Let me see that," the male officer said.

The female officer continued her questioning. "You say that suitcase belongs to a woman?"

"Yes, a hitchhiker. You should be looking for her, you have to find her," Jason urged.

Jason and the female officer both turned their attention to the click and pops of the opening latches on the suitcase. The case sprung opened. The male officer stood and jumped back, raising the back of his hand to his nose.

The other man said, "Jesus, what the hell is that?"

"Lord have mercy," the male officer said. His voice was calmer, more accepting of what he was seeing than the voice of the witness.

"Is that a body? A dead body?" the man asked, his voice climbing an octave.

For a moment nobody said a word.

"I think we found your woman," the male officer stated grimly.

"What? No, that can't be," Jason stammered.

"Blonde hair, stiletto heels, denim cut-offs?" the male officer relayed in question.

"Uh, yeah, but she was alive. I saw her here a few days ago. And again tonight," Jason said.

"I doubt that," the officer said. "Judging by the decomposition of her body, I'd say she has been dead at least six months. Perhaps even a year."

At that exact moment, a memory flooded into Jason's consciousness like a river breaking its banks. His mind returned to the dream that had begun on Saturday night. *The young woman tried desperately to extract herself from a car full of drunken men as they roughly groped and grabbed at her. She climbed out the back window and her shirt ripped as she fell to the ground. She ran off into the woods, screaming. Brian and Shaun jumped from the car and raced after her. When Cameron and Jason caught up to them, she was lying face down in the dirt, motionless. Shaun was holding a large rock in his hand.*

"I was just trying to stop her from screaming," he said. "She wouldn't stop, she wouldn't stop. I stopped her."

The rock Shaun held in his hand was dripping blood. Brian grabbed it and threw it into the woods. "Come on, we have to fix this. None of us are going to jail. It was an accident," he said.

At the car, Brian removed a tattered old suitcase and a hacksaw from the trunk. Jason couldn't watch the deed, so he stood as a lookout. Tears streamed down his face, and he winced at the sound of the saw cutting through bone and grizzle. After a few minutes, Brian emerged from the woods and handed Jason a small key. "You keep this," Brian said. "Hide it, swallow it, bury it. I don't care what you do with it. Just never let it be seen in daylight ever again."

After the initial shock, the female officer turned back to look at Jason, her gaze locking with his. She shined the flashlight into his distant eyes, searching for answers behind his far-off stare. Something within the deep recesses of Jason's mind told him that his next statement was true, so he just blurted it out. "Her name is Alice."

LATE ONE NIGHT AT THE LOCAL RADIO STATION, CIRCA 1984

TIM J. FINN

Dave Grayson gripped the plastic frame and yanked the picture from the lobby's paneled wall. He snickered as he read the photograph's caption.

"WHBT President Harvey Budd Taylor congratulates 1983 grocery sweepstakes winner Millie Solomon."

Even the decrepit golden agers that made up most of the station's listenership seemed grateful when he dumped the sweepstakes after Millie's win. Grayson smiled as he remembered their reaction to his replacement for the grocery giveaway. No one actually took it *all* off during his strip-poker tournament. The risqué round robin attracted a pant load of demographically desirable new listeners who stuck with the station after they discovered its updated, relevant format.

Grayson tossed the picture in the stuffed cardboard box at his feet. He shifted the ladder to the fireplace in the lobby's center. He swept the pictures and trophies from its faux marble mantel and dropped them into the carton. Grayson sniggered at the oil portrait hanging above the hearth—a bald man with fleshy jowls scowled back at him.

"Take a last look, Harvey Budd."

Grayson's extensive and varied broadcast resumé convinced Taylor to hire him for the station manager's position halfway through their interview. Grayson started to concoct his hostile takeover scheme before Taylor even finished his effusive welcome. Goosing the long-stagnant property into an accomplished and profitable success should put an exclamation point to his nose thumbing of all the butt wipes that ignored his innovative ideas and kept him in subordinate roles. Grayson often day-dreamed of being a Jeopardy contestant when Alex posed this answer: "The broadcasting industry and an aisle stocked with feminine hygiene products."

He would ring in with a quick reply. "Where are two places you can find a lot of douche bags."

Grayson gave Taylor the courtesy of asking the old man to sell him the station outright. Taylor replied to his multiple queries with a fatherly pat on the back.

"Buddy, you're already running the whole box of cookies."

Carte blanche at programming the on-air sound seemed to be absent from the tin. Grayson tolerated working at a few "golden oldies" stations during his climb up radio's barbed pecking order. The Taylor-originated "continued soft sounds of the suburbs" format featured moldy snooze inducers, outdated lyrics that skirted the line between quaint and offen-sive. Grayson thought the FCC's approval of his proposal to boost the operating power might goad Taylor into allowing him to update the stale on-air programming. His refusal to change wasted the lucrative possi-bilities created by the new signal's deep reach, deep into the surrounding high-tech belt. Grayson took his cue from the oft-requested Alice Cooper tune he played during his time at a hard rock outlet. He grinned at Taylor's picture and strummed an air guitar. "No more Mister Nice Guy."

Grayson bided his time until the station's license renewal application came due. He manufactured billing irregularities, falsified programming records, and made required engineering reports disappear. Grayson even created traces of the ultimate violation, the dreaded payola. He linked the infractions straight to Taylor. He reported the feigned contraventions to the FCC with the claim he uncovered them during his search for the proper renewal documentation. The agency yanked Taylor's broadcast authorization and allowed Grayson to operate the station under a temporary conservatorship. He later parlayed his goodwill with the bureau into full custody of the license. Taylor exhausted his money on failed appeals, forcing him to sell WHBT and all its fixtures to Grayson for scarcely pennies on the dollar. He retired in disgrace with a permanently soiled reputation among the local businessmen.

"Shouldn't have played with me, old man," Grayson told the portrait. "You didn't stand a snowball's chance in hell."

Static blasted from the lobby speaker and blanketed the station's signal. Grayson detected a vocal repetition amidst the crackle.

"Neither do you, buddy."

Grayson stared through the plate glass separating the on-air studio from the lobby. A paunchy man with a gray ponytail sat at the control board. He wore black plastic headphones and spoke into a microphone dangling from its pivot stand. His smooth baritone displaced the speaker's popping and hushed the muffled voice.

"Temps will drop into the lower fifties overnight. Tomorrow the sun pays another visit and brings in a high in the mid-seventies. Thursday, bid adieu to old Sol, rain returns with temperatures around sixty. Fifty-three current degrees as we go surfing on the rhythm of the night with Debarge. Jerry Morgan catching a wave here at WHBT."

The disc jockey finished his talk up as El Debarge crooned the song's opening line. He noticed Grayson looking at him and pointed a thumb up at him.

Jerry Morgan's main life achievement consisted of drinking himself out of a job at nearly every radio station in the area. Grayson remembered Morgan's industry-wide legendary bottle bouts when he first encountered him at the start of his career. The older disc jockey mentored Grayson during his lucid moments and provided him with insider information on the more sordid aspects of the broadcasting field, information that fueled Grayson's determination to succeed in the business. Grayson figured he squared accounts by rescuing Morgan from a dead-end gig babysitting the automation equipment overnight at a tiny religious station. He subsidized Morgan's rehab stint and put him back on the airwaves after he dried out. Grayson harbored doubts about his continued sobriety, but he figured Morgan owed him too big a debt to screw with him. Old equipment with faulty wiring probably picked up a strong ship-to-shore transmission or a signal from some stupid meathead fooling around with a nearby CB.

Grayson grabbed the shellacked frame around Taylor's portrait and pulled. The picture remained fastened to the wall.

"You never did know when to give up, you old bastard."

Grayson jerked the frame forward and stretched the coil holding the picture on its single hook. Morgan stepped from the studio and watched Grayson grunt and tug.

"You're getting it, boss."

The wire retracted with a snap and wrenched the picture from Grayson's grasp. He yelped when the frame's edges scraped his fingers. Grayson flailed his arms as he tipped backwards. He clutched at the mantel and banged his funny bone on its corner. Morgan rushed to the fireplace as the ladder toppled. Grayson tumbled into his outstretched hands. The disc jockey's legs buckled and they keeled onto the floor.

Grayson thought he heard the speaker chuckle as they fell. He rolled off Morgan, kicking his feet and holding his elbow.

"Shit fuck, shit fuck, shit fuck! I wish I knew the rest of Carlin's seven words so I could say them, too. Shit fuck."

Morgan moaned and sat up. He panted and rose to his feet in a slow, gingerly manner. He groaned and massaged his lower back. "Oh, my aching sacroiliac."

"You know that's a pre-existing condition, Jerry."

Grayson peeked at the man's medical records when he enrolled him in rehab. Morgan sustained the injury when he slipped while trying to sneak a case of bourbon past a distracted liquor store clerk. "What you did isn't part of your job description and nobody, like me, asked you to do it. Take a Tylenol and go buy a heating pad."

"It's cool, boss, I'm cool. A little massage, good as new. I was coming out anyway to tell you Mahoney Funeral Home just called."

"They know my policy. We don't air obits anymore. No more free plugs for those ghouls."

"That wasn't it," Morgan said. "They called to tell us that Harvey Budd died. They're doing up the arrangements and figured they should tell us of all people."

Grayson glanced at Taylor's crooked portrait. "Now your retirement *is* permanent."

"You want me to announce it?" Morgan asked. "Or just let Toby do it after the hourly AP?"

"It can wait for Oscar and the morning news block. We got the new format going strong, let's not screw with it by broadcasting any downers."

"I just thought, you know, he founded and more or less built this place and all..."

Grayson breathed an exasperated sigh at Morgan. "Shall I spell it out, Jerry? Do you really think *I* would want to give any extra props to *him?* You have just enough time to get back in there before you're playing the label."

Morgan ran back in the studio and hit the start button for the top slot of the triple-stack tape cartridge player. Explosions erupted from the speaker, followed by a deep, synthesized voice. "Your favorite music bursting right through your radio. The new W-H-B-T!"

Morgan activated the second turntable an instant before the jingle ended. The opening tones of Men At Work's *Overkill* shadowed the audio bumper. Morgan switched records on the first turntable. He cued the new disc and grabbed the blinking studio telephone.

Grayson reset the step ladder against the fireplace, checking its steadiness before he climbed to the top step. He pulled a hammer from his carpenter's apron and pointed it at Taylor's portrait. "Give me any more trouble, you old fart, and I'll use a machete."

Grayson reached for the wall behind the picture. The head on the nail holding the portrait's wire shrank when Grayson grabbed at it with the hammer's claw. He snatched at it again. The nail drilled itself into the wall, leaving only its thoroughly embedded head visible. Grayson blinked and tapped the side of his head. "All these frigging man hours are catching up with me and giving me the heebie jeebies. You're still finding ways to drive me crazy, you old son of a bitch, even with the worms chewing up your ugly old ass."

Morgan replaced the phone just in time to mix the final notes of *Overkill* into the stinger open of Shalamar's *Dancing in the Sheets*. He massaged his back as he shuffled to the lobby. "Got a problem, boss."

Grayson pantomimed a hammer toss at Morgan.

"Whoa now, I'm just the messenger. Toby called, said his car croaked on him. I tried calling the part-timer fill-ins, but the phone lines aren't working. They just make that whooshing sound you hear when the transmitter goes nighty night. Well, not our transmitter, I guess, we're twenty-four, broadcasting your favorite music all day and all night."

Grayson flipped Morgan the middle finger as he descended the ladder. He grabbed the telephone on the lobby's reception desk. Grayson banged the receiver down when he heard its vacuous hiss.

"I'd like to help you out, boss, but with all these twinges in my back, I should probably get it looked at right away. If I didn't because I had to stay and work, and it turned out I really did something to it, that could cause all sorts of problems all over the place."

"Put a cork in it, Jerry. You chose what flavor. Shit, nobody lives even remotely close, so even doing something stupid like asking over the air for one of them to come in isn't an option. Paying for a last-minute fill-in adds extra expense to my operating budget, anyway."

Grayson closed his eyes and pondered for a minute. "All right, everything good or bad that happens here falls under my purview. I wouldn't have it any other way. I planned to pull a near all-nighter so I could get rid of all traces of Harvey friggin' Budd."

Grayson addressed his last remark to Taylor's portrait. He dismissed the quick upturn he thought he saw around the corners of Harvey Budd's mouth. "You get a stay of execution, old man. I'll be following you, Jerry."

"Dynamite!" Morgan blurted. "DDG, Davey Dick Grayson back on the airwaves."

"Don't pop a woody over it," Grayson told him. "That name's been retired and it's staying that way. Call me, call me, Dan Mason. I bet I'm not too rusty to show up you guys."

"Whatever you say, boss. Oh, I mean *Dan*. Oops, there's my cue."

Morgan shambled into the studio and plopped into the swivel chair behind the console. He chatted over the next song's instrumental open. "This is Jerry Morgan, sliding on out of the captain's chair. Dan Mason is coming onboard with more of your favorites, taking you into the wee small hours. A quick round of calisthenics now with Olivia, at WHBT. Bye."

Grayson stepped into the studio as the opening lyrics of *Physical* warbled from the Bose speaker suspended above the console. Morgan grabbed a forty-five from the plastic bins lining the counter's left return. "You know, boss, you could just run these music tapes I found piled in the prod room. I always keep one cued up and ready. I can just replace my air check tape with another one."

Grayson wheeled to the ceiling-high equipment rack built into the back wall. A full reel wound around the spools of the tarnished silver Pioneer tape machine screwed into the top half. A scratched Revox set into the rack's bottom section held a similar load.

"What, you got a booboo on that tape you're trying to hide? Leave it right where it is and I'll see how badly you screwed the pooch." Grayson chuckled when Morgan flinched. "Don't get your panties in a bunch. I'm just teasing. You'll always be my hero."

Morgan guffawed and slapped his thigh. "You got me, boss, totally believed it. Those tapes run about an hour. You can fit the few late-night commercials in at the beginning, and you're not tied to the board all night."

Grayson shook his head. "The dog shit on those tapes isn't fit to be flushed, never mind aired. Harvey Budd's private stock. They're not even fit to be erased and reused. I should probably burn them, but that would just stink up the place. What am I kicking my shift off with?"

"A little Herbie Hancock, boss. *Rockit*. A stripper did a hot little g-string pull to it at Naked Wonders last night. Long and slow, in tune with the music. When the final beat popped, out popped her juicy, shaved clitoris. I gave her an extra dollar. She deserved it."

"I hope you didn't spend any other dollars boozing it up. Not with what I went through to get you clean and sober."

"No, no. They laugh at it, but I always stick to soda water. I don't forget what you did for me."

The speaker whistled and hissed. A hearty chuckle cackled through the static.

"And *I'll* never forget what you did. Buddy."

Physical boomed back on the speaker.

"Did you hear that, Jerry? Tell me you heard that."

Grayson tapped Morgan on the shoulder. He twirled the disc jockey around when he received no response to his query. Morgan remained fixed to the chair. His head with its scrunched face stayed straight and raised. Grayson leaned in and stared at Morgan's rigid countenance. The disc jockey twisted in an abrupt jerk and sneezed in his face. Grayson and Morgan both reached for the pop-up tissue box on the counter's right return. Grayson glared when their fingers touched. Morgan jerked his hand back and dabbed his nose with the sleeve of his Irish knit sweater. Grayson mopped his face with a wadded tissue.

"Oh, no, not the blackouts again."

"I've seen your blackouts," Grayson told Morgan. "That's not it. I don't suppose you heard that voice. It kind of reminded me of Harvey Budd's."

"No way. The only voice I heard was sweet Olivia's. Thinking about her in that tight workout gear she wears in the *Physical* video, I about gave myself a nice boner. I'd figured all that drinking kinda put a permanent kibosh on my nookie glands. It wasn't shaping up to be a full-fledged diamond cutter, but there was…"

"Spare me," Grayson told him. "And spare the dead air, the song's ending."

Morgan turned to the console and opened the microphone. "Your favorite music and the latest news… the new sound of WHBT, Marlford."

The clipped inflections of the anchorman trailed the blaring network fanfare.

Morgan popped from the swivel chair. He saw Grayson stare at his back. Morgan grabbed it and winced. "Shouldn't have done that," he said. "Got to get it looked at."

"Yeah, you wouldn't want it to just go away on its own"

Morgan frowned as he lifted a canvas tote bag from the counter. "Have a good show, boss. I'll be listening all the way home."

"Aw, that makes me feel all warm and fuzzy."

Morgan patted his back and shuffled out the front door of the station's compact ranch house. Grayson shook his head at the departing disk jockey and flopped into his vacated chair. He filed *Physical* in a yellow cardboard sleeve and shoved it in the back of one of the bins. Grayson snatched another disc and placed it on the empty turntable. He grabbed three cartridges from a rotating stand and plugged them into the triple stack's slots. Grayson scanned the teletype printout binder clamped to the console's copy holder. He checked the oval Seth Thomas clock tacked to the wall adjacent to the shuttered window. Grayson donned the headphones and waited while the network announcer concluded his report.

"I'm Mark Russo, AP network news. The radar forecast calls for clear skies overnight with temperatures hovering near fifty. Partly sunny tomorrow with the daytime high hitting the mid-sixties. Thursday's outlook calls for clouds and drizzle with temperatures in the low sixties. Clear skies now and fifty-two degrees. You're in tune with all your favorite music, the new sound of WHBT."

Grayson thumbed the turntable's remote start when he recited the call letters. His eardrums vibrated as *Rockit* boomed through the headphones. Grayson yanked them off and lowered their volume. "Damn it, Jerry, you're even more deaf than most jocks. Okay, it ends cold, a jingle bridge into the next song, piece of cake. I might even enjoy myself."

Grayson watched the tone arm and its needle play through the record's grooves. He nudged the button on the triple stack's top slot as *Rockit* throbbed to a conclusion. The tape clogged as it wound through the cartridge. Distorted music and garbled words oozed from the speaker.

"God damn hunk of crap." Grayson banged the triple stack. He barked when the machine's cooling screen sliced his palm and carved its imprint in his skin. "What the fuck, you bit me, you bastard!"

Static cackled from the Bose. Grayson cringed at the mocking giggles that reverberated through the studio. "Yummy, yummy, yummy."

Grayson wheeled back from the console. The tape slipped free and a bass announcer slurred the station promo.

"... it's here. The new sound of W-H-B-T!"

Grayson stared at the speaker for several seconds and willed it silent. He swiveled to the second turntable and held his breath as he clicked it into gear. The beginning of *The Safety Dance* popped, followed by the song's lengthy instrumental intro. Grayson crossed his fingers and watched the forty-five spin. He grinned when the female background vocalist trilled into her fourth rendition of the title.

"All right. Too many hours of work and too little regular eating. My sphincter doesn't even know whether to hold it or dump it. I should've made Jerry do a food run. Okay, get another record on and we'll be rocking and rolling."

Grayson pulled a disc from the bins. "BA added the single version. It might be a *monster* hit already, but it can't top *Billie Jean*. That's a classic."

Grayson donned the headphones and blended *Safety Dance's* repetitious fade into the new song's bombastic open. "Dan Mason sending out a big smooch on your ears. You think anyone predicted that little dynamo from the Jackson 5 would grow up to record the biggest album ever? Nostradamus even missed that one. Already a Halloween perennial, magic Michael raising some goose bumps with the *Thriller*, at WHBT."

Grayson high fived the air when Jackson's first "ooh" punctuated his words. "Hit the post without a preview or a hot clock. I still got enough to jock any of my announcers right under the table."

The screech of a sharp object shredding vinyl pierced his ears. Grayson flinched again and gaped as the tone arm's needle sliced through the spinning forty-five. He choked on the acrid smoke that wafted from the gouged record. The turntable ceased spinning. A heap of slivers covered its felt pad. The tone arm lifted and spat the needle into Grayson's right eye. He screamed as its point perforated his retina and speared the pupil. Grayson pawed at the ocular injury and attempted to pluck the needle. Blood-flecked tears drizzled down his cheek. Snickers resounded in the headphones.

"Keep listening, buddy. The broadcast is about to get very interesting, to quote Artie Johnson. Sorry I can't do the accent, but you probably don't know who I'm talking about anyway."

The headphones compressed and clamped to Grayson's head. He tugged on them as the earpieces squeezed. The headphones stayed adhered to his skin. He continued to pull, stretching the dermis until it frayed. He let out a cry as blood flowed from around his ears and down his neck. He grasped the plastic band connecting the foam pads and snapped it. Grayson gasped when the binding pressure stopped and his ears popped. He threw the twisted headphones on the counter. They chirped when they bounced on the scarred Formica. Grayson jammed his index fingers in his ears and gulped air while he massaged the tender canals. He felt thick moisture and removed his fingers. He scowled at the blood smeared on his fingertips. "Shit."

Grayson swiped at the cracked headphones. Their cord wriggled across the counter and jerked them beyond his reach. He grabbed again. The cord retracted and dragged the headphones behind the console.

"Pricks."

Grayson rose and leaned over the control board. He groped through the accumulated dust and grit behind it. When he felt a breeze sweep over his back he turned and looked above him. Grayson bobbed his head and ducked as the speaker whizzed by him. He scrambled to push himself off the console. The speaker twisted sideways and swung on a pendulous arc. The corners of it pounded into his ribs and shattered them. Grayson screamed until a bloody clump clogged his trachea. He collapsed into the swivel chair and hacked the sanguinary cluster onto the console. Taylor's voice scolded him from the Bose as the speaker rose back to its fixed position above the console.

"Buddy, that could seep through and short out the board. It's still the original wiring. I know 'cause I put it in and took care of it ever since we went on the air. It has my, what's that scientific, molecules term they're talking up now. DNA! My DNA is over it, just like it's all over every bit of this station, despite your slimy, slinky little coup. I even possess a piece of *you*. Judging by what you just yakked all over *my* board, a few more pieces must've been knocked loose."

Taylor's jeering laugh echoed through the studio. "It's your mess, but I'll clean it up. That's sort of what I'm here to do, anyway."

Grayson whimpered as he watched the bloody vomit thin and dissolve. The console glistened with a freshly polished gloss.

"You can even see yourself in it, buddy. And what a revolting development that is. That's right, you're only into what's current. You wouldn't recognize the reference. But I bet you can appreciate a real *new* revolting development!"

The microphone pivoted on its stand and bashed Grayson in the face. Grayson tried to scream but only managed a wet wheeze when its metal tip crushed his nose. Blood peppered with ground bone dribbled into his lap. Grayson rose and eyed the console as he backpedaled towards the studio door.

"Abandoning your post before your shift is over, buddy? Maybe I should report you to the FCC. But then, I guess *your* shift is definitely over!"

The three cartridges shot from the triple stack. One ricocheted off Grayson's forehead and stunned him. The second and third punched him in the chest and pushed him against the equipment rack. Both reel-to-reel players thumped on and unspooled their tape, lassoing Grayson's shoulders and ankles. The reels reversed and tightened the slack tape until it bound Grayson to the rack.

"I think I just found a good use for one of those stupid records you brought in here. *Buddy.*"

The Safety Dance whirled on the turntable. Grayson gawked as it revolutions sped past even the 78 rpms on the ancient turntables he jockeyed on at the start of his radio career. The record sailed off the spindle and winged towards him. Grayson opened his mouth and tried to scream. The whirring disc sliced through his Adam's apple. Grayson gurgled and gagged on his own viscera. The reel-to-reel machines rolled out loose tape and released him. Grayson splashed into the puddle of blood that swamped the floor.

The lobby telephone rang. Grayson dragged himself to the reception desk on his elbows. The carpet's fibers stiffened and pared bloody rug burns in his bare arms. The night-time answering machine picked up after the sixth ring. Grayson's one working eye misted red as he listened to an aged woman record her message.

"A big wet kiss for whoever put that beautiful music back on your station. Don't ever change again, please. Whoever bought in that crazy stuff can give me a kiss right on my big, wrinkled ass. I hope you got rid of them, too. I'm calling all my friends right now and tell them the good news."

"Looks like we're granting the listener's request, buddy. We returned to our original format as soon as you went on the air. So no one heard your last broadcast. Aw!"

Grayson heard a sharp squeak. He lifted his head and stared at the fireplace. Harvey Taylor's portrait creaked back and forth as it straightened. Grayson cringed when he saw Taylor's mouth widen into a toothy grin. He dropped his head again and slid into unconsciousness.

"Bye, buddy. And please, do let the door hit you in the ass on your way out!"

Grayson passed with peals of Taylor's laughter chiming in his ears.

IT ALL COMES AROUND IN THE END

JENNIFER WORD

The wind was chilly, a thick scud of gray clouds covering the sky. It whistled through the bare trees, seeming to taunt and tease, threatening rain at every shrill note. Rachael stuffed her hands deeper into the pockets of her Trilby coat. She should have brought her gloves, but they were sitting on the passenger seat of the green Fiat. They, at least, were warm. John was walking with the farmer, Kell O'Donough, asking questions like an excited schoolboy. Rachael shivered, sighed, then walked over to John, a grimace etched onto her face. Her lips were numb.

"Honey, this is amazing," John said, pointing to a headstone. "This tombstone is over three hundred years old."

Rachael smiled and nodded. Mister O'Donough smiled back, sympathizing. He had only agreed to bring the couple out here because John had offered him ten dollars, and Kell never refused easy money, especially from American tourists. Not that he'd ever had any knocking on his door before, but that was beside the point.

The tourists blew through town, marveling at the quaint little pubs, the architecture of the buildings, staying in the few bed and breakfasts along the row. Then they left and it never affected Kell at all, one way or the other. In town, he listened to the townsfolk complain about the "traffic," but he noticed they never complained about the money these tourists spent on their fine establishments. Now it was his turn to reap the benefits.

He'd taken over the farm after his father died, and his forefathers had done the same throughout the generations. *The graveyard had always been*

181

here, he mused. A fixture no more out of the ordinary than the trees surrounding his land. As it so happened, he was an expert on the site, so to speak. The stories, like the farm itself, had been handed down. No one had ever bothered to knock on his door asking about them, however, until today.

"There's older than that, fella. In the monastery down Cornamagh," Kell repeated. He had already told this man, John Engall, that this old, deserted graveyard was small business, if the American really wanted to see some ancient graves. John simply shook his head.

"Everyone looks at those. I want to see something no one else has seen."

Rachael sighed heavily, turning to head back to the car. Kell stopped her with his hand, smiling gently. She blushed and he lowered his hand to his side, feeling awkward.

"Now hold on, missus, if it's different you want to see, I can show you that much."

"I'm not the one who wanted to see anything," Rachael huffed. She perceived Mr. O'Donough's accent to be more of a Scottish persuasion than Irish, but then again, what did she know?

"Sorry, honey, but it's not every day we are in Ireland. We both picked this, remember? You wanted Europe," John said.

"Paris, Nice, *Rome*, John!"

Now it was John's turn to look embarrassed. He glanced quickly at Mr. O'Donough and pulled Rachael to the side, turning his back on the farmer. Kell pretended to look off, not hearing their conversation, although he heard every word.

"Honey, we went to all those places, like every other tourist, and the crowds," John sighed. "That's not real, that's what everyone comes to see. A McDonald's on the French Riviera! That's not Europe, Rachael. That's ridiculous. You agreed, we'd see some real parts of Europe, honey, remember?"

"Yes, but we've stopped at every small town for one hundred miles. They all look the same, and now you're stopping at random graveyards in the middle of nowhere… and I'm freezing!"

"I think I can settle this for the two of you," Kell said. He spoke low and gentle, as if sharing a special secret with his best friend.

"Now listen," he said, motioning to Rachael. "You're cold, and your new, eager husband is hungry. He wants to see something no one else has ever seen. Well, I can do that for you. I'll show you something no tourist has seen through these parts, and then after, you can check in at Bell's

Bed and Breakfast, 'cause I know it's not full tonight. She serves the best Shepherd's pie you'll ever taste, with a warm brandy to top it all off. Agreed? It'll only take ten minutes, and you can be on your way. I promise, you won't be disappointed."

John looked at Rachael, his eyebrows raised. She sighed lightly and nodded her head.

"All right, but after this, we check into the hotel and we're done for tonight. For the rest of the trip."

"Okay," John said. "We're done... for tonight."

"John!"

"Okay. If this is really as good as Mister O'Donough says, then fine. We can be done for the trip."

Kell led the couple past the larger headstones, down an overgrown path ripe with dead vegetation. They reached the edge of the graveyard, where the trees began to take over. John and Rachael stopped, but Kell motioned them to keep walking.

"Just a bit further on, through the trees," he said. They followed him ten more yards, into the thickening woods, Rachael grasping John's arm. Kell stopped short, arriving at a large headstone that stood alone. He turned to the couple, looking sinister, devilish. A small grin played at the corners of his mouth.

"This is the grave of a witch, so the legend goes," he said. "Sometime around 1380, or thereabout. Ashlynn Cass was her name. Her brother entered a wager-of-battle when she was accused by a man in town. The man said she bewitched him to sleep with her. He was married, see, but if he could prove he was bewitched, his wife could not hold him accountable. Back in those days, if a woman was accused, a wager-of-battle was sometimes fought. If the one fighting on the side of the accused won, the charges were dismissed, and the accuser paid a fine. If the accuser won, the witch was hanged."

"And so they hanged her," Rachael said, rolling her eyes, her voice sarcastic and annoyed.

"Now don't go thinking you know the story just yet, missus," Kell winked. John was looking rather interested now.

"Her brother fought the accuser in that wager-of-battle I told you about. A sword fight, it was. A drawn out affair, too. Lasted some thirty minutes or more, and by the end, both men were bloody and well cut up, but the brother stood, and Ashlynn's accuser was on the ground, without his sword. So Ashlynn's name was cleared, of witchcraft anyhow. The man paid a hefty fine, the likes of which broke his family, not to mention his wife was none too pleased with the infidelity. She killed herself, so the story goes, and her husband went mad not too long after. As you can well imagine, these events started some gossip amongst the townspeople. They began to say that Ashlynn was a witch after all, and that it wasn't suicide and madness that took out that married couple, but Ashlynn herself, using her craft. She was banished from town, living on the outskirts. Her brother died of illness some years later, and no one ever heard from her again."

"That's it?"

Rachael was not about to let the story end on that note. She motioned to the headstone, which bore no name or date on it. It was in pristine condition and contained odd-looking carvings etched into the gray stone.

"This headstone doesn't look that old to me. If this is supposed to be that woman's grave, that would make this headstone over six hundred years old. This stone is obviously much newer than that."

"Ah, now here's the part where the story starts to get strange," Kell continued. His grin expanded, causing Rachael to grab John's hand.

"Some years after all this took place, the town was growing, pushing outward in all directions. Some townsfolk took it upon themselves to pay a visit to the old Cass home, which no one had seen in years. Take it over, they probably thought. The money won in that wager-of-battle would have run out before too long. With Ashlynn not coming into town for supplies and the harsh winters we have in these parts, no one could fathom how she would have survived. They figured her home must be abandoned by now. They found her brother's headstone back yonder," Kell motioned behind him, back towards the graveyard.

"So they knew he was dead, but they couldn't figure how Ashlynn had put up such a nice marker on his grave. So they knocked on her door, 'cause they seen smoke billowing out from the chimney. Some twenty years had passed since the battle, so they were expecting an old woman to open the door, if anyone at all. What they got, instead, was Ashlynn herself, just as young and pretty as ever."

"Oh please," Rachael snorted, rolling her eyes. "Let me guess. She still lives out here somewhere, in the same little house, and at night, you can hear her cackling as she rides around on her broom in the moonlight."

"Honey, let him finish," John said.

"Now I told you, missus, don't go thinking you know the tale just yet. It was three folks from town, come back swearing Ashlynn was still alive out here, and just as young and beautiful as ever. That's how everyone finally learned that she really was a witch. That married man was telling the truth, and Ashlynn did bewitch him to lie down with her, and later, to lose his mind, and his wife to kill herself. So the people in town decided it was time to hang her as a witch, like they should have done all those years before. A group of men with torches and knives and ropes came back out that very night. Knocked on Ashlynn's door, and sure enough, a beautiful woman answered, looking confused. She was the spitting image of Ashlynn, see. Only she kept telling them all that her name wasn't Ashlynn, it was Criona, but they wouldn't believe her. She tried to take them and show them Ashlynn's headstone, which she said was in the cemetery, just yonder from her brother's. They dragged her from the house, into the waiting woods, threw a noose over a tree branch and hung her, as she cried and protested she was not Ashlynn, she was not a witch."

"And?" John was leaning forward, eager and waiting. Rachael also looked excited now.

"Well, you can't guess?" said Kell. "She died, the woman. And the men who hung her walked back out, through the graveyard, and on their way, they spotted the brother's headstone, with peculiar words writ upon it. It said, 'Angus Cass, loving brother and uncle'. His name was Angus, did I tell you that?"

Both John and Rachael shook their heads impatiently. Kell paused for dramatic effect, then delved on.

"The men were puzzled by the word uncle, so they looked for that other grave, the one 'Criona,' had said was not too far off from Angus. They found it, the next row over, another headstone. It had Ashlynn's name on it, and it said loving sister and mother on it."

Rachael gasped. John merely looked at Kell with a blank stare. Kell paused again, then continued.

"Ashlynn had been with child from that affair, and had born it on the outskirts of town. She named her 'Criona,' which in our language means 'my heart,' and that little girl had been raised by her mother and Angus, her uncle. Angus died, and later Ashlynn, and it was Criona that managed, somehow, to put up the lovely headstones. No one ever knew how she afforded it, or who crafted them, for it was none from their town, as far as anyone could tell. When those folks from town saw this beautiful young woman at the door, they thought it was Ashlynn, bewitched and still young, when it was really her daughter, who, as I said, was her spitting image."

"So that poor woman raised a child all alone, outside town, then her poor daughter was hung as a witch, all because of superstition and misunderstanding?" Rachael's cheeks were aflame. She breathed heavily.

John continued to look blank. Then his expression changed to one of doubt. "Now hold on, Mister O'Donough," John said. "You said the story got weird. So far it sounds like a series of simple misunderstandings and mistakes."

"It does sound that way, doesn't it though? Those men stood there, in front of Ashlynn's grave, and realizing their mistake, they went back to that tree, meaning to cut down the body of Criona and give her a proper burial, but when they got back to the tree, Criona's body had disappeared."

"This is ridiculous," Rachael said. "You're making all of this up."

"No, missus," Kell said, sounding insulted. "This story has been passed down in my family for over six hundred years. I'm not making it up, I'm only telling it the way I was told. The way my father was told. The way every O'Donough has told it since the first one broke ground out by this graveyard, where no one else would go, all those years ago, and my ancestors got the land almost free. It's the same story I told my son, and he'll tell it to his," Kell said, his voice cracking slightly.

"She didn't mean anything by it, Mister O'Donough, I swear," John said. "Right honey? Please, finish the story."

Kell took a deep breath and spoke. "Like I said, Criona's body was gone, but all the growth around the tree was dead, just below where her body had hung. The men were spooked. They ran back to town, crossing themselves. It was over a year later that people began moving further out, and the original idea took hold to use Ashlynn's old place. They knew for certain now it was empty. It was after a family moved into it, their son wandered out into the woods one day and found the headstone. Right on the spot where they hung Criona, where all that green growth next to the tree had died. The very headstone you are looking at now."

Kell stood silent, watching the Engalls. Rachael and John stared at the headstone. Rachael could feel gooseflesh spreading up both her arms and on the back of her neck. She shivered, her body shuddering. Then she turned to Kell. It was her turn to look doubtful.

"I don't mean to be insulting, but still, if this headstone is that old, wouldn't it be crumbling by now? This stone looks to be in perfect shape, as if it were placed here last week."

"That's the strange part, at least some of it," Kell said. "The headstone has remained in perfect condition all this while. Time seems not to have any effect on it. Angus and Ashlynn's graves are the same. Only difference is, this one's not marked. At least, not with anything that makes sense."

"What does it mean?"

Rachael stared at the headstone, feeling creeped out. The markings were dark, as if they had been burned into the stone itself. *How much heat would it take to do that*, she wondered? The markings were foreign. Odd shapes and symbols all over it, even along the outer edges. Symbols and etchings that made Rachael feel as if she might lose her mind if she stared at them for too long. The light was beginning to fade as twilight approached. John brought out his camera.

"Do you mind if I take some pictures of it?"

"If you can take a picture of that, it's yours to have."

"What do you mean?"

"Tried to photograph it some years back myself," Kell said. "None would take."

John looked at Kell for a few moments, trying to decide if the man was joking or not. He didn't know whether to believe his story or not, and yet, Kell seemed to be dead serious in telling it. John took several photos of the headstone, checking each digital image afterwards to ensure it was clear. Then he smiled at Kell, looking relieved. The pictures seemed to prove to John that the story was a fake. He no longer felt scared at all. He took Rachael's hand to walk back to the graveyard, but was met with resistance. He tugged on Rachael's hand, looking back at his wife with only slight concern. She stared at the headstone as if hypnotized.

"Rachael, honey, come on," John said. He shook her hand in his.

Rachael looked over at John, suddenly confused. "Huh?"

"Let's go, it's getting dark. I thought you couldn't wait to get back to town?"

"Sorry," she said. "I must have zoned out there for a minute."

"Happens all the time," Kell said, leading the couple out of the woods and back into the graveyard. He stopped momentarily to show them both the graves of Angus Cass and Ashlynn Cass, and John took photos of these as well. They both, indeed, looked brand new, although the other graves surrounding them were crumbled and broken. Many were so old the writing was worn too thin to read anymore.

They reached the house, and John shook Mr. O'Donough's hand, thanking him for the tale. Kell smiled.

"I hope I gave you what you were looking for, Mister Engall. It's definitely something no one else has seen before. My farm is not on most tourists' radar."

"You've never shown those headstones to anyone before?" Rachael asked.

"No, missus," Kell said. "The townsfolk all know about it, but they don't like to think about it. No one comes out here to look at it. I've only looked upon it three times in my life. As a child, when my father first told me the story, again, when I told the story to my son, and today, with you."

"But I thought you said you also tried to photograph the headstone," said John.

"Did I? I was mistaken. My son tried to photograph the headstone, and it wouldn't turn out." A shadow fell over Kell's face then. It was only momentary, so brief, John barely noticed, but Rachael stepped forward, looking concerned.

"Where is your son, Mister O'Donough?"

"In town, getting supplies," Kell answered quickly.

"What about her home," asked John, looking thoughtful.

"Her home?"

"Yes, you said a family eventually moved into Ashlynn's home, didn't you? And their boy was the one to discover Criona's headstone?"

"Yes, that's right," said Kell.

"Whatever happened to Ashlynn's home?"

"Why, you're looking at it," Kell answered simply. John and Rachael stared at Kell O'Donough for several moments, their mouths hanging agape. Kell stared back at them, unblinking. John was the first to speak.

"You mean, your family lives in Ashlynn's old home?"

"Yes, it were my ancestors who got this land near for free way back then, when no one else would have anything to do with this place. A far distant relative, a great-great-great-great-great-great grandfather, many times removed, Shamus O'Donough, who as a young boy first discovered the headstone in the woods, at the foot of that old tree. So you see, I tell you the truth when I say this story has been passed down in my family for generations. It's the truth, every word."

"Have you ever seen anything, or… you know… heard anything in your house?" John asked. He had a twinkle in his eye.

Kell grinned. "You mean ghosts? Sure, I got my fair share of those tales as well."

"You're kidding," John said. "Witches and ghosts? This is too rich."

"I ain't rich, Mister Engall, that's for sure," Kell laughed. "Stories I have, but money, not so much of."

"Well, you should really think about starting up a business with all this legend," said John. "I mean, you could charge people to look at those headstones and tell your story. Like a little tour. You could even open your own bed and breakfast. Let people stay in Ashlynn's home, like a tourist draw. You'd probably make a small fortune."

"I don't know about that, Mister Engall. I doubt if Ashlynn would like that much, having strangers come into her home all the time."

John stared at Kell for several moments, waiting for the joke, but Kell only looked back at him with a complete look of seriousness on his face.

"You're serious," said John. "Your house is actually haunted by the spirit of Ashlynn?"

"Undoubtedly."

John looked at Rachael, then back at Kell, then at Rachael again. Then he reached into his back pocket and pulled out his wallet, producing several fifty-dollar traveler's checks. He handed three of them to Kell.

"I'll pay you one hundred and fifty American dollars to allow my wife and me to sleep in your home tonight, what do you say?"

"John, are you crazy?"

"Shhh, Rachael, let the man think."

"Absolutely not, John. We are not pushing ourselves onto this poor man and invading his home. We've already bothered him enough."

Kell simply sat, staring, as if in deep thought. His mind was already made up.

"There's a guest room in the back. You can stay there tonight, if that's what you like."

"Awesome. Honey, let's do it."

Rachael pulled John away from the house, arguing with him beside the green Fiat. Kell watched them closely, smiling his slight grin. After several minutes of arguing, John opened the trunk of the car and produced two small suitcases. Rachael walked back up to the house, John following quickly behind with the baggage.

"Thank you so much for doing this. I'm really sorry about my husband. It's just… when he gets something in his head, he can be sort of stubborn and even kind of crazy at times."

"I understand, Missus Engall. We all get that way sometimes."

"Honey, think of the stories we'll be able to tell when we get back home. How many people come back from Europe and can say that they stayed in an actual haunted house? And I can show them the pictures of the headstones, and tell them the story Kell told us. Is it all right if I call you Kell?"

"That is my name, Mister Engall."

"John, please."

"All right, John."

Kell led the Engalls to a bedroom in the back of the house, where they deposited their bags. There was a bathroom directly across the hall. Kell explained that his and his boy's rooms were both upstairs.

"Used to be this was only a one story house. My family added the upstairs long after the Cass story unwound. That guest bedroom you're in, that was Ashlynn's bedroom."

The Engalls, who had been following Kell back down the hallway, stopped abruptly.

"We're sleeping in Ashlynn's bedroom?" Rachael looked at her husband nervously.

"You're not scared, are you honey?"

"Of course not," Rachael said, slapping John's arm.

Kell led the couple into the kitchen, which had a small dining table in the corner. The entire house was made from wood, the support beams visible near the ceiling. It was a humble home, and walking through it gave both John and Rachael the distinct feeling of stepping back in time some two hundred years. Kell put a large pot on the stove, which Rachael thought resembled a cauldron. She looked at John to see if he noticed this. John seemed oblivious. Kell poured water into the pot, then began chopping up potatoes and carrots. He pulled what looked like, possibly, a medium-sized hare out of the fridge, already skinned. He began to butcher this, throwing the pieces of raw meat into the pot as well. He looked sideways at the couple.

"Rabbit stew," was all he said. Rachael gave John a look. He shrugged back at her.

"I'm really sorry to be imposing on you like this, Mister O'Donough. I mean, Kell. We really shouldn't be putting you out like this. We can drive into town and stay at that bed and breakfast, really."

"And force me to part ways with one hundred and fifty of my new best friends?"

Kell raised an eyebrow at the Engalls, who simply stared for several moments. Then Kell laughed heartily. John laughed as well, although Rachael only smiled weakly.

"You know, I do believe I've spooked you a bit with my tale, Missus Engall."

"No, of course not. I'm fine. Besides, I don't believe in ghosts."

"Really," Kell said in a daring tone.

"Well, what kinds of things have you experienced living here, Kell?" John intervened.

"Oh, the usual," Kell said, sitting down to the table. "That will need to boil low for a few hours, steep the juices. She'll be ready just in time for supper. We can sit in the living room, by the fire, if you'd like, and I can continue my tale."

"Yes, that would be great, wouldn't it, honey?"

John put his arm around Rachael, rubbing her shoulder with his hand. He hardly even noticed how she bristled at his touch. The couple followed Kell into the small living room, where a fire was already glowing. Kell added two logs from a pile in the corner and stirred the embers up a bit with the poker. The couple settled on a couch directly in front of the fire, and Kell settled into a chair adjacent to them. The furniture smelled old and musty, yet it was comforting; a welcoming smell. The walls were bare, save for a portrait of Kell and what Rachael presumed to be his son. There didn't seem to be any Mrs. O'Donough.

"I hear crying," Kell said. Rachael frowned, straining to hear any wayward sounds. She heard nothing and said so. Kell smiled, understanding.

"At night, I mean to say," he explained. "In the darkness, laying in my bed at night. Sometimes I hear crying."

"Maybe it's the wind outside, or an animal, a fox?" Rachael said.

"No," Kell smiled again. "It is most definitely a woman. Crying inside the house. There are odd knocking sounds as well."

"That could simply be the house settling," John offered.

"Not the way these knocks come," Kell said, his face suddenly becoming dead serious. Rachael's heart skipped a beat, a cold chill coming over her. She suddenly didn't want to be in this house for another minute.

"You think it's Criona? Or is it Ashlynn?" John asked.

"Perhaps both," said Kell. "My son and I have also seen shadows moving on the walls. Shadows as if there are bodies in the room, but the bodies themselves are not visible to the eye, only the shadows they cast. You can hear them climbing the stairs sometimes as well, the steps creaking beneath their weight."

"Well, no offense, Mister O'Donough, but many of these things could be explained by natural occurrence, even a runaway imagination," said John. Rachael stiffened beside him. John did not notice. She expected Kell to take insult at John's remark, but instead he laughed again, heartily.

"These are the suggestions of one who has not yet experienced what I am talking of," said Kell. "But if you do intend to stay the whole night in my home, perhaps by morning you will have a different perspective on these things?"

"Perhaps," said John.

Rachael relaxed a little. She was suddenly angry and lost inside her own head. Damn John and his crazy need to have some unique adventure while in Europe. Europe itself wasn't enough. No, he had to go off looking for some quaint little experience that wasn't on the normal tourist destinations. He always had to veer off the beaten path. It was one of the reasons she had fallen in love with him. He never did things the way anyone else did. He was always coming up with last-minute changes of plan, or just flying by the seat of his pants. She usually loved that about him, but in this particular case, it was starting to wear her down.

Rachael had agreed on Europe, instead of Hawaii or the Caribbean. She had later even agreed to this unplanned side trip to Ireland, when John had become bored with their preplanned tour of Italy and France. "It was too 'touristy'," he had said. In some ways, she had agreed, although it did not irk her in the same way it did him. Now, here they were, in some small town in southern Ireland, she wasn't even sure what county they were in anymore. Heathmore, perhaps? John had the map, not that he'd been using it much. Kell continued to explain the spooky goings-on inside his home.

"They try to push you down the stairs," he said, his face growing shadowy again. "You can feel their hands on your back. And sometimes at night, you wake up feeling as if you can't breathe, and you'd swear they were trying to suffocate you."

"Are you serious?" John looked at Rachael with doubt.

"Hey, you're the one who wanted to sleep here, not me," she said.

"Oh, I'm sure you'll be fine," Kell assured the couple.

"Really?" John looked worried.

"Well, no, not really, you're the first guests to ever stay here, so who can really tell?" Kell said matter-of-factly.

When he saw the look on John and Rachael's faces, he bellowed a loud booming laugh that made Rachael jump. This made Kell laugh until tears rolled down his face. Then he excused himself to the restroom, leaving the couple alone.

After a few minutes, John left to get his camera from the bedroom, leaving Rachael alone to stare at the fire. She looked to her right, to the portrait on the wall. It was covered in glass, which reflected the firelight, as well as the dimming light from the window. She stood up and walked over to the picture to get a better look.

Kell's son was in the photo, standing on the right side of his father. The picture was taken in front of the house, and Rachael briefly wondered who had taken the photograph. She thought the boy looked bothered, something about the expression on his face looked troubled.

Rachael jumped, as she saw an image of a man in the portrait glass, reflected and moving. She turned in time to see John, frowning, holding the digital camera in his hands. He was scanning the photos he had taken less than an hour before.

"Honey, you're not going to believe this. None of those pictures turned out."

"What do you mean?"

Rachael had a sinking feeling, remembering what Kell had said earlier. Something about his son trying to take a picture once. His face had clouded over, that same troubled look she noticed on his son's face in the portrait.

"Look at this, they're all dark, like the lens cap was still on. I looked these over when I took them, they were fine then."

"Are you sure?"

"Of course I'm sure, I saw them. They were perfect when I checked."

"You won't get any pictures of that headstone," Kell said, startling Rachael and John. John actually dropped the camera on the floor, mumbling a quick "Shit!" and bending over to pick it up.

"You didn't believe me?" Kell said with a devious smile.

"Of course I believed you," John said, cradling the camera and sounding petulant.

"No, you didn't, but I don't blame you," he said. "It's a fair hard story to swallow. Sit back down on yonder couch and I'll finish the tale for you two."

"John, I think we should leave," Rachael whispered.

John looked at Rachael momentarily, considering her request. Then she saw that gleam in his eye, the one she knew meant he couldn't help himself. There was a mystery here, and John wanted to hear the rest of the story. Rachael sighed and followed her husband back to the couch, sitting on the far side, away from Kell, who was back in his chair.

"Now where was I? Ah, right. The bumps in the night, as they like to call it, eh?"

More hearty laughter came from Kell, and Rachael stiffened. John leaned forward, listening intently.

"She whispers to you in the night, while you lay in your bed." Kell seemed distant now, staring off into the fire.

His change in demeanor was so abrupt, Rachael again had that uneasy feeling. It stemmed from a basic impression that Kell was a man truly haunted. She began to feel as if eyes were on her, boring into her back.

She looked around the room, feeling paranoid, then foolish. She still couldn't believe any of this was real. Perhaps Kell had snuck into their room and deleted the photos John had taken? Then he replaced them with new snapshots that were dark, she reasoned. That seemed a plausible explanation.

Those headstones, they really did look brand new. Kell probably put them there, amongst the old ones, and made up the entire story. But why would he do that, she wondered? His farm was on the outskirts of town, his home the only one for miles. Surely he didn't get that many visitors, if any at all? If this was all some sort of ruse to part tourists from the cash in their wallets, it wasn't being advertised very well. John only stopped at the farm because he noticed the old cemetery and wanted to look at it, which had annoyed Rachael to no end. None of this made any sense. She sat on the musty old couch wondering now, how she had ended up here, in the middle of nowhere, in a man's house she barely knew anything about.

"She tells you to do things," Kell continued.

"She does? Wh-What does she tell you to do?" John looked at Rachael nervously, taking her hand.

"Wait," said Kell, looking John dead in the eye. "She tells me to wait. Says he'll be coming around soon."

"Who," John said, his voice shaking a bit. "You're son?"

"No," Kell spoke so quietly, they could barely hear him. "My son is dead."

At first John wasn't sure he had heard Kell right. He glanced at Rachael, a confused look on his face. Rachael only stared at Kell, a deep feeling of dread sinking into her. She was frozen in place, unable to believe any of this was really happening.

"What did you say?" John asked quietly.

"I said my son is dead. Pushed down the stairs. He didn't want to go along with it anymore, didn't want to stay here. Wanted no part of my family, and our cursed generations of the damned, living here alone like this. It's enough to drive a person mad, and many a man in my family went that way, you can be sure."

"Okay, this isn't funny anymore," John said, standing to leave.

"Sit down, Mister Engall, I'm not yet done with my story," Kell spoke forcefully. "You wanted something no one else has ever seen or heard, and you're going to get it, if it's the last thing I ever do. Now sit and listen."

John sat back down, looking at Rachael with fear and apology on his face. He took her hand and squeezed it tightly. His hand was ice cold.

"She been waiting, you see. All these centuries. Waiting for it all to come back 'round. It always does, you see? She knew that. It all comes around in the end, everything does. She drove that wife to suicide, and drove her lover mad, but they had a son, and he was shipped off to England to live with a distant relative. She had power, that woman. Ashlynn was right strong, but she had a child on the way, and was banished from the town. Had to put her focus on that, see? Then her brother died, and she took ill. She taught everything she knew to Criona, and Criona was stronger than even Ashlynn. Strong enough to survive death, in a way. To keep on in these parts, in this land, here on my farm.

"She was strong enough to keep my family going. Always a son, each generation. Always to keep it all going. Waiting for it all to come around. She knew, somehow. Didn't matter to her how long it took. And now, here you are. Showing up on my farm, the day after I buried my son. She knew you were coming, could feel you somehow, I suppose."

"What the hell are you talking about? What does any of this have to do with us?"

John looked at Rachael, panicked and confused. Kell looked only at John.

"Nothing to do with her," he motioned to Rachael, his eyes never leaving John.

"You're an only child, ain't ye, John?"

"Yes, but how did you..."

"What was his name?" Rachael interrupted, speaking urgently, but softly, looking at Kell with calm, cool eyes. The fear had settled deep into her, leaving her collected somehow. It was overload, and she sat frozen, unable to move, scarcely to breathe, awaiting the answer from Kell that she already knew in her heart.

"What was the name of the man Ashlynn had the affair with?"

"Ah," Kell smiled, settling back into his chair. "I was wondering when ye might be asking me that one."

John looked at Rachael again, imploringly. Rachael only closed her eyes, not wanting to see his face.

"His name was Connor. Connor Engall. His only surviving son was Riley Engall."

"Engall?" John said, his voice shaking.

"That's right. What I presume to be your great-great-great-great-great-great-great grandfather, many times removed. It don't matter much, though. Like she says, it all comes around in the end. Ashlynn's daughter was killed, but by that time, Ashlynn was no longer of this world.

195

Ashlynn's lover, Connor Engall had died in a crazy-house, and his son, Riley Engall was an older man with a son of his own, living too far off for her reach. So, Criona waited.

"Time's not the same in the spirit world, s'far as I can tell. It moves differently. To her, this has all been some sort of game, taking mere minutes to play out, for all I know. For my family, it's been centuries of madness, torture. Constantly haunted by her presence, and those damn headstones. All because my ancestors were the ones to take over this land, so cheap it was. We were the ones cursed to live out that witch's game! My son wanted out, thought he could end it all for us by simply leaving, but she would have none of it. She knew it was time, knew you were comin', even if you didn't know where you were goin' next, or how ye really got here. Drawn here, ye were. Drawn back to the place where your bloodline began. It all comes around in the end," Kell laughed, and Rachael felt sorry for him, even as sickened as she was.

John sat frozen in his place on the couch. Rachael stood, facing Kell O'Donough.

"So what happens now," she asked.

"Now ye go and pay your respects to Criona's headstone," Kell said to John, still not looking at her.

John looked at Kell blankly, then behind him at Rachael, who had stood up from the couch and was now backing away from him. She stopped when her back hit the wall, standing directly next to the portrait of Kell and his dead son.

"Rachael?" John looked infinitely hurt. "Honey?"

"I'm sorry, John," she sighed and closed her eyes, not wanting to look at him. Her hand subconsciously went to her abdomen and settled there. Kell looked at John, waiting. Behind him, the front door of the house opened slowly, creaking, allowing a cold wind to blow in.

"She's waiting for ye, Mister Engall," Kell said.

John walked towards the door on frozen feet, as if on autopilot. His mind told him this was all some kind of elaborate joke. He was floating, as if in a dream, and all of this did indeed feel completely surreal to him. He swam through the front door, carried by an unseen force, leading the way. The door closed behind him, leaving Kell and Rachael alone. There was no sound but the wood crackling in the fireplace and a slight whistling of wind down the chimney. Rachael stood where she was, frozen, for what felt like an eternity. Her hand still lay on her stomach. She felt ill. Kell smiled, still sitting in his chair.

Suddenly there was a loud piercing scream, which sounded almost like a small child waking from a bad dream, and yet, Rachael knew it was John. She stumbled over to the couch and fell into it, crumbling.

"Ye did the right thing, Missus," Kell said. "She would have taken him anyway. This way was better for everyone."

Rachael began to cry, cradling herself in her arms.

"It wasn't your fault," Kell said. "You know that, don't you?"

"It wasn't John's fault, either," she said bitterly. "He had nothing to do with any of this. It was six hundred years ago!"

"There's no need to yell, missus."

Rachael began to sob. Her head ached.

"There is one wee bit of business yet to take to," Kell said gently. "Your husband didn't know you were expecting, did he?"

Rachael looked at Kell through her tears, her heart suddenly skipping a beat.

"I–I don't know what you're talking about," she whispered.

"Course ye do, missus," Kell said gently. "You're carrying John's child in your belly. That's why you let him go, so as not to create a commotion, nothing to harm your baby, like a good mum would. I understand," Kell said, smiling at Rachael.

"You're crazy!"

She lurched from the couch and ran to the front door, trying to open it. It was locked. She turned the deadbolt, which should have unlocked the door, yet it was still sealed tightly.

"Can't get out, missus," Kell said sadly. "My son tried, and she took care of him. If she don't want you to leave, you won't. Besides there's business yet to take care of. I can still feel her around, her presence. She ain't through just yet. John was an only child, but..."

"No," Rachael said softly. "No."

"I'm sorry, missus. No choice, really. It all comes around in the end. She don't want you, like you said. You've got nothing to do with any of this, save for what you're carrying inside, and I expect she'll take care of that soon enough."

Rachael felt sick to her stomach. A sudden pain wrenched her abdomen, and she fell to the floor, doubled over. Cold, invisible hands squeezed her insides. Kell stood from his chair and walked into the kitchen.

"Help me," Rachael said, reaching her arm out to grasp his leg as he passed by. Blood was already beginning to soak the crotch of her pants, warm and sticky. Kell walked past, unscathed.

"Have to check on that stew," Kell said. "It should be ready any time now."

A knot popped in the fireplace and sparks of ember floated upward into the darkness of the flue. Outside, in the night, the chilly wind blew and whistled through the trees. All else was silent.

ABOUT THE AUTHORS

Brent Abell resides in Southern Indiana with his wife, sons, and a pug who believes mankind should be his foot stool. He has been published in a wide variety of publications from numerous presses and his debut novella, *In Memoriam* was released in late 2012. You can down some rum, smoke a cigar, and check out what is up with his written words at http://brentabell.hotmail.com.

Gordon Anthony Bean was born in Laval, Quebec, but has spent close to the last 20 years in New England. He is a licensed CPA and works in finance in private industry. He has been married for over 15 years and has a wonderful seven year old daughter and hyperactive black lab at home. In his spare time, he writes, reads, listens to music and enjoys films. Not surprisingly, horror is his favorite. He has a short story in the *Sinister Landscapes* anthology by Pixie Dust Press and is currently searching for a publisher for his debut novel, *Dawn of Broken Glass*, a dark tale of supernatural revenge.

Rose Blackthorn lives in the high mountain desert of Eastern Utah with her boyfriend and two dogs, Boo and Shadow. She spends her time writing, reading, doing wire-work and beading, and photographing the surrounding wilderness. An only child, she was lucky enough to have a mother who loved books, and has been surrounded by them her entire life. Thus, instead of squabbling with siblings, she learned to be friends with her imagination and the voices in her head are still very much present. She has published genre fiction online and in print with Necon E-Books, Flashes in the Dark, Stupefying Stories, Cast of Wonders, Dark Moon Digest, and the anthologies *New Dawn Fades*, *The Ghost IS the Machine*, *A Quick Bite of Flesh* and *Fear the Abyss*, among others. She is an affiliate member of the HWA, and suffers from an overactive imagination, but rather than complaining... she just goes with it. More information is available at: http://roseblackthorn.wordpress.com/ and http://www.facebook.com/Rose Blackthorn.Author.

Tim J. Finn is a member of the New England Horror Writers and is a graduate of Grinnell College, where he earned a BA in English. He has worked as a radio disc jockey, advertising copywriter, short order cook, office temp, and is currently employed as a branch receptionist for one of the U.S.'s top 100 design/engineering/consulting firms. His writing appears in the Massachusetts edition of Rymfire eBooks *State of Horror* series, the second volume of the *Satan's Toybox* trilogy from Angelic Knight Press entitled *Toy Soldiers*, Zombie Works

Publications *Monsterthology*, and Alter Press' forthcoming *No Holds Barred: Splatterpunk for a New Generation*. Finn is a near-lifelong New Englander and lives just outside of Boston. He can be found on Facebook and, very occasionally, on Twitter.

Scott M. Goriscak began writing in high school, but it wasn't until a conversation with Horror Writer Clive Barker did his writing turn to the dark side. Scott published his first collection of short stories, *Grim and Ghastly* in 2008. He followed up with a second collection, *Dead and Decaying* in 2009. Also in 2009, his short story "Home Sweet Home" was selected for the 2010 *Masters of Horror* anthology. The following year his story "Easy to Digest" was chosen for the 2011 *Masters of Horror* anthology *Damned If You Don't*. In 2011 he was published in numerous anthologies: *Soup of Souls* anthology—"No Man Left Behind"; *I Believe in Werewolves*—"Parenting-Not for the Faint of Heart"; *Satan's Toy Box*—"Playing with Dolls"; *Satan's Toy Box*—"The South Shall Rise Again"; *Post-Apocalyptic Raids*—"Who are the Faithful"; *Spirits of the Night*—"Lost and Found"; and "Field of Shrieks" in *The Spirit of Poe*, which all proceeds of the publication go to keeping the home of Edgar Allan Poe open to the public due to the city of Baltimore budget cuts. Angelic Knight Press published Scott's third collection of horror in 2012 entitled *Horrorism*. The Horror Society Published Scott's fourth collection, *Welcome to the Dark Side* in October 2012. He is currently putting the final touches on his first novel, *The New Jersey Devil*. Founder of THE HORROR SOCIETY 2012.

Marianne Halbert is from Central Indiana. Her dark fiction has appeared in dozens of anthologies (by such publishers as Evil Jester Press, The Four Horsemen, Wicked East Press, Pill Hill Press, Blue River Press, and more) as well as magazines such as *Necrotic Tissue*, *Midnight Screaming*, and *ThugLit*. Follow her at www.halbertfiction.webs.com. Her collection, *Wake Up and Smell the Creepy* is available as an eBook and in print.

Jeffrey Kosh (born October 28, 1968) is the pen name of an author turned Digital Nomad. He had various art experiences, before discovering his love for writing fiction. His different careers have led him to travel extensively worldwide, causing a passion for photography, wildlife, history, and popular folklore. All these things have had a heavy influence on his writing. His works include the novel *Feeding the Urge*, and various short stories and novelettes. Jeff currently travels in South East Asia with his wife. For more info: http://www.authorsdb.com/index.php/component/content/article/8-authors/38-jeffrey-kosh.

Lisamarie Lamb loves to write horror. She has written and published a horror novel (*Mother's Helper*) and a collection of short stories (*Some Body's At The Door*).

She has recently completed her second novel (*At Peace With All Things*), and she is writing the second draft of her third, *Perfect Murder*. Dark Hall Press has published a collection of her short stories, entitled *Over The Bridge*. Her work can be found online at http://www.themoonlitdoor.blogspot.com, and within many anthologies including books from Angelic Knight Press, Cruentus Libri Press, and Sirens Call Publications. A complete list is available on her blog. She has edited a collection of short stories (*A Roof Over Their Heads*) set on and around the Isle of Sheppey, Kent (U.K.), where she lives with her husband, daughter, and two cats.

Mark Leslie and **Carol Weekes** write primarily in the Horror, Dark Fantasy and Crime/Suspense genres and have written several short stories together over the years. Mark's most recent book is the non-fiction ghost story book, *Haunted Hamilton*, and he is the editor of such anthologies as *Tesseracts Sixteen* and *Campus Chills*. His novel, *I, Death* is forthcoming later in 2013. Carol's latest book, *Dead Reflections*, which contains a full novel, five short stories, and two poems, was published in February 2013. Carol is also the author of the novels *Terribilis*, *Ouroboros* (co-written with Michael Kelly), and *Walters Crossing*.

Edward J. McFadden III juggles a full-time career as a university administrator and teacher, with his writing aspirations. His first novel, a mysterious, dark thriller called *The Black Death of Babylon*, is now available from Post Mortem Press. His steampunk fantasy novelette, *Starwisps*, was recently published in the anthology *Fantastic Stories of the Imagination*, his story *Breaking Down* is forthcoming in the print edition of *Abandoned Towers Magazine*, and his novella *Anywhere But Here* is scheduled for publication in 2013 by Padwolf Publish. He is the author/editor of six published books: *Jigsaw Nation, Deconstructing Tolkien: A Fundamental Analysis of The Lord of the Rings* (to be re-released in eBook format Fall 2012), *Time Capsule, The Second Coming, Thoughts of Christmas*, and *The Best of Pirate Writings*. He has had more than 50 short stories published in places like *Fantastic Futures 13, Apocalypse 13, Hear Them Roar, CrimeSpree Magazine, Terminal Fright, Cyber-Psycho's AOD, The And*, and *The Arizona Literary Review*. Over the last seven years he has written six novels, all of which are at various stages of rewriting and submission for publication. He lives on Long Island with his wife Dawn, their daughter Samantha, and their mutt Oli. See EdwardMcFadden.com for all things Ed.

Adam Millard is the author of thirteen novels and more than a hundred short stories. Perhaps best known for his post-apocalyptic fiction, Adam also writes horror/fantasy for children. His work can be found in collections from Evil Jester Press, Sirens Call, Angelic Knight Press, Bizarro Press, Bizarro Pulp Press, Rymfire Books and many more. Adam is a member of the British Fantasy Society.

David North-Martino's fiction has appeared in *Epitaphs: The Journal of the New England Horror Writers*, *Extinct Doesn't Mean Forever*, *Dark Recesses Press*, and *Afterburn SF*, among others. He is also hard at work on his first novel. A graduate of the University of Massachusetts, he holds a BLA in English and psychology. When he's not writing, David enjoys studying and teaching martial arts. He lives with his very supportive wife in a small town in Massachusetts.

Jeffrey C. Pettengill is a New England native whose mild-mannered cover as a hospital's financial analyst keeps others from suspecting what lurks within his imagination. Since beginning seriously writing five years ago, he has had eight short stories published, including one in the Bram Stoker Award nominated anthology *Epitaphs*. In addition to writing, he expresses his creativity by cooking, creating spreadsheets, and by role-playing. He also loves movies, the theater, and his wife.

Nelson W. Pyles is the author of several short stories and is also the host of The Wicked Library—a podcast featuring up-and-coming horror writers. His work has appeared with the likes of Harlan Ellison, F. Paul Wilson, and Jack Ketchum. For more information, go to www.nelsonwpyles.com or follow him on Twitter @nelsonwpyles. Nelson currently resides in Pittsburgh PA—the zombie capitol of the world.

Michael Thomas-Knight lives in Long Island, N.Y., down the block from a famous Amityville house and just east of Joel Rifkin's lovely home. Growing up, his family lived in a real haunted house and his childhood babysitter was shot by Son of Sam. No doubt, these strange events influence his tales. His recent horror fiction has been published in *Twisted Dreams Magazine*, *Infernal Ink Magazine*, and at *Microhorror.com*. You can find Michael at his blog, *Parlor of Horror*, which deals with all things horror—movies, books, and articles for the horror enthusiast. Check it out at: http://www.parlorofhorror.wordpress.com.

Robert W. Walker is an award-winning author and graduate of North-Western University. He created his highly acclaimed *Instinct* and *Edge* series between 1982 and 2005. Rob since then has penned his award-winning historical series featuring Inspector Alastair Ransom with City for Ransom (2006), *Shadows in the White City* (2007), and *City of the Absent* (2008), and most recently placed Ransom on board the Titanic in a hybrid historical/science fiction epic entitled *Titanic 2012 — Curse of RMS Titanic*. The original Ransom trilogy straddles the Chicago World's Fair circa 1893, and has had enthusiastic reviews from Chicago historians and the Chicago Tribune, which likened "the witticism to Mark Twain, the social consciousness to Dickens, and the ghoulish atmosphere to Poe!" Rob has since published *Dead On*, a PI's tale of revenge as a reason to live—a noir set in modern day Atlanta, followed more recently by *Bismarck 2013*, an historical horror title, *The Edge of Instinct*, the 12th book in the *Instinct* series, and a short story collection entitled *Party of Eight — the one that got away*. Rob's historical suspense *Children of Salem*, while an historical romance and suspense novel, exposes the evil in mankind via the politics of witchcraft in grim 1692 New England, which one professional editor reviewed as: A title that only Robert Walker could make *work*—romance amid the infamous witch trials. Robert currently resides in Charleston, West Virginia with his wife, children, pets, all somehow normal. For more on Rob's published works, see www. RobertWalkerbooks.com, www.HarperCollins.com, and www.amazon.com/kindle books. He maintains a presence on Facebook and Twitter as well.

Cynthia Ward (http://www.cynthiaward.com) has published fiction in *Asimov's Science Fiction Magazine* and *The Mammoth Book of Comic Fantasy II*, among other anthologies and magazines. She has published nonfiction in *Weird Tales* Magazine and *Locus Online*, among other webzines and magazines. Her story "Norms," published in *Triangulation: Last Contact*, made the Tangent Online Recommended Reading List for 2011. With Nisi Shawl, she coauthored *Writing the Other: A Practical Approach* (Aqueduct Press), which is based on their diversity writing workshop, Writing the Other: Bridging Cultural Differences for Successful Fiction (http://www.writing-theother.com).

Jay Wilburn lives with his wife and two sons in beautiful Conway, South Carolina. He has written many horror and speculative fiction stories including his novels *Loose Ends: A Zombie Novel*, *Time Eaters*, and *The Great Interruption*. Follow his many dark thoughts at JayWilburn.com or @AmongTheZombies on Twitter.

Jennifer Word is an award-winning poet and editor in Southern California. She holds a B.A. in Psychology from Pepperdine University. Her Science & Speculative Fiction trilogy series *The Society, Book One: Genesis* is now available c/o Stony Meadow Publishing, and can be purchased at Amazon and Barnes & Noble online. Her short fiction and poetry has been featured in *The Storyteller* Magazine, *The Klondike Sun*, *Dark Moon Digest*, *Dark Eclipse e-Magazine*, *Surreal Grotesque* Magazine, *eFiction* Magazine, and the *Frightmares* and *Slices of Flesh* anthologies. She is also the author of "*The Poe Toaster*," "*All Because of the Cat*", and "*Higher Love*", available on Amazon and in the Smashwords Premium Catalog as e-books. Her website: www.Fiction-spook.com . Her debut horror e-novella, *Rain*, is now available from Dark Moon Books and can be purchased for the Nook and Kindle at Amazon.com and www.barnesandnoble.com.

Made in the USA
Middletown, DE
10 March 2018